SOUR CHERRY TURNOVER

SOUR CHERRY TURNOVER

AUNTIE CLEM'S BAKERY #7

P.D. WORKMAN

ISBN: 9781989080740 (IS Hardcover)

ISBN: 9781989080733 (IS Paperback)

ISBN: 9781989080702 (KDP Paperback)

ISBN: 9781989080719 (Kindle)

ISBN: 9781989080726 (ePub)

pdworkman

ALSO BY P.D. WORKMAN

Auntie Clem's Bakery

Gluten-Free Murder

Dairy-Free Death

Allergen-Free Assignation

Witch-Free Halloween (Halloween Short)

Dog-Free Dinner (Christmas Short)

Stirring Up Murder

Brewing Death

Coup de Glace

Sour Cherry Turnover

Apple-achian Treasure

Vegan Baked Alaska

Muffins Masks Murder

Tai Chi and Chai Tea

Santa Shortbread

Cold as Ice Cream

Changing Fortune Cookies (Coming soon)

Hot on the Trail Mix (Coming soon)

Recipes from Auntie Clem's Bakery

Reg Rawlins, Psychic Detective

What the Cat Knew

A Psychic with Catitude

A Catastrophic Theft

Night of Nine Tails

Telepathy of Gardens

Delusions of the Past

Fairy Blade Unmade

Web of Nightmares

A Whisker's Breadth

Skunk Man Swamp (Coming Soon)

Magic Ain't A Game (Coming Soon)

Without Foresight (Coming Soon)

Zachary Goldman Mysteries

She Wore Mourning

His Hands Were Quiet

She Was Dying Anyway

He Was Walking Alone

They Thought He was Safe

He Was Not There

Her Work Was Everything

She Told a Lie

He Never Forgot

She Was At Risk

Kenzie Kirsch Medical Thrillers

Unlawful Harvest

Doctored Death (Coming soon)

Dosed to Death (Coming soon)

AND MORE AT PDWORKMAN.COM

For when things don't turn out quite the way you had planned.

CHAPTER 1

*E*rin arranged the cupcakes carefully in the display case, carefully adjusting the space between them and making sure the icing shapes would all be oriented right-side-up for her customers.

"Well, if it isn't your favorite person in the world," Vic drawled.

Erin didn't need to look at her assistant to know who was approaching. She raised her eyes to look through the glass of the display case to the young woman about to walk through the front doors of Auntie Clem's Bakery, the muscles of her stomach clenching into a hard knot. She tried to school her expression to keep a pleasant smile on her face, and smushed the cupcake in her hand against the bottom of the shelf above it.

She groaned and pulled it out. It was a good thing there were no customers in the shop at that moment.

"Sorry." Vic gave a little grimace and a shrug.

Erin grabbed a damp cloth to wipe the smear of icing from the shelf, then straightened to greet her half-sister.

"Hi, Charley."

"Oops," Charley looked at the cupcake in Erin's hand. "Looks like that one didn't make it."

"No." Erin chucked it into the garbage can. She put her hands on her hips, unconsciously retreating into a defensive stance. "What can I help you with today?"

Charley smiled. Having only recently met Charley, Erin still found it disconcerting to see the dark hair and delicate features she was used to seeing in the mirror on someone else's face. And she knew that particular smile was just as fake as her own.

"I came to see if I could borrow a muffin pan," Charley said. "Every time I turn around, there's some other piece of equipment I am missing. The Bake Shoppe should have been fully-stocked. I'd really like to know who has been taking stuff home with them. If I could afford it, I'd hire help from the city instead of Bald Eagle Falls, just so I could be sure I wasn't hiring back whoever has been helping themselves to everything!"

Erin wavered between sympathy and irritation. She knew that she would have been pretty angry if she'd found someone had been stealing from her, especially when the bakery was her livelihood, but she was also increasingly annoyed with Charley and dearly wished that she wouldn't reopen The Bake Shoppe. And not just because she would be in direct competition with Erin's bakery.

"You must be madder than a wet hen," Vic said, without a trace of sympathy in her voice.

Erin avoided looking at Vic.

Charley nodded. "You bet I am. Half of Angela's recipes use weights for flours instead of measuring cups, so you'd think there would be an electronic scale in the place, but do you think there's any sign of one?" She sighed. "Anyway, I need to whip up some muffins before opening and I really don't have time to go into the city to get a jumbo muffin pan, so I wondered if I could borrow one of yours just for a couple of days and then I'll bring it back to you."

Erin had already explained enough times that she shouldn't have had to tell Charley again. "I can't, Charley. They would be contaminated with gluten and I wouldn't be able to use them again."

"I'd clean them really well. And it would be cooked, so it shouldn't cause a problem for your *special* clientele. Please, Erin, this will be the last thing that I ask for."

"It doesn't matter how well you clean it, there could still be microscopic traces of gluten or other proteins on the pan, enough to trigger a reaction in someone. None of the equipment I use has ever been used for gluten-containing batters. Nothing is cross-contaminated, so people who are celiac or allergic don't have to worry about reacting to my baked goods, no matter how sensitive they are."

"But like I said, it will all have been cooked anyway. So they shouldn't be allergic."

"Baking doesn't denature gluten proteins enough for someone to stop reacting to them."

"I had a friend who was allergic to eggs. She couldn't eat them scrambled or boiled or fried up for breakfast, but she could eat cake and cookies that had egg in them, because baking changes them."

"Some people can tolerate eggs that have been baked," Erin agreed, "but it's not the same with gluten. Or they'd be able to eat regular bread and there wouldn't be any need for specialty baked goods! I can't use pans that have been used for regular muffins. Even though you scrub the pans and they look perfectly clean, there could still be microscopic amounts of gluten that would get into my baking. I'm not willing to risk it."

Charley folded her arms across her chest and pressed her lips together, clearly irritated. "Can't you help me out just this once?"

"I'll help you any way I can," Erin promised, "just not in any way that will endanger the health of my customers."

She suspected that, like a large portion of the population, Charley figured that anyone who claimed to be gluten intolerant was just trying to get attention, and that they didn't really have any health concerns at all. While some people did avoid gluten some of the time just because it was a trendy thing to do or they thought it would help them to lose weight, Erin had customers who could end up in hospital if she glutened them. She wasn't about to take chances with their health.

Erin looked over at Vic. As usual, Victoria Webster had her long blond hair put up and corralled inside a baker's cap. Her makeup was perfect in spite of the Tennessee heat and she could have just as easily walked off a runway as out of the hot kitchen. Vic arched one eyebrow at Erin. She knew how much Charley had been driving Erin crazy as the reopening of The Bake Shoppe approached. Her advice had been to stop helping Charley. Family or not, Erin wasn't under any obligation.

"So you're going to make me drive all the way into the city to pick up new muffin tins, when you could just loan me a tray for a few days," Charley accused.

"Sorry, I can't."

"Thanks loads."

"Sorry."

"You're lucky you don't have employees who steal from you." Charley looked at Vic for a moment, then back at Erin. "If I knew who was stealing from me…"

Erin imagined the former organized-crime soldier could have made some pretty good threats, but Charley didn't put them into words. "Do you think someone is stealing from you now, or is this stuff that disappeared before you got The Bake Shoppe?"

"It's still theft, whether they knew they were taking it from me, or decided to take things home after Angela Plaint died and the bakery closed. It wasn't theirs to take."

"No," Erin agreed. "You're right. I just wondered whether you were still having stuff disappear."

Charley shrugged. "I don't know. All I know is that for what should have been a turnkey business, there are an awful lot of things missing!"

Erin nodded sympathetically. "Maybe you should do an inventory before you go into the city, make sure you get everything you need in one run."

"The trouble is, I don't really know what's missing until I go to make something and it's not there."

Erin nodded. That was exactly her point.

"You should make a list," Vic suggested. Her face was smooth, no sign of the laughter bubbling under the surface. She was always teasing Erin for her endless lists. But Erin couldn't imagine trying to run a business—or her life—without them.

Charley rolled her eyes at Vic and didn't bother to comment. While she didn't bully Vic for her transgender identity like some of the Bald Eagle Falls townsfolk—knowing how Erin would react if she did—Charley clearly didn't intend to take any advice from Erin's eighteen-year-old employee, no matter how on-point it was.

"So that's it?" Charley asked Erin. "That's your final answer, you won't help me out?"

"I can't help you with your muffin tin problem."

"Fine. You have yourself a nice day." Charley shook her head and stormed out of the store, making the front door bells tinkle wildly.

Erin didn't say anything immediately. She just stared after Charley. Eventually, she spoke. "Is it just me, or..."

"Is your sister on the verge of a mental breakdown?" Vic suggested, cocking her head.

"I don't know if I'd go that far, but she does seem to be a little... stressed."

"And you weren't before you opened Auntie Clem's?"

"Well, yeah." Erin thought back to the days before she had reopened her late aunt's tea shop as a specialty bakery for those with celiac disease or allergies. "I was pretty nervous... but I had my lists."

Vic giggled. "She didn't seem to appreciate the suggestion. Really, when I think about the two of you being sisters... I don't know if I could find two people less alike."

"Charley is a little... rough around the edges. She just has some... maturing to do."

"She's older than I am."

"*Everybody* is older than you are," Erin teased. "But you're remarkably mature for your age. Charley is still in a sort of rebellious stage..."

Vic polished a few smudges off of the display case of baked goods. "I think my family would tell you I'm right in the midst of my rebellious stage too. Running away from home, coming out as a girl..."

"You being you is not a stage," Erin said firmly, looking Vic in the eye. "Don't let them get to you."

Vic hadn't said anything about having had contact with her family recently, but she normally didn't mention them in conversation unless she'd heard from them. They weren't exactly supportive of her transition.

"Thanks," Vic said softly. She looked down at the glass and polished away another invisible smudge. "And my advice to you is to make sure all of your pans and equipment have your name on them."

Erin smiled. "I'm not exactly worried about *my* employees walking off with them."

"I was thinking more about Charley," Vic said, with a nod in the direction of the door. "It would be a lot less work for her to raid your kitchen than it would be to drive into the city."

"She doesn't have a key."

"Maybe not, but having worked for the Dyson family, I suspect she probably wouldn't need a key."

Erin thought about that. "Well… you might have a point there. Do you think Willie has engraving tools?"

"Sure. I'll tell him you need him to mark everything he can?"

"Yes. It's probably a really good idea even without Charley in the equation. If we had a break-in, or even did a catering job and left something behind, it's a lot easier to recover if everything is marked!"

Vic nodded. She tapped her temple. "I'm putting it on my list."

CHAPTER 2

*E*rin was more tired than usual at the end of the day and wondered whether she was coming down with something. Or maybe it was just the additional stress of having to deal with Charley and worrying about a competing bakery opening in Bald Eagle Falls.

She had said from the start that there was enough business in Bald Eagle Falls for two bakeries, but it had been a lot easier to stay in the black when she was the only one. People who wanted to get freshly-baked treats had to either go to her bakery and get gluten-free, or to go into the city. Now anyone who didn't have special diets to deal with would have the option of a regular bakery, and Erin was a lot more worried than she let anyone know.

She didn't have much appetite for supper, opting for just a day-old roll from Auntie Clem's and a cup of ginger tea. Vic was out with Willie, so Erin didn't have anyone to nag her that she needed to eat a well-rounded meal. Or at least as well-rounded as anything that came from a box in the freezer could be. She took her tea into the living room. Orange Blossom followed her to the couch and made a place for himself on her lap, meowing and yipping chattily about how he had passed his day in her absence. Erin encouraged his story with *mm-hmms* and ear scratches until he got settled. Marshmallow, the toasted-brown and white rabbit she had rescued nibbled at the pant leg of her pajamas and snuffled her bare toes, and then eventually flopped down on top of her feet.

Erin wiggled her toes. "Do you really think I need foot warmers in this heat?"

Of course, she had air conditioning, so it wasn't like she had to put up with the outdoor temperatures. Marshmallow just stared at her out of one eye, his nose wiggling busily.

Erin tried to focus on the job at hand, which was brainstorming what areas she could specialize in; what reasons people had to choose Auntie Clem's Bakery over The Bake Shoppe. The top ones were, of course, people who required special diets. Sufferers of celiac disease, allergies, and intolerances. Vegans. And... nothing else was coming to her. There were other untapped possibilities, such as those who followed special diets with acronyms like SCD or FODMAPS, who had PKU or other digestive enzyme disorders, were trying to lose weight or gain muscle, were sugar-free, fat-free, or low carb. But she couldn't cater to them all.

She could possibly develop a low carb line; paleo recipes were popular, but they tended to revolve around almond or coconut flour and eggs, which were bad for her allergic clientele. She had been nut-free from the beginning and didn't want to leave those who had potentially fatal nut allergies in the lurch. That meant she was choosing a smaller customer base over the larger one, which was not a particularly good business decision.

There was a knock at the door. Erin glanced out the front window and saw the squad car parked at the curb. Removing the animals from their comfortable spots, she got up to open the door for Officer Terry Piper—Officer Handsome, as Vic had been known to refer to him—and his partner, K9.

"Personal safety check, ma'am," Terry said, affecting more drawl than usual, "just wanted to make sure you're safe and secure."

Erin laughed. Terry wasn't usually so playful. She liked seeing that side of him. "I could use some personal protection," she breathed, putting her arms around him and giving him a kiss. They stayed like that for a moment, just looking into each other's eyes. K9 interrupted the tableau with a high-pitched whine followed by a low grumble, as if to say, "Oh, please!"

They both laughed. Erin drew back, allowing her personal protection to enter the house. He closed and locked the door behind him.

"On that note," he said in a more serious tone, "I didn't see you check the peephole before opening the door."

"I didn't," Erin agreed. She motioned to the window. "I could see your car from the couch."

"How did you know it wasn't some *other* police officer?"

"Because my date with the sheriff isn't until Friday."

Terry chuckled. He took his place on the couch, making a motion to K9 that indicated he was allowed to lie down and no longer be on guard. K9 did so, sprawling like a teenager. He nosed Marshmallow, snuffling curiously. Marshmallow wasn't in the mood to play, and kicked K9 in the nose with a back foot. K9 sat up, affronted, and sneezed. He looked at Terry and gave a snort.

"If you're going to poke your nose where it doesn't belong, you risk getting kicked," Terry said unsympathetically. "You go doing that to a porcupine or skunk, and you'll really regret it."

"Or even Orange Blossom," Erin contributed. "He'd probably take your nose off."

K9 approached Erin. He bumped up against her leg and nosed at her hands. Erin scratched his ears and was rewarded with a lick, but that wasn't what he was after.

"Oh," Erin scratched his neck and chin. "You're looking for a treat."

Both Orange Blossom and Marshmallow perked up at this suggestion, looking at Erin to see if she were going to give them something.

"He doesn't need a treat every single time he comes over here," Terry pointed out. "You spoil him."

"It's my house, I'll spoil him if I like." Erin patted K9's head and walked toward the kitchen. "Come on, boy. You can have a cookie."

He went with her eagerly, tail waving back and forth in wide arcs. The cat and the rabbit followed close behind. Erin picked a gluten-free doggie biscuit out of the cookie jar for K9, some soft treats from a snack can for Orange Blossom, and a stick of celery for Marshmallow. She handed K9 and Marshmallow their treats directly, but for Orange Blossom, skimmed the treats along the kitchen floor, making him go careening after them in wild pursuit.

"Doggie treats," she murmured as she went back to the living room and sat down next to Terry. "That's another thing."

Terry raised his eyebrows. "What's that?"

"I was trying to think of all of the reasons people come to Auntie Clem's

Bakery, and that's another one. Grain-free doggie treats. A lot of dogs are sensitive to grains and the grocery store doesn't stock grain-free biscuits."

Terry nodded. "Right. We'd have to go all the way to the city to get them."

"And that's not something Charley is going to want to stock, is it? She just wants a regular bakery, and most bakeries don't do treats for dogs, gluten-free or otherwise." She picked up her list and wrote the thought down.

"What else have you got on there?" Terry looked down at the short list. "What about the ladies' tea?"

Erin had revived Clementine's tradition of an after-services tea Sunday mornings for the churchgoing ladies.

"There's nothing to stop Charley from doing a ladies' tea," she countered.

"Well, I suppose not, but people will go to yours because that's where Clementine's Tea Room was. Having it somewhere else wouldn't be the same."

"But you don't think they'd choose Charley over me if she did offer one? Because I'm an atheist and she's... not?"

"Charley isn't exactly religious herself. Does she even attend services?"

"I wouldn't know, since I don't go," Erin teased. "But seriously, no, I don't think she ever has. And I don't think she goes into the city or back to Moose River for services. But she's Christian in name, and that matters to people around here. Better a Christian who beats his wife and goes fishing every Sunday than an atheist."

"I don't think they're quite that bad."

Erin considered. "Maybe not quite," she admitted. She held up her fingers, pinched close together. "But it's close."

"Has someone been getting on your case?"

"No more than usual. I think they've adjusted to the idea that they're not going to convert me, but they're not happy about it and people still... make comments."

"You're never going to get people to stop talking."

"No."

They sighed in unison, then laughed.

"Does it ever bother *you* that I'm not a Christian?" Erin asked.

He raised his brows. "Me? Not a bit. Never even crossed my mind."

"It doesn't bother you that I'm not going to your heaven?"

"You might be surprised where you end up! No, it really makes no difference to me what you believe. I'm not entirely sure what it is that I believe. I'm born and bred Christian and have never considered myself anything else, but do I believe the whole thing?" He shrugged. "That the Bible and everything in it is meant to be taken literally? I don't know about that. I'll take it on faith for now... and see what happens."

"Hedging your bets? Making sure you're covered just in case it is all true?"

"Our society is built on the Ten Commandments and the Bible. That's where our most basic laws stem from. So... yes. I'll do my best to keep the top ten and uphold the law. Whether that will get me anything in the afterlife or just keep me on the right path in this life, I don't know."

Erin shook her head. "Okay..."

"What does that mean?"

"I thought one of those top ten was going to church on Sunday, and you don't do that. You go to work like usual."

Terry looked away, grimacing. "Well, it doesn't exactly say that..."

"Oh."

"It says to keep the Sabbath day holy, and I..." he trailed off.

Erin waited for him to finish. He didn't come up with anything.

"You'll take that one under advisement?" she suggested.

"Well, maybe I'll do better at that one when I'm retired."

"Sounds good to me."

They sat in silence for a few minutes while the animals gathered back around them and found comfy places to nestle. Erin added the ladies' tea to her list and read over it again. There still wasn't enough there to keep a business running. If everybody who didn't have to eat a special diet decided to go to The Bake Shoppe, Erin's business was going to be in trouble.

CHAPTER 3

S o while you're trying to figure out how to deal with your sister," Terry said, nodding to the list, "I'm still trying to figure out what to do about your former foster sister."

"Reg?"

Terry was clearly about to say something smart to her like 'how many foster sisters do you have?' and then stopped himself as it came to him that she did, in fact, have a lot more than just Reg. Reg was the only one he had met and would have brought up, but she did have others.

"Uh, yes. Regina Rawlins. We haven't been able to track her down."

Erin shrugged. "She's had plenty of experience with disappearing. She'll be living halfway across the country under a new name. You might as well not waste your time."

"You haven't heard anything from her?"

Erin considered her answer, which made Terry straighten and look at her more closely.

"You *have* heard from her?"

"Well, sort of. Just one quick phone call, and it didn't make a lot of sense."

"Where was it from? When was this? Do you still have the number in your call log?"

"I tried it again later and it didn't work. So just a burner phone, probably."

"Where?"

Erin was reluctant to give him any information. She hadn't liked having Reg around and had refused to get involved in any scams with her, but she wasn't a snitch. She'd expect her friends and old foster families to keep quiet and protect her if she were in trouble. It was the code.

"Where was she calling from?" Terry repeated. "What was the area code?"

"Florida," Erin said finally. But that was all she was going to tell him. There were lots of people in Florida, and Terry wasn't exactly going to drive there himself to go looking for Reg. He could call it in to the locals or the FBI, but no one was going to care about solving the case of a small-town cop looking for a swindler who had walked off with certain pieces of jewelry belonging to her clients. It wasn't like his investigation was going to go anywhere.

"Florida," Terry repeated, thinking about it. "I had one query from Florida. I didn't think anything of it, because the officer never returned my call when I called her back. Figured she must have sorted things out on her own. I'll have to pull it out and have another look at it."

"You're not going to find Reg if she doesn't want to be found. Why don't you just let it go?"

"She stole from your friends. You don't think they deserve some justice?"

"I just know Reg. You're not going to find her. And... I don't know... she sounded kind of strange. Wasn't making a lot of sense."

"Drunk?"

"Maybe. I never knew Reg to get like that when she was drinking before, though."

"What exactly did she sound like?"

"Kind of... hysterical. Upset or excited. Not slurring her words or anything."

"You ever know her to be like that before?"

"Well... maybe." Reg *had* behaved strangely before. Sometimes Reg's behavior could be very bizarre. "There have been a couple of times when she's... gone off the rails."

Terry leaned in closer, frowning in concentration. "Off the rails? What does that mean?"

"She's been hospitalized. For... things like depression or... hallucinations."

"Psychosis? Is she schizophrenic?"

"No. I mean, she's had a lot of different diagnoses over the years, and I wouldn't doubt that schizophrenia is one of them... but she's not. She's just... different."

"So, when you called her back, it was to check on her? To make sure she was okay?"

"Yeah. But like I said, the number wasn't in service anymore. She knows not to keep the same number for long. She probably just bought it for that phone call, or to make a bunch of one-off calls, and then she tossed it."

"But if she's trying to run a business passing herself off as a psychic or whatever she's up to now, she'll need to have a number people can reach her at."

Reg nodded. "But I doubt if it will be anything you can track. You might as well just not waste your time."

Terry studied Erin. She knew he thought she was just trying to protect her friend.

And maybe she was.

CHAPTER 4

*E*rin was happy to see Mary Lou Cox come through the door the next afternoon. Mary Lou had been keeping a pretty low profile since her husband had been arrested for the murder of Joelle Biggs. He was still in hospital or some other facility being evaluated so they could decide how to deal with him. Erin hoped that he didn't end up in prison. It seemed obvious to her that he didn't have all of his faculties.

"Hi, Mary Lou. How's it going?"

Mary Lou was neat and well-tailored as always, her gray hair in a sleek, short style. She gave Erin her usual pleasant-but-reserved smile, then glanced back over her shoulder as if she were worried someone else might have followed her in. She turned back to Erin, the smile a little less certain.

"I'm as good as ever. Things have just been so busy lately, I haven't been able to get around…"

"Busy at the General Store?"

"Well, that and home life and… just everything. I've been keeping myself busy."

"Well, good." Erin gestured to the display case. "What would you and the boys like today?"

"Campbell has gone away for a while, so it's just Josh and me. Going from four people down to two… I admit, I'm not doing much meal planning anymore. We just fend for ourselves, mostly. But I feel like I've

15

neglected Josh a little, so I thought…" Mary Lou gazed over the day's offerings. "Everything just looks so good. Maybe some of those cranberry muffins for breakfasts. And m&m cookies for a treat."

"Sounds good," Erin agreed. She let Mary Lou finish browsing over the contents of the case and deciding how many of each item she wanted, then started to package it up. Vic walked in from the kitchen.

"Hello, Mary Lou. I hope your day is going well."

Mary Lou's smile at Vic, who she was usually uncomfortable around, was a fraction warmer than usual. Maybe she was getting more used to Vic and appreciating the fact that unlike some of her older friends who were not supporting her, Vic hadn't turned against her and started treating her like a pariah during her recent trials.

Or maybe she appreciated that Vic hadn't asked her how she was doing. She probably got tired of people being overly interested in her life and in having to come up with an acceptable answer as to how she was doing when her life was in shambles.

"Nice to see you too, Vic."

Vic went over to the cash register and started to punch in Mary Lou's order while Erin got it all packaged up.

"Where is Campbell, then?" Erin asked. "I hadn't heard that he was leaving."

"He's… pursuing other options. I'm not sure what he's going to do… he always did so well in school, but since Roger… he just seems to have lost the will to put in any effort."

"Maybe he's been having trouble with the other kids," Vic suggested, not looking up from the register.

"I expect the boys have had at least as much trouble as I have, and that has not been pretty. I always thought… I don't know. People suddenly seem very shallow. I thought we were such good friends, but suddenly other things have become much more important in their lives."

Erin shook her head. "Well forget them. We will always be there for you, Mary Lou. And anyone who isn't, they just aren't really a friend, are they?"

"I know. It's just a little sad to find out that the people you thought were real friends… well, that they aren't."

"I know," Erin agreed. She'd been through it herself. People pretending to be friends, acting like they cared, and then suddenly they were gone when they were needed the most. It was easy to say just forget about them, but Erin suspected that Vic too had lost her share of friends when she had transitioned. She glanced over at Vic. Vic flushed a little pink and nodded, as if she had read Erin's mind.

"I know it's not easy to just forget about them. But it's still good advice. You can't eat yourself up over someone who never really cared in the first place."

Mary Lou sighed. "Of course you are right. And I'm sure it will all turn out just fine. Opposing forces increase strength."

"We are refined by fire," Vic agreed.

Mary Lou paid the bill, nodded at them each, and headed out. Just as she left the shop, Charley came in. Her face was flushed pink and she looked happy for once instead of stressed and irritated.

"Hey, Charley," Erin greeted.

Charley marched up to the display case. "You are so good at this," she said. "You always have something new in there that I haven't seen before."

Erin warmed at the compliment. "Well, thank you. I'm always experimenting with something new."

"And it seems like they all turn out! Even things like this," she pointed at the pastries. "I've never seen gluten-free turnovers anywhere else. I would have said they couldn't be done. But those look just like regular turnovers. I would swear you were using wheat flour."

"They're pretty tricky. They take a lot of fiddling. I found that if I freeze the butter, and then grate it fine between each layer, and then roll the layers just as thin as I can... something like this can take twenty layers, and if it gets too warm, it won't work, so you have to keep stopping and chilling it..."

Charley shook her head. "I can't imagine the patience. I buy the pre-made filo pastry, and pre-made fillings, and put them together. They turn out pretty good. But you can't buy pre-made gluten-free pastry like that."

"Nope. Maybe someday, but until then, if people want gluten-free turnovers, they're going to have to come here."

Charley grinned. She pulled out a small spiral notebook and, looking into the display case, started jotting down notes. Erin looked at Vic, who was frowning.

"What are you doing?" Erin asked.

Charley didn't look up from her notes. "I'm just writing down what you're selling. You have such a good variety of different things. I want to be able to do the same kind of thing at The Bake Shoppe."

Erin remembered one foster mother telling her repeatedly that imitation was the sincerest form of flattery. It had driven Erin crazy when the younger kids would mimic her, and she would run to her foster mother complaining.

So what if Charley was planning to copy her lineup? There was nothing wrong with two bakeries having similar offerings. How could they not be similar?

"You have to find your own thing," Vic told Charley. "What's your specialty going to be?"

"I don't need a specialty. There's already a specialty bakery. I'm the one who is going to carry the *normal* baked goods."

"I've got to check on some cookies," Erin announced, and retreated to the kitchen. She didn't really have anything she had to check on, but she washed some dishes and stayed out of the way for a few minutes while she tried to regain her equilibrium. She knew she should go back out front when she heard the front door bells jingle. Either someone else had come in and Erin should help wait on them, or Charley was gone, and she didn't need to hide out anymore. But Erin wasn't in any hurry to get back out to the counter.

"Are you okay?" Vic asked, entering the kitchen.

"Oh, I'm fine."

"No offense, but that sister of yours shore rubs me the wrong way sometimes. The nerve of her, coming in here just to copy your lineup!"

Erin looked up from her dishes. "So I'm right, that was weird, wasn't it? Who does that? Is she really planning to offer exactly the same foods as I am, or is she just gaslighting me?"

"I don't think she's that subtle. And yeah, it is weird. She should be making her own specialty, not baking goods *just like Erin, only normal.*"

Erin shook her head. She dried off her hands and went back out to the front of the shop with Vic. "I just have visions of all of my customers going over to her bakery. Even the ones who have to eat gluten-free. That's what Carolyn was like. She just wanted to be normal and eat normal food. We didn't have all of this kind of thing. Our foster mom tried, but all we had were these loaves of rice bread that were always so dry. Or she would try to make a birthday cake, and it would be so gritty, so obviously not normal. Carolyn wanted so much to just eat normal food. So she did."

Vic grimaced. "Some people want so badly to fit in... they'll do anything. Even when they know it's foolish or dangerous."

"She knew it made her sick, but she didn't care. It was more important to be sick and normal than to stay healthy."

"And in the end, her system was too messed up to recover." Vic had heard Carolyn's story enough times to know how it had ended. Carolyn was the reason Erin had learned to do gluten-free baking in the first place. Trying to make nice things for her foster sister or for others who were in the same position.

Vic put her hand on Erin's shoulder. "You are doing exactly what you set out to do. You're making life better for people like Carolyn. Look at little Peter Foster. He adores your baking. Without Auntie Clem's, he would have to rely on packaged gluten-free goods from the city. He wouldn't get any of this nice stuff. He wouldn't have any choices. And when he went to friends' birthday parties, they wouldn't have anything for him to eat. The Fosters are not going to go to The Bake Shoppe when it opens. They're going to keep coming here."

"Mrs. Foster will come here to get things for Peter, but what about the rest of the family? It will be cheaper for them to go to The Bake Shoppe. And I don't think I can survive if only the people who have to come here do."

Vic gave her shoulder a squeeze and let go. "That's not going to happen. People don't just come here because they have to."

"They come here because it's the only bakery in town. The grocery store can't carry everything they need and doesn't have freshly-baked goods, and they don't want to drive all the way to the city for it, so they come here. But when there is a normal bakery available, they're going to go there."

"Some of them will," Vic admitted. "But a lot of them are going to keep coming here, because you've made a place for yourself here. I loved my Aunt Angela, but going to The Bake Shoppe when she ran it was not like coming to Auntie Clem's. You didn't go there and visit and get the latest gossip. You went there to get your bread or your birthday cake, and then you got out. There were no teas or children's parties or dog biscuits. People didn't linger and get something for tomorrow's dessert too, or lemonade slushes to beat the heat," Vic nodded to the new freezer case. "And you want to know why?"

Erin knew what Vic was getting at. She had met Angela only a couple of times before she had died, but she had been a hard woman. She hadn't been able to work inside The Bake Shoppe anymore because of a late-onset allergy to wheat, but she had continued to own and manage it. Erin had never been there when it was running, so she could only imagine what kind of atmosphere pervaded the place.

"But Charley isn't your Aunt Angela. She's going to do all of the things I'm doing. She's going to copy everything I do that makes me successful. And she naturally has the bigger market."

"We'll make it work, Erin," Vic insisted. "Don't let her get you down."

"But… what if we can't?"

CHAPTER 5

$\mathcal{E}$rin wouldn't have thought that things could get any worse as she dreaded the reopening of The Bake Shoppe. There was no way of knowing whether her worst fears were going to be realized, or whether she had reason to be optimistic like Vic said and to believe that people would keep coming for the good food and gossip rather than just going to The Bake Shoppe with its normal fare. Charley had done little to endear herself to the residents of Bald Eagle Falls, but if she had cheap fresh bread, did anyone really care about her interpersonal skills?

Erin knew who Don Inglethorpe was. She had seen him around town, but he hadn't been a regular customer at Auntie Clem's. Maybe he had bought one or two emergency purchases there, but he hadn't been a frequent visitor. She knew he was a lawyer, one of the three trustees who administered the Trenton Plaint estate, which currently held The Bake Shoppe in trust for Charley and her half-brother Davis Plaint, who was in prison. Erin's own lawyer, James Burgener, was one of the others, along with a woman who wasn't often in town.

So she was surprised to see him walk in the door while she was working a Wednesday afternoon shift with Bella, but at the same time, it wasn't anything that rang alarm bells for her.

"Good morning, Mr. Inglethorpe," she greeted him as he approached the counter.

He was a middle-aged man, white, slightly balding and overweight. Not someone who stood out in a crowd. He was wearing a blue button-up shirt and seemed uncomfortable. Maybe that was just because he hadn't been to Auntie Clem's very much. The early-morning rush had died down, but there were still a few other customers coming and going, and maybe he'd been hoping it would be quieter. Some people couldn't make decisions when there were other people waiting on them.

"Here you go." Erin handed Melissa her purchase, a box of muffins for the police department break room. "Have a good day!"

Melissa nodded, her brown curls dancing, and smiled her wide, easy smile. "I'll say 'hi' to Terry for you."

Erin had been sure to include a couple of blueberry muffins in the selection, knowing it was Terry Piper's favorite flavor. Though he always complained that he shouldn't be eating so much sugar, he walked it off during his patrols with K9 and he hadn't put on any noticeable weight in the time she'd been running Auntie Clem's.

"What's your turnover?" Inglethorpe asked, looking into the display case.

"These ones are sour cherry, and these are blueberry," Erin told him, pointing to them even though they had clear signs in Vic's neat printing. "I have some apple turnovers in the oven, but you probably don't want to wait or come back for those…"

"Uh… that's not what I—"

"I think he means finances, Erin," Bella said, with a bubbly laugh. "What are your annual sales?"

Inglethorpe looked at the teenager in surprise. He nodded. "Yes, exactly."

"My… what business is it of yours?" Erin blurted before she could come up with a more tactful response.

"Just wondering what a bakery in this town can make."

Erin stared at him. Bella looked at Erin.

"Did Charley send you here?" Erin asked finally.

His eyes gave nothing away.

"Are you going to get something? If not, I'd appreciate it if you'd step aside so others can order."

"You've said for some time that there's enough business in Bald Eagle

Falls for two bakeries," Inglethorpe pointed out. "So I don't see why you'd have any problem sharing information."

"The only turnovers I'm going to talk to you about are these ones," Erin pointed to the pastries in the display case. "Would that be cherry or blueberry?"

He stood there for a minute looking at her. He looked back down at the turnovers. "I'll take three of each," he said finally.

Erin was surprised, but she just nodded and put six turnovers into a box for him. He paid for them without a word. Bella gave him his change.

"You have a nice day, now, Mr. Inglethorpe," Erin said politely. He gave a nod and walked out of the bakery. Erin shook her head.

"You handled that pretty well," Bella complimented. "You sure put him in his place."

"Well, I made a sale. I don't know whether he got anything out of it."

"Sure he did. He got six of those turnovers."

Erin forced a smile. "Which is six times what he was looking for, right?"

"That's right."

"He's got some nerve coming around here scoping out my business and fishing for information."

"He wasn't exactly covert."

Erin shook her head. "Well, I guess I'd rather he was obvious about what he was doing."

Willie was working, so Vic had joined Erin for the evening, and they were sitting in the living room with the animals, Erin making her lists for the next day and Vic paging through the weekly paper for any local news they might have missed. She stopped, staring at an advertisement.

"Holy crap."

Erin looked over at her. "What?"

Vic turned the paper around to show it to Erin. It was a full-page advertising circular for the opening of The Bake Shoppe, advertising "traditional baked goods, made the time-honored way your grandma made them, with no trendy or unorthodox ingredients." There were pictures of various kinds of baked goods, sweet cherry turnovers featuring prominently. The lineup replicated almost exactly the current offerings at Auntie Clem's Bakery.

There were a number of call-outs with notations such as "healthy foods, not health food" and "traditional family recipe."

Erin swore under her breath, making Vic giggle. Erin swatted at the newspaper.

"Take that away. I don't want to see it. In fact, it wouldn't hurt my feelings if you burned it."

"At least you know you're doing something right. She wouldn't be copying you so closely if she didn't think so."

"She mimics me and attacks me in the same ad copy! Who does that? I never did that when I opened Auntie Clem's."

"No, I know," Vic agreed, growing more serious. "You advertised your specialty and offered a free cookie or muffin for each customer. I remember."

Erin cocked her head. "You weren't even around yet."

"I was around. We just hadn't met yet. I went in, you know, and got a cookie from you."

"You did?" Erin was floored. "I don't remember that!"

"I picked a time when it was really busy, so I could hide in the crowd and you wouldn't notice me. Nobody really did; it was pretty chaotic. It was just you, working all by yourself, but you had a great big smile and were so friendly with everyone. I only went because I wanted free food. But I liked it," Vic ducked her head, turning a little pink. "I liked you. I thought you were cool."

"You never told me that! I thought the first time we'd met was that day I caught you at the bakery."

Vic shrugged and shook her head, getting still redder.

"Well, I'm just glad you decided to stay," Erin declared.

"Yeah, me too. I never would have guessed, when Aunt Angela turned me away, that things would turn out the way they did. That you'd take me in and become such a good friend to me."

There was a lump in Erin's throat. She patted Vic's knee, and sat back to look over her lists to make sure she hadn't missed anything, not wanting to get all teary.

CHAPTER 6

There was a knock at the door and Erin got up to answer it. She didn't look out at the curb to see if Terry's squad car was there, and she didn't look out the peephole. Vic was there with her, and despite all she had been through during her time in Bald Eagle Falls, it didn't occur to her that it could be anyone but Terry, Willie, or one of their friends at the door.

She was startled to see a stranger in a long, dark coat that flapped in the wind, along with long hair that obscured his face at first. Erin's stomach clenched, and her hand tightened on the door, preparing to shut it again and shoot the bolt.

The young man pulled his hair back from his face, fighting the wind, and gave her a smile.

"Hullo, Miss Erin. I'm sorry to bother you, but I wonder if my—"

"Jeremy!" Vic was on her feet and pushing past Erin to reach her brother. "What are you doing here? Why didn't you tell me you were coming?"

Jeremy Jackson gave her a big hug. "I didn't know how you'd feel about it, so I figured it was easier to get forgiveness and you wouldn't turn me down if we were face-to-face."

"Come inside, out of the wind," Erin ordered. She shut the door once Jeremy was inside.

"I wouldn't turn you down?" Vic repeated. "Turn you down for what?"

"Well…" He scratched his head, looking sheepish. "I'm looking for a place to stay. Just for a few days, while I get on my feet…"

"Sure, of course," Vic agreed immediately. "There's a fold-out couch. I'm not sure how comfortable you'll be—I don't have a lot of space—but of course you're welcome."

"We have the whole house too," Erin put in. "He doesn't have to stay in the loft. I'm the only one here, so you could have your own room with a real bed."

It didn't even occur to Erin that she had just barely gotten rid of Reg as a houseguest. Jeremy might be even more annoying than Reg had been. Who knew what bad habits he might have? But he was Vic's brother, and the only one who had treated Vic with tolerance and love, so Erin wanted to do something for him.

Jeremy laughed. "Two offers, when I wasn't even sure if I would get one. You're both so generous! Thank you."

"Come and sit down." Vic practically pushed him into an armchair. "Tell me why you're here. What's going on?"

Jeremy got back up to take off his coat, moving slowly. He was, Erin thought as she watched his eyes, coming up with his answer on the spot. He hadn't arrived with an explanation worked out and was stalling for time.

"I decided to leave the farm," he said finally. "I had enough of the expectations, so I thought I'd take a page from the book of my little bro—sister and get out on my own. Make something of myself. I decided I'm not cut out for working the Jackson farm. It's just not for me."

Vic's eyes were wide with surprise. "You always loved the farm. I thought if anyone was a natural farmer, it was you. You loved the animals and the fields and everything about it."

"Things change. I'd like to be something… more."

"Wow!" Vic sat back, amazed. "Who would've guessed!"

Jeremy glanced over at Erin and then back at Vic. "If you could keep this all on the down-low. I didn't tell anyone where I was going, and I want some time before Pa—before Mom and Dad know where I am. Time to think and figure out what I want to do with myself."

Vic nodded vigorously. "Of course," she agreed. "They'd be out looking for you and have you back there before you knew what hit you. We'll keep it a secret, won't we, Erin?"

Erin shrugged. "I don't need to tell anyone."

"You guys are awesome, thank you so much," Jeremy said. He let out a long stream of air. "I've been all wound up, worrying about it. Thank you."

"I'm so excited to have you here!" Vic exclaimed. "It'll be just like old times."

Erin laughed. "You guys are too young to have old times!"

"You're not that much older," Vic countered, "and you and Reg had old times."

"You're babies compared with me." Erin smiled at them. "So, tell me what you did in the old days. And what changed?"

Jeremy and Vic looked at each other.

"Just guy—kid stuff," Jeremy said. "Playing games outside with the others. Climbing trees, shooting, helping Pa on the farm. Vic and me shared a room, being the two youngest. We'd stay up late talking when we were supposed to be asleep. We played cards. Tried to scare the pants off each other with ghost stories."

Erin smiled. There had been few foster siblings that she'd been close to. But sometimes things just clicked, even though they had completely different backgrounds. Those relationships had always been temporary, fleeting, and she had no idea where any of them were anymore.

Jeremy looked at Vic again, soberly. "And then... I don't know what happened. We stopped talking. Around about tenth grade. Maybe I thought I was too grown up." He raised an eyebrow at Vic. "Was I a jerk to you? Did I act like I didn't want my little brother around anymore?"

"No, I don't think so. I just... was going through a lot of stuff. I knew you wouldn't understand."

"Well... I guess you're probably right. If you'd told me you were a girl instead of a boy, I probably wouldn't have been real understanding." He scratched his ear and looked down fixedly at a spot on the carpet. "Is that when you decided? When you knew...?"

"I always knew." Vic was looking at her big brother, blinking rapidly. It had meant so much to her the previous Christmas when he had visited her, and she knew that she had one person in the family who could accept her for who she was. "But that was when I decided... that I couldn't live like that forever. I couldn't keep pretending to be something I wasn't to keep everybody else happy."

"I must have had my head in the clouds," Jeremy admitted, "because I didn't have any idea. Not for a couple more years."

"It wouldn't have been safe for me to come out. I knew that once Pa knew… I'd have to leave."

"Yeah."

Erin noticed the time and started to gather up her papers. "The two of you can talk, if you like, but I need to get ready for bed. Morning comes early for bakers!"

Jeremy looked at the clock. "I guess you've got to get to bed early too, Vic. So…"

"Where do you want to stay?" Vic asked. "In the loft on the couch, or in the house with your own bed? I know which I'd choose."

"You wouldn't be insulted if I chose the bed…?" Jeremy asked tentatively. "If you want me at your place, I'll stay with you…"

"I'm here just as much as I am over the garage. I'll see you at breakfast. Actually, who am I kidding? You're not going to be up before the rooster. You can come over to the bakery for some lunch. Or I'll see you after we close."

Jeremy nodded. "Okay. And you're sure it's okay with you, Erin? I'm practically a stranger."

"No, you're not. You're family."

"And… your boyfriend is the cop, right? He won't… maybe it's best if he doesn't know I'm here. Does he stay over…?" Jeremy looked around. "Maybe I should stay with Vic."

Erin shook her head slowly. "No, he doesn't stay overnight. And he won't be by tonight, because he knows I'll be heading to bed." Erin hesitated. She looked at Vic. "Let me just walk Vic out…"

Erin and Vic walked into the kitchen, slowed, and stopped at the back door in the growing shadows.

"Is he in trouble?" Erin asked Vic. "If he's on the run from the police…"

Vic shook her head. "Not Jeremy," she said with certainty. "I know him, and he wouldn't get into anything serious."

"They're all involved with the Jackson clan, aren't they?"

"Can't help but be. But that doesn't mean he's done anything. He would have stayed away from anything real bad…"

"So, you think it's safe to have him here?"

"Jeremy wouldn't do anything to hurt you. And nobody but you and me are going to know he's here."

"I don't like the idea of hiding it from Terry."

"It's too late to make any other arrangements tonight. If you don't want him in the house, just say the word, and he'll come to the back with me. Tomorrow we can sort everything else out."

"I'm okay with him here tonight."

"Okay." Vic gave her a hug and left by the back door to go to her own apartment over the garage.

Erin armed the burglar alarm. She turned around and just about tripped over Orange Blossom, who had decided that if Erin was in the kitchen, it must be to feed him. He yowled when she stepped on his tail, even though she knew she'd just gotten the fur at the end and hadn't stepped on the tail itself.

"Oh, hush," she told him. "Jeremy will think I'm killing you." She got him a couple of treats from the can and slid them across the floor past him. He chased after them excitedly and gobbled them up. He looked disappointed when Erin didn't give him more or stay to play with him.

"All settled?" Jeremy asked, giving Erin a charming smile. "Do you want me in here or out back?"

"You can stay in here," Erin said. "I'll show you your room." She led Jeremy down the hall to the bedroom that had first been Clementine's, then Vic's, and then Reg's.

"This isn't your room?" Jeremy asked, looking around it with quick eyes. "This is the master, isn't it?"

"Yes, but I like the smaller room. Plus, I have a sewing room and the attic hideaway, so all in, I do have more space than you do."

"Okay. If you're sure. I don't want to be taking your bed."

"Sheets are clean. It's all yours."

"That's not what I meant, but thank you. This is very generous of you, taking in a near-stranger who just shows up without any warning. I really appreciate the help. I would get a hotel room, but…"

"You'd have to go to the city for that, there are no hotels in Bald Eagle Falls."

"Yeah, so I discovered."

Jeremy went into the bedroom. Erin stood in the doorway for a minute longer, wondering if she should ask him what kind of trouble he was in. Then she shrugged. It was none of her business. He would tell her when the time was right.

CHAPTER 7

$\mathcal{E}$rin returned to Auntie Clem's after dropping a platter of treats off to Naomi at The Book Nook for the Book Club.

"Okay, I wanted to get some more pastry sheets started for the new batch of turnovers," she told Vic. "You'll be okay out front for a bit?"

"It's quiet," Vic confirmed. "Nothing I can't handle. You'll be done before the afterschool crowd."

"Definitely."

Erin went into the kitchen and pulled the chilled dough out of the fridge. She set it on the counter, floured the rolling surface, and reached for her rolling pin.

Her hand hovered over an empty space on the counter.

Erin looked around, wondering if she had somehow misplaced it. It wasn't on any of the counter surfaces, which were gleaming and bare. It wasn't hung up on the utensils rack. She opened and closed a couple of drawers without any luck. Not in the sink. She even looked in the fridge and freezer, thinking she might have put it there absentmindedly, or in an effort to help keep the dough cold while she worked with it. There was no sign of it anywhere.

Erin went out to the front and looked at Vic. Vic raised her brows questioningly.

"You haven't seen my rolling pin, have you?"

"No. On the counter, last I saw. Isn't it there?"

"I don't think I could have missed it."

There were only a couple of customers there, and they hadn't made their choices yet, so Vic poked her head into the kitchen and looked around. She frowned. "Well, that's odd."

"I looked everywhere. A rolling pin doesn't just go walking off by itself."

"No, it would need someone with two legs to carry it."

A wave of anger washed over Erin. Vic immediately saw what she was thinking. "You don't think that…"

"Charley. Who else would it be? She decided she needed a rolling pin, and knew I wouldn't lend her one, so she just came over here and took it. I can't believe her!"

"I'm sorry," Vic looked around the kitchen. "I was out front when you went over to The Book Nook, and the back door must have been unlocked. I didn't hear anything."

"Sometimes I wish I had never found her!"

"She's your baby sister," Vic said. "You had to."

"Well, I'm not so happy about having found her, now. I'll be back as quickly as I can."

Vic nodded. Erin hung up her apron and exited through the front of the store, crossed the street, and went down to The Bake Shoppe. She tried the door, but it was locked. She banged on the glass.

"Charley! Open up! It's Erin!"

She probably didn't need to say who it was. Even if Charley didn't recognize her voice, she very well knew who was going to be looking for her. There was no answer. She was pretending not to be there, hoping that Erin would just go back to Auntie Clem's.

"I know you're in there! Let me in!"

Erin banged as loudly as she could on the glass. She didn't want to have to go all the way around the back. She knew from her previous visit to The Bake Shoppe that all of the stores were attached, and she had to go all the way down the block to get around to the back of the store. Chances are, that door would be locked too.

"Charley! Open up! You want me to call the police?"

People up and down the street were starting to pay attention to what was going on, stealing glances in her direction. Erin banged a few more times, but to no effect. She was going to have to try the back door.

She marched down the block, marching at an angry pace but taking care not to trip over the uneven sidewalk blocks. Around to the back of The Bake Shoppe. She stopped outside the door, her hand on it, remembering. The last time she had been there, she had spent hours administering CPR to a dead man. Not the best of memories. But she needed to confront Charley. Erin banged on the back door.

"Charley! I'm coming in."

She tried the door and found it unlocked. Swallowing her anxiety, Erin marched forward, composing her speech in her head. Charley was going to get a real talking to. Erin was done with being nice to her. She was done with being reasonable and explaining and trying to humor and help Charley. Stealing Erin's bakery equipment was going too far!

Erin stomped into the kitchen and stopped short. Her brain took separate, unconnected pictures. Flour smeared on the counter. A newly-purchased electronic scale. Erin's marble rolling pin on the floor, dirty and contaminated with who-knew-what. It appeared to be smeared with the red filling of the sweet cherry turnovers in Charley's ad. There was a sticky pool of the red filling on the floor. And there was a man, apparently drunk, sprawled across the floor.

Erin's throat closed as she looked at him, her breath whistling through the constricted pipe. A large man in a button-up shirt, spattered with the red pie filling. Balding, his face gray. She could hardly bring herself to look at his face.

Don Inglethorpe. What was he doing passed out in The Bake Shoppe? Erin supposed that he had gone there to meet with Charley. He did represent the estate that held the bakery in trust for Charley and Davis, so it would make sense for him to be there, checking up on the asset to make sure that everything was in order for the opening.

And where was Charley? Late getting to the meeting, Erin supposed. And Inglethorpe had passed out while waiting for her.

Erin had come for the rolling pin. It was on the floor. She bent down and picked it up automatically. Then the gears in her head ground and seized up, unsure what to do next. The part of her brain programmed with her schedule said that the next step was to return to Auntie Clem's to make the turnovers, like she had planned to do. That was the next thing on her list. But the problem-solving section kept her from leaving. The rolling pin was contaminated and couldn't be used in her bakery again. She would need to buy a new one.

And there was the additional problem of the man on the floor.

She couldn't just leave him there. She should wake him up, make sure that he was okay. But she couldn't bring herself to bend over and shake him. She'd dealt with drunks before. She knew that if she woke him, he might be angry and violent, and she'd have to be prepared to get out of his way.

She could just let him sleep it off there, leave him for Charley to deal with.

And then there was the little voice that told her Don Inglethorpe wasn't drunk and he wasn't going to wake up or be violent toward her.

Because, of course, he was dead.

CHAPTER 8

"Freeze! Hands up!"

Erin didn't freeze or put her hands up. She turned around and looked at Terry, not comprehending anything that was going on. He had his gun out, pointing at her in a two-handed stance. His eyes were wide, and his jaw dropped when he saw who it was.

"Erin!"

Erin looked back at Don Inglethorpe's body again. "I just… I was looking for my rolling pin."

"You need to put it down, Erin."

"What's going on here? What happened?"

"Erin."

She stared down at Inglethorpe's body, leaning closer to get a better look, feeling nauseated as her brain allowed her to absorb more of the details and to fully comprehend that it wasn't a movie, it wasn't an act or a prank, but that Don Inglethorpe lay dead in the kitchen of The Bake Shoppe, and she was standing over him with the rolling pin.

She looked at the rolling pin in her hand, not sure what to do with it. It was part of a crime scene. She wasn't going to be able to take it back to her bakery. Not that she could anyway. How could she use an implement that had been contaminated in her kitchen?

"Just put it on the floor, Erin. Away from the puddle, if you can."

She stared down at Inglethorpe, tasting acid in the back of her throat. It wasn't cherry pie filling. Of course it wasn't. Don Inglethorpe had been bludgeoned and she was holding the murder weapon in her hand. Someone had taken her rolling pin and had used it to kill the man. Charley? Would Charley intentionally implicate Erin? But why would Charley kill Inglethorpe?

Terry holstered his weapon. He ordered K9 to sit and stay so he wouldn't contaminate the crime scene. He walked over to Erin, reaching into one of the pouches on his belt to pull out a pair of blue gloves, which he tugged on over his hands.

He took the rolling pin out of Erin's hand and laid it carefully on the floor, away from the sticky red pool of what Erin now knew was not pie filling. His fingers closed around Erin's forearm in a gentle but firm grip, and he gave her a little tug.

"Come with me."

Erin's feet moved of their own accord, following his lead.

CHAPTER 9

$\mathcal{E}$rin was sitting in a car sideways, her feet out the door, as someone helped her to sip from a cold bottle of water. It was too cold. Erin shuddered, goosebumps raised on her flesh.

"It's going to be okay."

"I..." Erin looked around her, trying to orient herself. "What happened?"

"Drink some more."

"No." Erin pushed it away. She didn't want any more water sloshing around in her stomach. She didn't know what to do. She was supposed to be making turnovers. She would have to go to the grocery store and pick up a new rolling pin. It wouldn't be a good one, like the marble one that had been stolen, but she could work with a wooden rolling pin until she could get to the city and replace it with something of quality. "I need to get back to the shop."

"You're not going anywhere. Have some more water."

"I can't drink any more." Erin wiped her forehead, dripping with sweat, with the back of her arm. How could she be sweating and shivering at the same time?

"Maybe you should put your head between your knees. You're still looking pretty pale."

"What happened?"

"You fainted."

"No, I didn't," Erin objected, though she couldn't remember what had really happened. She was sure she hadn't fainted. She didn't faint.

"Okay, maybe you didn't technically faint. I don't know if you completely lost consciousness. But you... collapsed and you couldn't talk to me."

"Where is Charley?"

"We're looking for her. You don't know where she would be?"

"She's not here. This is her bakery and she's supposed to be opening tomorrow. Is it tomorrow?"

"She might have to put her grand opening off for a few days. Why did you come over here?"

"To get my rolling pin."

"What made you think it was here?"

Erin tried to recapture her mental processes. She was feeling disoriented, out of sync with the present. "Charley took it. So I came to get it back."

"Why would Charley take your rolling pin?"

"Why?"

She realized that it was Terry talking to her, not just a disembodied voice. She looked at him, saw him there in front of her, his face concerned, but set into that serious, no-nonsense expression he took on when he was investigating a crime. She looked down at her hands, encased in plastic bags. She wiggled her fingers to make sure that she was really seeing them and that they were connected to her body.

"We need to preserve any trace," Terry said. "Anything you might have touched in there."

"I didn't touch anything."

"Okay."

"I think..."

Terry waited for her to finish her thought. When she didn't, he raised his brows and prompted her. "What do you think?"

"I think... that was Don Inglethorpe in there."

"Yes, it was."

"And he was... dead."

"Yes. Not that he's been declared yet, but there isn't anything we can do for him."

"It wasn't something he ate."

Terry's eyes searched her face. "No. Not this time."

"Did she use my rolling pin?" Erin shook her head, angered. "That was a really special tool. It's marble."

"You're sure it was yours?"

"Yes!"

"Why would anyone take your rolling pin? Charley must have her own."

"She said people had stolen things from the bakery. It was fully-stocked when Angela was running it, but people must have taken things home when it closed down. They probably didn't think it would ever open again and no one would know the difference. Charley kept discovering that things that should have been in the bakery, weren't."

Terry nodded. "Did she borrow yours? Did she ask for it?"

"She asked for other things, but I told her no. They couldn't be contaminated with gluten flours."

"And you think she went into Auntie Clem's and took it anyway?"

"Yes! Who else would have?"

"Did you see her? Did anyone see her?"

Erin shook her head. "I went over to The Book Nook. The back door was unlocked while I was gone. Vic was in the front."

"So, anyone could have walked in."

"Yes. But no one else would have wanted it. Just Charley."

"Do you have a security camera?"

"No."

"We'll see who else on the block has one. Maybe we'll get lucky." Terry offered her the water bottle again. "Have another drink."

"I don't want any more water. Unless you want me to throw up on your shoes."

"Not particularly." The corner of Terry's mouth twitched, and the dimple appeared in his cheek. Erin wanted to reach out and touch it, but it wasn't appropriate. She *couldn't* be a murder suspect again. After all that had happened, how could she be sitting in his car, her hands wrapped in plastic, the central suspect or witness in another murder investigation? It couldn't be happening.

Sheriff Wilmot approached. "Scene's secure." He looked down at Erin, a fan of fine wrinkles appearing at the corner of his eyes. "You feeling a bit better, Miss Price?"

Erin wanted to scratch an itch on her temple, but didn't think she should with the bags over her hands. She might tear a hole and compromise the evidence.

"I… I guess I'm okay."

"You're still white as a ghost. But you're talking sense and that's an improvement."

"I'm just a little… it doesn't feel real."

Terry took her by the arm and touched a couple of fingers over her radial pulse. "I would think that with the number of bodies you've come across, this would be old hat."

"It's not."

He let go of her. "Why don't you tell Sheriff Wilmot what happened while I go get a collection kit?"

"Okay." Erin watched him walk away, feeling a little insecure. She wanted him to stay by her side and reassure her. She forced herself to turn to the sheriff, and started her description of having left Auntie Clem's to find the rolling pin.

"And why did you assume that Charley Campbell had it?" Sheriff Wilmot asked.

"She kept asking to borrow other stuff. She couldn't seem to understand that I couldn't allow any of my equipment to get contaminated. So, when I reached for it and it wasn't there… and I checked the whole kitchen and couldn't find it… I figured she had popped in the back door while I was at The Book Nook and took it."

He nodded. "Okay. Go on."

Erin told him about knocking on the front door and getting no response, then going around the back way.

"Did you cross paths with anyone else going from the front to the back? Anyone who might have been coming from this direction?"

Erin thought about it. She shook her head. "I don't think so. I saw other people on the street, but no one in the alley or the side street. But I kind of had tunnel vision. I might have walked right by someone without really registering it."

"Did you knock on the back?"

"I knocked and then tried the door. It was unlocked, so I went in."

"Tell me what you saw when you walked in."

Erin described the fractured impressions she'd had on walking into the scene. She shrugged, her face getting warm. "I just thought... I'd been thinking about cherry turnovers, and I just thought it was all cherry sauce."

He smiled. "Our brains do funny things sometimes, trying to come up with explanations for things that we don't want to believe. I've heard the same thing described many times. People who thought they had walked into a TV set or a prank of some sort. The victim was just pretending. Can you tell me what you did? What you might have touched?"

"Nothing. I didn't touch anything."

"Terry said you were holding the rolling pin."

"But it's my rolling pin."

"Right now, it's evidence. Where was it when you picked it up?"

"I don't know." Erin tried to replay it. "Just... on the floor. Near his head. Not in the... pool. Just to the side."

"Good. Why did you pick it up?"

"It's mine."

"But you know you can't touch evidence at a crime scene."

"I just wasn't thinking. That was what I came for, so I picked it up. It was automatic."

"What happened next? Did you see or hear anything that might have indicated someone was still here? Smell any perfume or body odor?"

The question triggered a memory, not of perfume, but the scent of blood. Even though her eyes had been trying to tell her it was just cherry pie filling, her nose had known that it was not. Erin gagged. The sheriff took a step back from her, getting his feet out of the potential splash zone.

"Sorry," he apologized. "What was it?"

"Blood." Erin swallowed, trying to settle her stomach. "Ugh. So much."

He nodded and spoke soothingly. "The door to the basement was ajar. You didn't go down there, or see or hear any sign of anyone?"

"No."

"Until Terry came in."

"Yeah."

"Tell me what he did when he came in."

Erin looked at Sheriff Wilmot, frowning. Terry had surely told him what had happened from the time of his arrival. "Um... he told me to stop. I think he told me to put the rolling pin down. But I was kind of stuck."

"Then what?"

"He told K9 to stay, he put on gloves, and he took the rolling pin away from me and put it down. After that... I'm not sure."

"I gather that's when he brought you out here and called for backup."

"I guess. I don't remember."

"Okay."

Erin saw the sheriff nod to someone outside of her field of vision, and then Terry returned. He put down what looked like a tackle box full of various swabs, packages, and plastic bags.

"You'd better take this part," he told Sheriff Wilmot.

The sheriff nodded. He put on a pair of gloves and removed the bag from one of Erin's hands. She watched as he swabbed the skin with several different swabs, putting each into a different container or bag. When they were sealed, he and Terry both scribbled their initials over the seals. Then there were sticky strips of paper that were stuck to Erin's hand, peeled off, and then preserved in evidence bags.

"How about this spa treatment?" Sheriff Wilmot joked. "A wash, a peel, and now I'm going to give you a manicure."

Erin laughed, but Sheriff Wilmot next scraped under each of her nails and clipped a couple of them back, preserving his findings in a small bag. He and Terry marked each of the bags and then repeated the same procedure on Erin's other hand. Sheriff Wilmot released her hand.

"You can have this back now."

Erin rubbed her hands together. "I'm done?"

Sheriff Wilmot looked her over carefully. "I don't see any blood or other transfer on your clothes, so I don't think we need to take those." He looked at Terry. "What do you think?"

Terry shook his head. "Don't think so. There's no spatter, nothing on her knees; I don't think she touched the body."

"I'm sure we'll have follow-up questions. We know how to reach you," Wilmot told Erin.

She smiled and nodded. The smile felt strained and unnatural.

"You don't know where Charley is, do you?" Wilmot asked casually.

"No... I'm sure she has a lot to do before her grand reopening. But..." Erin realized belatedly how everything she said had pointed a finger at Charley. "I'm sure... Charley didn't do this. She couldn't have. What reason would she have?"

"We'll look into that, I can assure you. We'll see where the evidence leads. But Charley will obviously need to be interviewed, just like anyone else connected with this business."

CHAPTER 10

*E*rin said that she was just going to go back to the bakery, but Terry wouldn't hear of it.

"Vic can manage on her own. You're not in any shape to be working right now."

"I'm okay. It wasn't that bad."

"Tell that to someone who wasn't there. Maybe they'll believe you. I'm taking you home. I'll pop into Auntie Clem's later, help Vic close up, and bring her home. You can spend the rest of the day cuddling with the animals."

Erin sighed. "Well, I guess. If you won't let me go back to the bakery."

"Nope. You need some quiet recovery time, not gossipy customers. They'll all find out what happened soon enough."

Erin closed her eyes for the few blocks back to her house. Terry parked the car. "I'll walk you in."

Erin suddenly remembered about Jeremy. "No, that's okay. I'm fine." She opened her door, jumped out, and was halfway to the house before Terry could get out to follow her. He stood beside his car, looking bewildered. Erin gave him a cheery wave and let herself into the house, swinging the door shut behind her.

She hoped that Terry would take her strange behavior as resulting from her traumatic experience and not be offended by it. She didn't want to push him away, but she didn't want to damage her friendship with Vic by betraying her brother to the police after promising to keep his presence 'on the down-low' either.

Erin moved away from the door and went to her bedroom, hoping that if Terry were watching, her movements would seem natural. She paused in the bedroom, watching his car through the slatted blinds until it pulled away from the curb. A moment later, she heard the door to the master bedroom.

"Erin?" Jeremy asked in a low voice.

"Yeah, it's me."

They both poked their heads out their bedroom doors to look at each other. Jeremy nodded and let out a breath. "What are you doing home? I know you started early, but I didn't expect you to be home before four."

"Oh…" Erin realized she was going to have to explain it to Jeremy, and wasn't sure she was up to it. "Well, something happened."

"Is everything okay? Where's Vic?"

"She's still at the bakery. Terry will drop her off later. Though now I'm not sure that's such a good idea. She should probably tell him she wants to walk, because if he brings her home, he's going to expect to come in."

"Terry is the cop?"

"Yeah."

"This is more complicated than I expected."

"A bit," Erin admitted.

He took a step toward her. "So, what happened? Are you sick?"

"No," Erin denied her queasy stomach, knowing that it wasn't the result of a virus. "I just… well this lawyer in town, Don Inglethorpe… he was in The Bake Shoppe…"

Jeremy nodded, his eyes narrowing.

"I went over there to get my rolling pin from Charley, but she wasn't there, and he was, and…"

"Who is Charley? She's the other girl who was with you when you came to the farm?"

"Yeah. My half-sister. She's opening up the other bakery, The Bake Shoppe."

"The other bakery?" he repeated blankly.

"When my rolling pin was missing, I knew she was the one who had taken it. Or I figured she was. So I went over there to confront her."

"And found Don Inglethorpe there instead."

"Yeah."

Jeremy waited for more. "And…?"

"I just… I guess it gave me a turn. I wasn't expecting that. Terry said I shouldn't go back to Auntie Clem's, but I should come home and relax…"

"This Don Inglethorpe… did you have a fight? Or you just don't like him…?"

Erin stared at Jeremy. She rewound the conversation, trying to figure out how it had gone off the rails. "No… he was dead."

At that, Jeremy looked staggered. His eyes got wide and he grasped the doorframe, knuckles turning white. "Who was dead? Don Inglethorpe?"

"Yes."

"What happened? Was he shot?"

"Shot? No. He was…" Erin suddenly couldn't frame the words. It seemed so brutal, so violent and intrusive even to say what had happened. "The rolling pin…" She made a little clubbing motion with her hand.

"With the rolling pin? He was beaten?"

Erin nodded.

"To death?" Jeremy checked, disbelief in his voice.

She nodded again.

Jeremy swore. He reached out a hand toward Erin. "Are you okay? No wonder the cop told you not to go back to work. You discovered this guy?"

"Uh-huh."

He used both hands to push his shaggy blond hair back from his face. It was strange to see him so serious, when she had usually only seen him smiling and laughing. "I should do something," Jeremy mused, talking to himself. "Should I get you a drink? Tea?"

"Actually, tea does sound good." Usually it was Adele or Vic who made Erin tea, if she wasn't the one making it. She wasn't sure what she thought of the tall young man rattling around her kitchen.

"Tea," Jeremy agreed. "That's what my mom would say." He went into the kitchen.

Erin followed him and when he started opening and closing drawers and cupboards, indicated the proper cupboard.

"Ah," Jeremy pulled down a tin of assorted teas and handed it to Erin. "Pick out what you like. There's the kettle. I'll get the water on."

He talked like he was coaching himself, giving himself the steps one at a time. Erin pictured Mrs. Jackson trying to teach her sons some civility, walking them through various little services, drilling them on what they would do in different circumstances. *What do you do if someone is ill? What do you do if they've had bad news? How do you make a cup of tea for a lady?*

Jeremy's hand hovered over the teacups in the same cupboard as the teas and service. "Do you have a favorite? Which one do you want?"

"The blue one," Erin suggested, selecting a cup with a wide, shallow bowl. It would cool more quickly than a deeper cup, so she'd be able to drink it sooner.

Jeremy took the cup carefully down from the shelf. He took down the tea tray and lifted the lid from the sugar bowl to make sure it was filled. "Do you want milk? Cream?"

"No. Just sugar is fine."

He started to take the tray over to the kitchen table, then hesitated, listening to his mother's unheard prompts in his ear. "Do you want to take it in here? Or the parlor? Or do you want to lie down?"

"Here is good, Jeremy. You're doing just fine, thank you. I appreciate it."

She selected a ginger tea from the tin and put the rest back away. Then she sat down at the table to give Jeremy a chance to finish his service without interference. They waited for the kettle to boil.

Orange Blossom came into the kitchen, sniffing the air and looking at Erin with confusion, clearly wondering what she was doing home already. He meowed loudly a couple of times, demanding an explanation and soothing words and pats from Erin.

"Silly kitty," she told him. "You should just be happy mommy is home early!"

Jeremy watched her with the vocal cat. "You have a very loud cat," he told her.

"Oh, you noticed, did you?"

"He doesn't like closed doors."

Erin laughed. "No, he doesn't. He wants to know everything that is going on in this house. Curious as a cat." She scratched the cat's ears. "Were you giving Jeremy a hard time, Blossom? You should be a nice boy. Let him sleep!"

"I was afraid the neighbors were going to be coming over to see what was wrong. He's like an alarm bell!"

"Well, at least you can be assured that it wouldn't be the first time one of the neighbors complained about him being too loud. It's a regular occurrence. Not just because you're here."

"Well, that's good," Jeremy agreed.

Erin watched him pour boiling water into the teapot, and then he placed it before her.

"There you go. Would you like anything else?" He looked around the kitchen, evaluating. "A cookie?" He moved toward the cookie jar.

"Uh, no. Those are dog biscuits, actually." Erin poured water into her cup and swirled the teabag around.

"Dog biscuits. Well, I guess it's a good thing I didn't help myself to one for breakfast. But you don't have a dog, do you?"

"No. Terry does."

"Oh, right. I remember that whole thing at Christmas. K9, right? He's recovered from his experience?"

Erin nodded. "He's just fine. No ill effects."

She grew self-conscious under Jeremy's gaze. She motioned to the tea. "Help yourself to a cup. Don't make me drink alone."

He hesitated.

"Or if you do want a cookie, there are some in the freezer."

Jeremy gave a sheepish grin and went over to the fridge. He opened the freezer door. There was always plenty of baking in Erin's freezer. He looked over the variety. "Is there something particular I should have?"

"Anything in there is fair game. In case you forgot, I run a bakery. There are always leftovers."

He looked through the zip-sealed freezer bags and settled on a couple of chocolate chip cookies.

"Put them in the microwave for thirty seconds," Erin advised. "They'll be just right."

He put them on a small plate and followed her directions. When the microwave beeped, he sat down across the table from her to eat.

CHAPTER 11

*E*rin should have known that word of the murder and Erin's part in finding the body would get around town before Vic even got home. The doorbell rang shortly after she had finished her tea and Jeremy ducked back into the bedroom while Erin went to answer it.

It was Adele, Erin's friend and official groundskeeper of the woods on the property Erin had inherited from Clementine, including the summer cottage Adele resided in. Adele had needed somewhere to live, and Erin had needed someone to keep an eye on happenings in the woods, so it was a mutually beneficial relationship. Erin had grown closer to the tall, reserved woman over the previous few months.

"Hi, come on in."

Adele accepted the invitation. Her eyes went to the kitchen, then around the living room. Erin had a feeling Adele picked up on a lot more than she gave away. Adele sat down in one of the chairs, her back straight and stiff.

"Are you okay, Erin? I heard... I thought I'd come and see if there's anything you need."

"I'm okay. Everybody is treating me like a china doll, but I'm really not. I don't need to take the afternoon off, and I can do most things for myself even if I did have a shock. I barely even knew the guy, so..." Erin trailed off, not sure what that proved.

"You've already had yourself a cup of tea," Adele had either seen the dishes on the kitchen table or had smelled the ginger tea, "and probably all you want to do now is lie down for a rest. You don't need to be entertaining company right now."

"I don't mind…"

"But you don't need it," Adele said firmly. "The last thing you need is a house full of guests."

Erin was careful not to look toward the master bedroom where Jeremy was keeping himself hidden.

"If you want to talk or need anything else from me, you know how to reach me." Adele rose to her feet.

"I'll be okay, Adele," Erin assured her. "Really."

"If you need anything, call. I'll be over here in a jiffy. Okay?"

Erin nodded.

Adele leaned in and gave Erin a brief hug around the shoulders, something she did not normally do. Adele whispered in Erin's ear, lips almost touching.

"Anything, okay?"

Having received Erin's text, Vic told Terry that she wanted to walk home, so it was a little later than usual when she arrived. Terry had helped with clean-up as he had promised, but it didn't go as quickly as when Erin and Vic were working together, following the routines that had become habit.

"Whew, what a day!" Vic dropped her bags on the floor and gave Erin an exuberant hug. "Are you okay? Let me look at you." It was a minute before she could take a look at Erin, as she was holding onto Erin too tightly and had to release her and step back. "You look okay. Did you end up being bored all afternoon? Or did you have a nap?"

Jeremy had come out of the bedroom. He laughed and gave Vic a quick squeeze around the shoulder. "Erin had me to look after her, so she's just fine."

"Oh, what did you do? Demand that she wait on you hand and foot?"

He raised his eyebrows, putting his hand on his chest. "Me? Just because I used to order my little brother around, that doesn't mean I'd do that to Erin! I even made her tea."

Vic gave a gasp. "Tea? You?" She turned to Erin. "Should I take you to the hospital now or later?"

Erin laughed and shook her head. "He did just fine. He was very helpful. Be nice to him."

"I'm always nice to him, aren't I, Germy? So, where's my dinner?"

"You'll have to make your own. I used up all of my domestic skills boiling water."

"I have the solution," Erin interposed. "Bread and jam."

"We *do* have frozen dinners," Vic said, their other fallback when they were too tired at the end of the day to make anything else, which was most of the time.

"I can't manage a full dinner today. I'm going for bread and jam. How about you?" Erin asked Jeremy. "You can choose what you want. There are frozen dinners in the fridge, or some leftovers from the bakery today. And we still have a few jars of Jam Lady jam."

"Can I have a dinner *and* bread and jam?"

Vic laughed. "That's my brother."

Vic and Jeremy mostly discussed their family and childhood over dinner. Erin listened in, appreciating a new window into her friend's former life. Vic normally didn't talk much about her family, and when she did, it was in relation to their estrangement and how they did not accept her transition. It was nice to hear more about the good times she'd had with her brothers, the fond memories of Mom's home cooking, and helping Pa with the running of the farm.

Jeremy was cheerful, his wide grin and laughing eyes brightening Clementine's kitchen. But every now and then, the smile dropped away, and he looked troubled. Erin could see the concern in Vic's eyes for her brother, but neither of them demanded an explanation. If he was comfortable with them, then sooner or later he would tell them what was going on.

Vic leaned back in her chair, sighing with satisfaction. "Now. What's the scoop on Don Inglethorpe? What are we going to do about him?"

Erin raised her brows, surprised. "Well, since he's dead, there's not much we can do to help him."

"Except bring his killer to justice. Isn't that your other specialty?"

"No, absolutely not. I told you, I'm not a detective. Leave the investigating to Terry."

"Terry's not going to be able to investigate it. Not when *you* were discovered standing over the body with the murder weapon. He's going to have to bow out of this one too."

Jeremy looked back and forth at them, as if watching a tennis game. "Uh, exactly how many murder investigations has he had to bow out of because you were a suspect?"

"Only one!"

"He investigated the previous ones," Vic said, "since they weren't a couple yet for those ones."

"This sweet thing?" Jeremy gestured to Erin. "What is this, a Steven King novel? The baking serial killer?"

"I didn't kill anyone. I was just... suspect for reasons beyond my control."

"Why did you pick up the rolling pin?" Vic demanded. "That seems like just about the stupidest thing you could have done. You know not to touch evidence."

Erin felt her face flush. "I wasn't exactly thinking. I'd gone there to get the rolling pin, and when I got there, I was so shocked, I couldn't really understand what was going on, and I just picked it up automatically. It wasn't even conscious, really."

"You're lucky you do have friends in the police department, or you would have spent the night in a jail cell for sure."

Erin frowned, but she wasn't thinking about spending the night in jail. "Whoever did it must have gotten blood on them. There was..." she choked, "a *lot* of blood on the scene."

"I thought he was beaten," Jeremy said.

"Yes... but there was a lot of blood." Erin swallowed and tried not to think too much about the scene she had stumbled into.

"Head wounds always bleed like the dickens," Vic said. "The scalp has lots of blood vessels close to the surface. I would guess something like a rolling pin would break the skin pretty easily." She cut her eyes toward Erin. "I don't know whether he was just hit once, or more than that."

"It's a marble rolling pin," Erin told Jeremy, not answering Vic's implied question about how many times Inglethorpe had been hit. "It's heavy and hard and the ends have sharpish edges."

She could see him revising his opinion. Not just a light wooden or plastic rolling pin. An implement that could do some real damage. A deadly weapon, wielded by the right person. He nodded seriously.

"Yeah, okay, I guess I can see that."

Vic leaned forward. "But who do you think did it? You think it was Charley?"

"I... I guess that must be what everyone is thinking, but what motive would Charley have to kill him?"

"It was in her shop. Who else had access?"

"The back door was unlocked. Just like ours was. Anyone could have walked in. Someone stole my rolling pin, and someone walked into The Bake Shoppe and killed him."

"You make it sound like a frame-up," Jeremy contributed. "Do you think someone was intentionally trying to implicate you?"

Vic frowned and nodded. "Yeah, why else would they bother to take a rolling pin from our kitchen? Why not just use a frying pan or something else handy at The Bake Shoppe?"

Erin hadn't thought about that, but they did have a point. "Unless it was Charley who stole the rolling pin, like we originally thought, so it was handy at the scene."

"Where did Charley go? Why wasn't she there? I would think that with the grand reopening, she would have been busy baking and getting everything arranged."

"I don't know. No idea where she went. The police were looking for her. Maybe they'll know something else by morning."

"You don't think anything happened to her?" Jeremy asked. "That she was kidnapped, or she was hurt too?"

"Charley can take care of herself," Erin said, hoping it was true and looking at Vic to see what her thoughts were. "She had a gun and she knew how to use it."

"A gun isn't always a protection," Jeremy said.

"Why would anyone do anything to hurt Charley?"

"Why would anyone do anything to hurt Don Inglethorpe?" Vic countered.

They were all silent. Erin had to confess she didn't know too much about Inglethorpe or who would have a motive to kill him.

"Who was he?" Jeremy asked, in the dark about Bald Eagle Falls affairs.

"A lawyer, like most of the Inglethorpes," Vic told him. "Old money. Lots of history in these hills. He was one of the lawyers who made the decisions on Trenton Plaint's estate, right Erin?" Vic looked at her for confirmation.

Erin nodded. Jeremy would know who Trenton Plaint was, since the Plaints and the Jacksons were cousins.

"The Bake Shoppe was part of the estate," Vic resumed speaking to Jeremy. "The estate hadn't been settled or distributed or whatever you call it yet, so these lawyers were the ones who decided what to do with the assets until it was."

"It was to be split between two people," Erin supplemented. "When Trenton died, that just left his brother Davis, but if it can be proven that Davis conspired to kill Trenton, he won't be able to inherit it. But then we discovered Charley Campbell, a sister neither of them knew they had. Charley is the one who was living in Moose River and working for the Dysons, not knowing she was actually born into the Jackson clan."

"So there *is* a connection between Inglethorpe and Charley."

"Yes, but…" Vic looked at Erin. "Originally, the lawyers said that Charley couldn't reopen Aunt Angela's bakery. They were just going to hold it as an asset until who was going to inherit the estate was settled. But Charley wanted to open the bakery."

"She said it was losing value if it just sat there closed," Erin agreed, "and eventually, she managed to convince them."

Vic drummed her fingers on the table. "Don Inglethorpe was the swing vote."

"What does that mean?" Jeremy asked.

"He originally voted *against* opening the bakery. So, it was two-one against. But Charley was able to talk him into changing his vote. If it weren't for him, she wouldn't have been able to open the bakery again. It would have just sat there empty, waiting for some resolution of whether Davis could inherit from the estate."

"Then she wouldn't want to kill him. He did what she wanted him to."

"Yeah." Vic's eyes flashed to Erin.

Erin understood the look without Vic voicing it. "But if there was a business that might be damaged by The Bake Shoppe opening, then *that* business owner would have reason to be upset about Don Inglethorpe changing his vote," Erin said for her.

Jeremy look from one of them to the other. "You mean you. You'd have motive to kill him. And you had the weapon and were at the scene. That doesn't look good for you, Erin."

"They haven't arrested me yet," Erin said blithely. But there was a knot in her stomach. She could see how the police investigation would go. Terry and Sheriff Wilmot might not think she was involved, but when the evidence started to pile up, they'd be forced to act on it...

"Killing Inglethorpe might not change the way the trustees vote, though," Vic said. "Now it will be deadlocked, but Charley has already been given permission to open and has been getting everything in place so that she could. They won't be able to reverse their decision unless they both come down on the same side or they get a new tie-breaker who votes against reopening The Bake Shoppe at the eleventh hour. Charley is still going to be able to open the bakery, whether Don Inglethorpe is alive or dead."

Erin blew out her breath. "Yeah, you're right. Me killing him wouldn't change anything."

"Unless you just wanted revenge," Jeremy suggested. "You were mad at him for changing his vote, so you killed him, even though it wouldn't change anything."

"I wouldn't do that!" It occurred to Erin belatedly that she hadn't said earlier that she wouldn't kill Inglethorpe to keep The Bake Shoppe closed either.

"We know you didn't kill him," Vic said firmly. "We're just talking about the evidence. *Somebody* killed him. He didn't bludgeon himself to death."

"The police will sort it out," Erin said. She wasn't going to get involved. She was just going to let justice take its course and not interfere. She wasn't going to get in the way of the investigation or put herself or anyone in her circle of friends into harm's way.

Not this time.

CHAPTER 12

*E*rin was back at Auntie Clem's bright and early as usual the next day. She knew she was going to have to deal with an increase in gossip and curious questions for a few days. Until some other news took over, like an engagement or elopement. In the meantime, it would bring her an increase in revenue, as people had to cover their curiosity with purchases from the bakery. No one would want to look like the only reason they had gone to Auntie Clem's in the first place was just to gawk at the murder suspect.

There was a method of increasing revenue that Erin hadn't considered when she was making her lists. Putting herself at the center of yet another murder investigation. If she kept doing that every few months...

Erin chuckled.

Vic glanced over at her with an eyebrow raised.

Erin shook her head. "You don't want to know."

They had everything freshly baked and out in the display case when it was time to turn the sign to 'open' and unlock the front door. As usual, there were a few customers already outside, ready to get their morning muffin or Danish on the way to work. Early mornings were one of the busiest times of day.

Erin was surprised to see Mrs. Foster with Peter and the young girls as part of the morning rush. Usually, Mrs. Foster dropped the older children at school first so that she only had to deal with little Traci while she was at the bakery. The Foster children were normally well-behaved while at the bakery, but were always excited and eager to get treats, and Mrs. Foster was much more relaxed if she didn't have to deal with all of them in the chaos of the morning rush.

Erin was trying to deflect questions from a couple of other regulars about the Don Inglethorpe situation. Mrs. Foster's eyes widened as she took in the questions. It was obvious she hadn't yet heard of the murder and was not one of those who had come for the sole purpose of getting the latest gossip and talking to the prime suspect. Erin saw Mrs. Foster's panicked look at her children. She couldn't clap her hands over the ears of all of them at once, and there was no way she was getting them back out of the bakery once they were in. Not without their cookies.

"Uh…" Erin fumbled to dam the flow of the conversation. "It's really not the best time."

Mrs. Urquhart looked at Erin with a frown, not understanding why Erin was trying to stop them from talking. "Whatever do you mean? I was just asking—"

"Little pitchers," Vic interrupted. She made a nod toward the children. "Li'l pitchers got big ears."

Mrs. Urquhart turned around slightly and saw Mrs. Foster's little brood. She patted at her cheeks. "Oh, dear. Of course." She gave Erin a little nod. "We will have to talk later," she said conspiratorially.

She and the other ladies quieted to whispers and the children waited impatiently for their turns at the counter without being any the wiser. As they discussed the options with each other, pointing and pressing their noses and fingers to the glass of the display case, Mrs. Foster gave a relieved nod to Erin and Vic.

"I had no idea," she whispered.

"Sorry about that!" Erin apologized.

"No, it's not your fault. I just don't want them hearing…" She looked at Peter in particular, Erin's best and most loyal fan. Erin got the feeling that not only did Mrs. Foster not want the children to hear any of the grisly details of Inglethorpe's death, but she didn't want Peter to hear that Erin was a suspect in the murder. He would find out soon enough that his heroes were not perfect.

"Mom, can I have two things?" Peter asked hopefully.

"No, Peter, you know better. Just one."

"I was just thinking that since I'm sleeping over at Bobby's tomorrow night, maybe I could have a muffin for breakfast. Bobby's dad usually makes pancakes, and they won't be safe for me."

Peter was an expert negotiator, and it wasn't long before he'd talked his mother into a cookie, a muffin, pizza shells for their dinner, and bagels that had something to do with a social studies project at school. Erin couldn't help grinning as Vic rang it up.

Mrs. Foster rolled her eyes. "That boy will be the death of me!" Then she flushed. "Oh! I shouldn't have said that, I'm sorry…"

As she herded the children out of the shop, Erin could hear Peter demanding to know what she was sorry about.

Later in the morning, Vic had whispered to Erin that Charley was back in town, but they didn't see her until it was almost closing time. After the after-school and supper rush had faded to a trickle, Charley slipped in the door, looking up in irritation at the jingle of the bells as if they had just announced her visit to the whole town.

"Charley! How are you? Is everything… okay?"

Charley's usually fresh face was drawn with fatigue. "Ugh. I just spent most of the day talking to your beloved and the rest of the police department. I wouldn't recommend it as entertainment, by the way."

Erin's face heated at the mention of Terry in such a flippant way. She was surprised that Terry would be involved in the investigation in any way with Erin as a potential suspect. She wouldn't have thought he'd be questioning Charley. Maybe that meant that they had ruled Erin out as a suspect, so Terry was not conflicted.

"Well, they didn't put you in jail," Erin said. "That's a good sign, right?"

"They didn't put you in jail either, and you were the one who was caught with the murder weapon in your hand. They tried ten ways to Sunday to stick a motive on me, but I didn't have any reason to kill Don. Having someone killed in my store doesn't mean I'm guilty." She looked at Erin. "As you well know."

"No, of course not."

Charley sat down in one of the chairs at the front of the shop. "I don't suppose you could bring me a cookie and a cup of tea, could you? I'm just so wiped out."

"Sure, of course," Erin agreed. "Chocolate chip?"

"Molasses?"

Erin nodded and got a cookie out for Charley. The teakettle was warm, so it didn't take long for it to come back to a boil. A few minutes later, Charley was sipping her tea. Erin suspected that Charley wanted her to sit down for a chat, but she didn't have time so close to closing. There were always a few last-minute customers who were trying to squeeze their errands in before closing time. Then Vic and Erin would need to clear out the display case, wipe everything down, and clear the till.

Vic was already in the kitchen preparing batters and doughs for the next day's offerings. They would turn out better if allowed to soak overnight and it would help them get the baking in the oven more quickly in the morning.

Erin served the final stragglers and turned the door sign to 'closed.' Charley was still at the table. Erin didn't rush her out. If she needed to talk about what had happened, Erin was curious enough to listen.

"You want to come to the back while we finish up? Or do you just want some quiet time to think?"

Charley got up, picking up her teacup to return it to Erin. "If *you* want to talk," she said, as if Erin were insisting upon it. She sighed loudly when she chose one of the kitchen stools and sat down.

"You're okay?" Erin asked, not sure where to start.

"Yeah, of course, I'm made of pretty stern stuff. But it was just a bit too much like being questioned after Bobby died... I kept thinking they were going to put the cuffs on and take me away. I'll tell you, I did not enjoy my time in those lovely digs."

Charley had only been jailed for a few days before bail was granted, and she had never said much to Erin about what it had been like.

"Well, you're still free, so at least I don't have to look after Iggy."

Charley's pet, Iggy, was not a cuddly kitten or puppy, but a chameleon. While Erin was impressed with how quickly he could tongue-zap a cricket, he still gave her the willies. Bugs and lizards were not her thing.

"I'll give him an extra big worm for you," Charley teased, her mouth quirking up slightly.

"Grrreat. Tell him it's from Auntie Erin."

"Why did you call your bakery Auntie Clem's instead of Auntie Erin's?"

"It was left to me by my Aunt Clementine. I just thought… it was a good way to honor her."

"Oh," Charley nodded. "Makes sense."

"You didn't want to change the name of The Bake Shoppe to something else?"

Charley grunted. "The trustees didn't think it was a good idea. Goodwill already established under the old name, people would be confused, blah, blah, blah."

"Maybe they're right. You want people to associate it with Angela and the bakery they were already used to going to, instead of thinking you're a brand-new start-up."

"If I can ever get it opened."

"You will. This might be a bit of a setback, but you'll still be able to open it."

"The other lawyers won't return my calls. I'm thinking that means I'm out of luck. They're going to change their minds and either liquidate it or just leave it sitting closed until it's not worth anything anymore."

"They wouldn't do that, would they?"

"It's a bad risk now. They're spooked. People won't want to go to a bakery where the last three owners have been killed, more or less. First Angela, then Trenton, then one of the trustees of the estate. People are superstitious around here."

"But you aren't asking them to become owners, just customers. People are curious. It will drive them there. You know how much more business we get when something bad happens? People want to talk about it, they want to see the place where something happened, they want to see and talk to the people involved. We've had a ton of extra business today because I was the one who found the body."

"Yeah?" Charley sat up a little taller. "I'll tell them that. Maybe that will help."

Erin was happy to help, but also irritated that she felt the need to. Did she *have* to keep helping her competition? Charley had just told her that she wasn't going to be able to reopen The Bake Shoppe, which would have been the best decision for Erin, and instead of simply commiserating and letting that decision stand, Erin was helping Charley to fight back.

She caught Vic's gaze on her and gave a helpless shrug. She just couldn't seem to stop herself.

Erin tidied away the washed and dried kitchen implements, putting the cheap wooden rolling pin she'd picked up at the grocery story away in a drawer.

"Did you take my rolling pin?"

Charley turned toward Erin, her expression a mask. "Why would I take your rolling pin?"

"I thought maybe you'd found that yours was missing, so you thought you'd borrow mine until you could get one. You asked about using some pans."

"I wouldn't just come in here and take it."

"Okay."

"So, who did?" Vic asked.

Neither of them had an answer for her.

"Somebody who wanted to set me up," Erin said. "They wanted to implicate me."

CHAPTER 13

*E*rin was glad to separate from Charley and go home. She tried to
love her sister, but Charley was abrasive, and they had little in
common. They probably wouldn't ever have become friends without a
family connection. Erin was ready to go home and stop talking about Don
Inglethorpe's murder. She'd had enough of it for one day.

"Hello?" Erin called out as she closed the front door behind her. There
was no answer. She heard Orange Blossom jump down from her bed, but he
was the only one who came to the door to greet her.

Erin picked him up and scratched his ears, listening for any other sound
in the house. Marshmallow lollopped silently over. Erin couldn't hear
anything else.

"Jeremy?"

There was no answering call or noise. Erin walked through the house,
putting Orange Blossom down in the kitchen, and went out through the
back door. Vic was just opening her door in the apartment over the garage.

Erin didn't want to say anything about Jeremy to Vic where a neighbor
might overhear them.

"Vicky?"

Vic turned around to see Erin standing there. Erin pointed back at her
house, then gave a dramatic shrug. Vic frowned. She opened her door and
poked her head inside. She went into the apartment, leaving the door open,

then came out again a minute later and shook her head. Erin waited while Vic descended the stairs and walked across the yard, apparently also wary of shouting anything that might be overheard.

"Did he tell you he was leaving?" Erin asked quietly.

"No. Not a word. I'll check my email and see if he left a message, but I did check it at noon."

"Come in for a minute. Or do you want to shower and change first?"

They both walked into the house and shut the door. Erin leaned against one of the kitchen counters. "Did you find out why he was here?"

"No. And I didn't push it. I figured he'd tell me sooner or later on his own. He just said he wants to get out on his own."

"Have you talked to any of the others? Did he have a fight with your parents? Get kicked out?"

"I haven't talked to them. Jeremy's the only one who's wanted anything to do with me."

Erin thought from her visit to the Jackson farm that the other boys just didn't know how to take the changes in Vic. They hadn't seemed antagonistic toward her, just awkward and uncertain. Only her father had been threatening.

"Is there one of them that you could ask? What if something happened to him? If we don't say anything, it might put him in more danger than reporting it."

"We don't have anything to report right now. He was out of the house when we expected him to be home. He's not missing."

"You don't think you should talk to any of them?"

"No," Vic shook her head with certainty. "He said we needed to keep it quiet that he was here. He's not just striking out on his own. He's hiding. And maybe there's a reason he's hiding from the others."

"If he doesn't show up again…"

"He will. Or he'll let us know where he is. We're not going to report him missing."

Erin breathed out in a puff, frustrated. But she knew what it was like to want to disappear. She'd pulled up stakes and left all of her troubles behind more than once. Or she had tried to leave all of her troubles behind. It had never actually worked out that way.

If Jeremy was in trouble, she had to assume he knew the best course of action to take for himself.

～

They were still talking when they were interrupted by a knock on the back door. Vic startled, then smiled. "There he is."

But it wasn't Jeremy who opened the door and poked his head in, it was Willie Andrews.

"Oh!" Vic jumped up. "Is it that late already?"

"I was expecting to pick you up from the loft. You aren't ready?"

Willie had cleaned up as much as he could, his skin always stained dark from his mining and refining activities. He was a rough-looking character, but always pleasant and happy to help.

"I just need a quick shower and change. Sorry, we got talking and I lost track."

Willie shook his head. "You've got all day to talk with each other. I don't know how you could have anything else to talk about at the end of the day!"

"My fault, Willie," Erin apologized. "I don't want to talk about all of this stuff about Don Inglethorpe in front of the customers."

Willie accepted this. "That makes sense. Murder isn't good for business."

Vic gave Erin an amused look, but neither of them argued the point as they had with Charley. Erin gathered Vic hadn't told her boyfriend that Jeremy was in town. Willie would have kept Jeremy's secret, but if he didn't know, there wasn't any way it could slip out accidentally.

"Have a good day tomorrow. I'll see you for sure on Monday," Vic advised.

They would likely see each other several times before then, but Erin was working with Bella on Saturday, and Vic was working with Bella Sunday morning, so they wouldn't both be at the bakery at the same time.

"See you then. Have a good weekend."

Vic quickly was out the door and hurrying to her apartment to get ready. Willie didn't follow her immediately.

"You okay, Erin?"

"Yeah. I'm fine, thanks, Willie. It's almost becoming routine stumbling across dead bodies."

He wasn't fooled by her bravado. "I hear you fainted."

"Don't listen to Terry. He lies."

Willie chuckled. "I am sorry you had to deal with that. Sounds like it was a pretty messy scene."

Erin tried to remain stoic. There was no need for her to visualize the scene of the crime, to think about what she had seen and the smell of the congealing blood. She put her hand over her mouth.

"Yeah, it was."

"You need anything? Is Terry coming over tonight?"

"I wouldn't be surprised if he stopped by, but no specific plans. I might just hit the sack early."

"Okay, well, take care. You know you can call on me if you need anything."

Erin nodded. "Thanks."

He backed up out of the doorway. "Lock the door and arm your burglar alarm."

"I'll arm it before I go to bed."

"There's a killer out there who is trying to send trouble your way. I think you should arm it now."

Erin gave a shudder. She hadn't thought about it that way.

"Okay. I will."

CHAPTER 14

*E*rin did arm the alarm and she did go to bed early, without Officer Terry Piper having come by for a visit. She knew he was on call and he had probably ended up having to deal with a nuisance report of some kind. She didn't hold it against him. That's just the way things worked when dating a small-town police officer.

The sound of the burglar alarm blaring woke her out of a sound sleep. Erin jumped out of bed, grabbed her phone, and crept toward her bedroom door, listening for the sounds of an intruder, trying to decide whether to go out to see what had set the burglar alarm off or to hide in her room and call Terry.

Was some crazed killer coming after her, disappointed that she hadn't been arrested at the scene of Don Inglethorpe's murder? Someone who wanted her out of the way and wasn't going to wait to see where the investigation led?

There was swearing and a male voice calling her name. "Erin? Are you home? I'm sorry..."

Erin hurried down the hall toward the alarm control panel without identifying who it was. She hit the disarm code on the panel and the alarm was silenced abruptly. Erin turned around to see Jeremy, his face bright red. She hadn't bothered to talk to him about the burglar alarm, not anticipating that he was going to take off—and then return at night without contacting her first.

She shook her head at him and went to the front door. She looked back and forth at her neighbors' houses. Mrs. Peach was looking out her doorway, phone in hand. Erin waved at her.

"Sorry! False alarm! Everything is okay."

The older woman nodded and retreated into her house, muttering to herself. Erin looked around for any other concerned citizens and didn't see any. She repeated the procedure, going to the back door and checking to make sure the siren hadn't awakened Vic. There was no sign of life in the apartment, all lights out and no movement that Erin could see. Vic and Willie appeared to be out. Erin wasn't sure what time it was or how long she had been asleep. She shut and locked the door, then turned to face Jeremy.

"The polite thing would be to let me know that you were going to be out, and when you planned on coming back. Or maybe given me or Vic a text that you were here, and would we open the door for you."

"Yes," Jeremy nodded vigorously, "I'm sorry. I should have done that. I should have let you know ahead of time. I just… I didn't want to disturb you. That was the wrong thing to do."

Orange Blossom wound around Erin's legs, staying quiet for once, but wanting to be close to her with all of the unusual activity.

"How do you even have a key?"

"Uh…" Jeremy hesitated, then opened his hand to reveal a key. It was narrow and looked as if all of the teeth had been filed down. "It's called a bump key. It's…"

"For burglarizing houses! Now I don't feel bad at all that the alarm went off! What are you doing with a bump key?"

"It's just…" he shook his head. "Sometimes you need to help a friend who has locked himself out…"

"I might be naive, Jeremy, but I'm not that naive."

His Adam's apple bobbed. "Uh…"

Orange Blossom sat back to wash.

"What are you doing sneaking in here in the dead of night?" Erin was still holding her phone, and she looked down at the screen for the time. "Well, maybe not the dead of night, but still. You don't just burglarize people's houses after they offer you their hospitality."

"I wasn't stealing anything, I was just letting myself in to go to bed. I didn't want to disturb you because I knew you'd already be in bed. I'm really sorry, Erin. Please, I won't ever use it again. I'll call you if I get locked out."

"I should turn you over to Terry."

"Yes." His voice was small, and he stared down at his shoes, looking like a little boy facing his principal. "You should. I should never have used this. If you call him, I won't run away. I'll face the music. Whatever you think is right."

Erin knew she wasn't going to turn Jeremy in to Terry, but she was not happy with him thinking that he could just break into her house instead of calling or ringing the doorbell. She studied his shamefaced attitude for signs that he was just dramatizing for her sake, and decided he was sincerely embarrassed and penitent.

"You won't ever use it again?"

"No. I'll call you or Vic, I won't use the bump key."

Erin nodded. "Fine, then. Where have you been?"

Jeremy raised his eyes from his shoes to look at her. He weighed his words, and she saw the mask come over his face. "If I'm going to be on my own, I'm going to have to find a job. A place of my own. Stuff like that. I'm not going to get anywhere just hiding out here all day."

So he wasn't going to tell her why he was really there or what he had been doing. Erin kept her eyes on him for a few extra moments, letting him know that the explanation didn't fly with her. She was not that naive. Jeremy lowered his eyes again.

"Find anything?" Erin asked.

"Uh… no, not yet."

"Did you try the General Store?"

"Well, no. That's kind of out in the open."

"The grocery store?"

"No."

"Where, exactly?"

"Just did some asking around," Jeremy said, with a hint of irritation in his voice.

"What is it you do? What kind of work are you looking for? I could help."

"I doubt you'll hear of anything as a baker. I'm not exactly looking for the same kind of job as Vic."

"What kind of job?" Erin persisted.

"I don't know. Bouncer at a bar. Courier. Something… not too high profile, but I don't have a lot of skills. Born and raised to work on the farm."

"There are farms around here. Maybe one of them would be willing to take you on as a farm worker."

"I don't want to work on a farm. If I wanted to work on a farm, I would have just stayed home."

Erin pushed a lock of hair away from her eyes. "Why didn't you?"

"You don't know what it's like to live there."

"No," Erin agreed. "I don't." She hadn't liked what she had seen of Vic's father, an angry, abusive redneck. And they were all part of the Jackson clan, which turned out to be a sort of Tennessee crime syndicate. She wouldn't have wanted to stay there. She would have wanted to get out as fast as she could. "What exactly are you running away from?"

"I'm not running away."

Erin waited.

"Vic is the one who ran away. I just… wanted to try something else."

"Vic didn't run away. Vic got kicked out. Did you?"

"No!" Jeremy flushed, as if Erin had suggested that he might also be transgender. "I'm not… I didn't…" He forced himself to stop protesting, and used a calm, firm voice. "Look. If you don't want me here, just say so. I will find something else. I mean, I'm going to anyway. If you want me out of here…"

"You can stay for now," Erin said, "as long as it's not going to get me in trouble to have you here. But I think I deserve to hear the real story at some point."

He shuffled his feet uncomfortably and didn't offer an explanation. Erin nodded to his bedroom door.

"It's bed time. Please keep me updated on your schedule."

He nodded obediently. "Yes, ma'am."

Erin scooped up Orange Blossom, and they each went to their rooms without another word.

CHAPTER 15

The bakery opened a little later on Saturdays. Bella drove in at the same time as Erin and they went in together. Bella had worked there long enough to know the routine, so she and Erin got started without the need for detailed instructions.

"I heard about Mr. Inglethorpe," Bella commented, looking sideways at Erin to see what her response would be.

"You and everybody else in a two-hundred-mile radius. Yes, I was the one who discovered his body. And yes, it was... horrible."

"It must have been," Bella agreed. "I can't imagine." She tucked her long blond curls into a net and put on her hat. "And is it true that it was done with... your rolling pin?"

"Yes. It's true. I mean, there hasn't been an autopsy completed yet, so we can only assume that was the cause of death. Either way... he was hit more than once with my good rolling pin."

"Ouch. Now you're going to have to get a new one."

"Yes," Erin agreed, smiling slightly that Bella's concern was for the rolling pin rather than the man. "I've got a wooden one for now, but I'm going to need a proper replacement. It's just not the same."

The light wooden rolling pin meant she needed a lot more muscle power to roll dough out, and it didn't stay chilled when rolling pastries like the marble did. A wooden rolling pin was fine for quick cookies.

"Who do you think killed him?"

"I don't know. I don't know who might have had motive. Do you?"

Bella pursed her lips as she considered the question. She had lived in Bald Eagle Falls all her life and might have a few more insights than Erin.

"He's not someone I knew really well. He wasn't mom's lawyer and didn't have any kids in school. Didn't go to church. Those are the people that we tend to know. I knew who he was, but I didn't really know him personally."

"You didn't hear anything about him? I gather he wasn't married?"

"No. But I never heard any gossip about why not. He just wasn't…" She shrugged. "I mean, he was kind of geeky, right? Not someone women chased after. So, if he didn't have his eye on anyone…" She shrugged. "Lots of perfectly good guys stay single."

"Was he involved in anything? 4H? Block Watch?"

"Not that I know of. He was a lawyer. They're always busy."

Erin nodded.

"I saw him with some out-of-towners last week," Bella commented. "He must take on files from outside of Bald Eagle Falls too."

"Really? Who did you see him with?"

"I didn't know them. Like I said, they had to be from out of town. A man and a woman. They didn't act like they were too happy. Maybe they got sued."

Erin nodded slowly as she flattened cookie balls onto trays. "It might be a good idea for the police to look into who he was seeing last week."

"I'm sure they're already doing that," Bella said. "They've got all of his electronics and his planner and everything. They'll be talking to everyone, won't they?"

"Yes. Of course. But they might not know that he had this fight with these out-of-towners."

"Well, it wasn't exactly a fight. Just… a heated discussion."

"It just doesn't make sense to me. I mean, Charley's right; she didn't have any motive to kill him. Unless someone can show that he had changed his mind about allowing the bakery to open. The one person who was negatively affected by the opening is me."

"But you didn't do it. So someone else must have a motive too. Maybe he screwed up on some file. Made someone lose a bunch of money."

"Yeah. That's a possibility." Erin sighed. Again, something for the police to investigate. Not something that she could find out on her own. "How does it work? Do most people get a lawyer in Bald Eagle Falls? Or go to the city?"

"Probably depends how big a thing it is," Bella said. "If it's just like a will or selling your house, why go to someone in the city for that? But if it was something big, you might want to go to a lawyer in the city to be sure. Or if it was something really specialized."

Erin nodded. Clementine had used a local lawyer. Angela Plaint had.

"What if a lawyer had two clients whose interests conflicted?" Erin mused. "That could happen a lot in a little town like this."

"I don't know. I guess they'd tell you."

"They'd have to, wouldn't they? They'd be in big trouble if they played clients off against each other or told confidential things about one to another."

Bella nodded vigorously. "That would be really bad."

"I wish I knew more. It's making me really anxious to think that there's someone out there trying to set me up. Somebody violent."

One of the first customers into the store was Melissa. Erin was surprised to see Melissa and Mary Lou together. Not because they weren't good friends, but because Melissa had been hanging out more with Charley lately, and Mary Lou had been more solitary since Roger's arrest. Erin couldn't understand why people were shunning Mary Lou. It wasn't her fault that Roger had gone off the rails. She'd been the best wife and mother she could be, but she could only spread herself so thin, and she couldn't monitor her ill husband twenty-four hours a day while trying to work to support the family and to take the boys to their various activities. She had done the best she could to get Roger the help that he needed before things had gotten so bad, but all of the professionals had said that he was fine. Erin was glad to see Mary Lou and Melissa together again.

"Morning ladies," Erin greeted. "Good to see you."

"I wanted to see how you were doing," Melissa said in a long, sympathetic drawl. "It must have been so awful for you, finding Don Inglethorpe like that. Just shocking!"

Erin nodded. Melissa did some admin work at the police department, and sometimes revealed a little more than she ought to.

"It was pretty horrible," Erin agreed. "I hope they're making good progress in figuring out who did it."

"Don't like being the prime suspect in another murder?" Melissa teased.

Mary Lou gave her a reproachful look. "Melissa! Really."

Melissa covered her mouth as if she were embarrassed, but Erin suspected she was enjoying the reaction. She loved to dramatize and be right at the heart of the action. That was, Erin was sure, the reason she liked to work for the police department. It gave her immediate access to anything exciting going on in town.

"I didn't mean to upset you," she told Erin. "I just meant, it's an awful predicament you're in, and if it was me, I'd want to solve the case and prove my innocence as soon as I could too."

"What did you want today?" Erin asked, turning her attention to the display case. She wasn't going to give Melissa's attention-getting behavior any mind until the woman started giving up some information. "Cookies for the church exchange?"

"Oh, I almost forgot all about that!" Mary Lou said, her eyes getting big. She would normally have made her own batch of cookies, but it had apparently fallen off her radar. It was less than twenty-four hours before the exchange, so time was quickly running out. "Oh, dear… yes, I think I'm going to have to go with bought cookies this year. I really don't see any way around it." She looked at Erin. "I *always* make my own. I have every year. But this year…"

"You've had a hard time," Erin said. "Give yourself a break. These were made fresh today. It isn't like they're packaged cookies from the grocery store."

"Store-bought are perfectly acceptable," Melissa agreed, though she had a bit of a smirk that told them both that she had already made or had plans to make her own.

"What would you like?" Erin asked Mary Lou. She helped her to pick out what she would like to take to the exchange.

When she looked up, Melissa was practically bursting, she wanted so badly to spill whatever news she had about the murder.

"And what would you like today, Melissa? Are you looking for something for breakfast? Dinner? You said you already have your cookies for the exchange tomorrow."

"Oh," Melissa looked impatiently over the baked goods on display in the case. "Maybe some of those cheesy pizza crusts for supper. They look awfully good. And a muffin for breakfast. Double chocolate."

Erin wasn't sure how Melissa could eat things like double chocolate muffins for breakfast and extra cheesy pizza for dinner and still maintain her figure.

"They've requested all of Don Inglethorpe's files for the investigation," Melissa confided, leaning closer but not actually lowering her voice.

"Have they? Do they think it was one of his clients, then? Something to do with one of his cases?"

"They've asked for everything, not just Trenton Plaint's trust. I don't think they know what it was about."

"At least they believe it wasn't you," Mary Lou said.

Erin nodded. "I hope Terry knows me at least that well by now. I hate it when he gets all suspicious."

"Well, I don't think you need to worry about that now," Mary Lou said in her most soothing voice. She gave Erin a smile that was just a little bit sad. Erin had her man looking out for her, but Mary Lou had lost hers. She'd lost him by degrees over the past few years, ever since he had lost an investment with Angela Plaint and tried to take his own life.

"Thanks." Erin gave a nod, but what she really wanted was to take Mary Lou by the hand and give her a squeeze and to tell her that everything was going to work out okay. And not just because that was what Mary Lou wanted to hear. She really did want things to get better for Mary Lou, but she had no idea how it would come out in the end.

"So, they haven't got the files yet?" Bella asked. "They've just asked for them?"

Melissa nodded. "Things take time. It's not all instantaneous like on TV, with warrants being granted at all hours of the night and police breaking down doors and grabbing files like it's a home invasion. They ask, and it takes time for the law office to respond, and they want to photocopy everything before it's out their doors, then the police have to actually go through every box and every piece of paper and decide whether it's anything that's helpful to their investigation or not. That's slow, tedious work, let me tell you." Melissa gave a little sigh, as if she had done it many a time and knew how very taxing it could be. In reality, she'd probably just transcribed a report of the police department's search of a file, not something that was very difficult at all.

"I hope they figure it out quickly," Erin said, "I don't like the idea of the killer wandering around Bald Eagle Falls free."

"It doesn't mean anyone else is in danger," Mary Lou put in. "There's no hint that anyone else was an intended target. Whatever Mr. Inglethorpe got himself into, there's no reason to think that any of the rest of us need to be concerned for our safety."

"Except for me," Erin said. "I was intentionally framed as his killer, so they must have something against me too."

"Must be someone who wants to open a third bakery," Melissa laughed. "Kill two birds—or businesses—with one stone."

Erin thought about that, but there didn't seem to be any merit to it. What was the benefit to anyone of closing down the two existing bakeries? Maybe it was someone who wanted to open a bakery for their own, but they must have kept their dream to themselves up until that point, because Erin hadn't heard any rumor of anyone else who wanted to open a bakery. Not unless Bella or Vic wanted to break out on their own. Erin looked over at Bella.

"You're not planning on starting up your own place any time soon, are you?"

Bella laughed, showing her even white teeth. "No, it's going to be a while before I've got the capital to open up my own business. And when I do, I don't know that it's going to be a bakery. And I need to get my degree first."

Erin shrugged at Melissa. "Nope, doesn't look like it. Unless you have a suspect."

"No, not me. I'll leave that job to the guys."

CHAPTER 16

$\mathcal{E}$rin headed over to The Book Nook to pick up her trays from Naomi. It was hot, as always, but she took a deep breath of the warm, muggy air and sighed. It smelled like home. She might not like the heat, but on a clear summer day, she could almost see herself as a child, walking to the river with her father to paddle in the water and pick up rocks. It had been a long time ago, but it was a happy memory of her early childhood, and she didn't have many of those.

So Erin just stood there and breathed and pictured it and felt the warm, happy feelings she'd had then. As she stood there, she saw a couple of people down the street who must have just had a fender bender. Both had stopped in the middle of the road and were getting out to inspect the damage and to talk to each other. Erin didn't recognize the cars or either driver.

The woman was blond, maybe around Erin's age, late twenties or early thirties. She wore a camouflage hat with her hair in a ponytail out the back, an army green t-shirt, and camouflage cargo pants with lots of pockets that made her look broader than she was.

The heavyset man wore a black t-shirt and blue jeans, a black cap turned around backward, and sunglasses which he had pushed up onto his head in order to glare at the woman who had rear-ended him. Erin couldn't hear their words, but their body language said it all. They were both confronta-tional, both of them sure that they were in the right and ready to defend their opinions to the end. Neither one was ready to back down. Physical violence seemed a very real possibility.

Erin inched closer, wanting to hear what was being said. Normally, little dings in Bald Eagle Falls didn't require any kind of police intervention. People apologized, traded insurance information, and went on with their lives. There were occasional bumps along the way, but no one was ever so confrontational.

As Erin got closer, she could see movement from the nearby shops as well. People pushing back curtains and opening windows to hear what was being said. People coming out of the stores and standing around trying to look natural, as if they were waiting for the bus or making a phone call. But all eyes and ears were on the man and woman.

Erin wasn't sure how close she could get to them. She didn't want them to think that she was somehow involved in the accident and bring her into the argument. Then she heard barking, and saw Terry approaching them from the other direction, K9 straining against the collar Terry was holding on to.

"Let's take a step back and cool things off," Terry suggested. "Everybody just take a deep breath. Looks like we just had a little accident?" He inspected the bumper of the man's car. "It doesn't look like there's very much damage."

"You should arrest her for reckless driving," the man growled. "There are what, two stop lights in this town, and she rear-ends me? She's a menace."

The woman was chewing a wad of gum. At least, Erin hoped that it was gum and not tobacco. She couldn't understand anyone chewing tobacco, but especially a woman. The blond woman was calm, her face was like a mask. She observed everything around her, completely detached emotionally. The man could rant and scream and threaten all he liked, and the woman would just keep chewing her gum and looking at him.

"Ma'am, you're the driver of the station wagon?" Terry asked.

"Yep."

"You were following too close."

She shrugged. "Apparently."

"Have the two of you exchanged insurance information?"

"She rammed me!" the man ranted. "She did it intentionally!"

"Do the two of you know each other?"

"No." He muttered something under his breath that Erin didn't hear, but suspected was along the lines of "thank goodness."

"And you think that someone you don't know would intentionally ram your car?"

"Yes! Obviously, because she did."

"I see. And why would she do that? Was there something that happened earlier? Something that escalated?"

"No, she just came out of nowhere and rammed my car."

"Okay. If you would come over here, sir, I'm going to ask you to fill out an accident reporting form."

He skillfully separated the two potential fighters, herding the man to the sidewalk where he could start filling out paperwork. The woman stayed where she was, watching them, chewing her gum like a cow chewing its cud.

Once Terry got the man going on his paperwork, he returned to the woman. "I'll need you to fill out your report as well. Anything to say? *Did* you ram him intentionally?"

"Why would I do that?"

Terry shrugged. "People's stories can be pretty outlandish when they're upset. You also need to fill out a form. Do you have your insurance papers?"

She walked over to her car with Terry and in a couple of minutes, had handed him whatever she had in the car. He copied down the information he needed and handed the papers back. He approached the man's car.

"Insurance papers in the glove box?" he asked.

"Stay away from my car!" The man came immediately to life. "I haven't given you permission to search!"

Terry stopped. He raised his brows. "I wasn't going to search it, I was just asking you about your insurance papers. Would you like to get them out for me?"

"Just get back."

Terry took a couple of steps back from the car. The man relaxed. He sat down in the driver's seat of his car and reached for the glove box, then looked over his shoulder at Terry, hesitating.

"Maybe I overreacted about all this."

"Maybe you did."

"If there isn't really any damage, maybe we could just each go our separate directions and forget about it."

"No, at this point the police department is involved, and I would like to see the proper paperwork filed. So, if you would get your insurance papers, please."

"I just realized I left them at home."

Terry continued to gaze at the glove box. "Why don't you just check? Maybe you have an old document in there that has the policy number on it. Then we can call the agent to confirm it is still valid."

"No, no. There's nothing in there. I just got this car. All of my insurance papers are at home."

"You need to provide proof of insurance."

"I'll call my agent, okay? He'll confirm it to you. Fax or scan you a copy. Then we can get on our way. If you really think you need to go through with this. I think we can just chalk it up as lesson learned and be on our way."

"Do you have proof of valid registration?"

"I have my plate and stickers."

"But no registration papers?"

"Uh, no. Not here."

"You sure you don't want to check the glove box?"

"No. They're not in there. Give me a ticket, if the plates aren't enough."

Erin leaned against a power pole, getting tired of standing in one place. But she didn't want to make any movement to draw attention to herself. She kept waiting for Terry to insist on searching the car or at least seeing what was in the glove box, but it became apparent that he didn't have enough cause to insist on it.

"If you'll finish your statement and track down a copy of your insurance for me then, please. I'll take a look at your driver's license while you're doing that."

The man sighed and pulled his wallet out of the back pocket of his pants. He slid out his driver's license and handed it to Terry, then went back to writing out his witness statement.

The woman was writing her statement and had given no sign that she was listening to the rest of the conversation going on between Terry and the male driver. But when neither of them was talking, she looked up, scanning the area. She met Erin's eyes, then looked away again, deciding Erin wasn't anyone important. She continued to chew.

Eventually, both of the strangers had filled out their paperwork to

Terry's satisfaction, and far from wanting to have a fight with each other, they were both eager to just get back into their cars and, presumably, out of Bald Eagle Falls.

Terry watched them both drive away, and then resumed his patrol with K9. K9 had seen Erin and drifted away slightly to go to her. Terry said a sharp word to bring him back to heel, then spotted Erin.

"I didn't see you there. What's up?"

"Oh… I was just going to The Book Nook to get some serving platters when…" Erin circled her finger to encompass the street and the cars that had previously been there. "All of this happened, and I just kind of hung around to see what was going to happen."

"Happy to provide entertainment."

Erin felt her face flush, but tried to remain nonchalant. "It was all very exciting. What exactly do you think he was hiding in his glove box?"

"Either a weapon or drugs. Or both. But he was determined not to give me any opportunity to find them."

"Did he have any warrants?"

"If he had, I would have arrested him and searched the vehicle. But he didn't have anything outstanding."

"Does he have a record?"

"Yes, he does."

Erin raised her brows questioningly, not asking the next question.

"I'm afraid I can't really share any of that with you." Which Erin already knew. "But suffice to say… I'm quite sure he had something in his glove box and wasn't just embarrassed that he'd forgotten his papers or that his cubby was messy."

From Terry's previous comment, she assumed he had previous arrests for drugs and guns. Not the kind of person they wanted hanging around Bald Eagle Falls.

"Why do you think he was here?"

"Hopefully, just passing through. I don't want to see his type hanging around here. We try to keep them moving right through."

"There aren't any major problems with drugs in Bald Eagle Falls, are there?"

"No. Not really. It's mostly confined to the city, and any of our people who go to the city to party or bring back enough for personal use. Not a lot of dealing going on, other than maybe some pot and prescription meds to school kids. Not the huge problems with meth and crack and some of these other nasty drugs that you get in the city."

"And we want to keep it that way," Erin summarized.

"Exactly. Walk you to The Book Nook?"

It wasn't far. Just half a block. But Erin didn't get to spend much time with Terry during the day, so why not? They walked side by side down the street, back toward The Book Nook and Auntie Clem's Bakery.

"You need any water?" Erin asked.

"Not yet. Might stop by for some later." They reached the front of The Book Nook. "You take it easy, right Erin? I don't want you getting involved in anything…"

Erin wondered what he was thinking of in particular. The murder? Covering for Jeremy? The two strangers having a collision in the middle of Main Street? She wasn't involved in anything. He was welcome to do the investigating, she didn't want anything to do with it.

CHAPTER 17

*E*rin thought all afternoon about the strangers suddenly showing up in Bald Eagle Falls. They didn't get a lot of tourist traffic through the town. A few people who wanted to stop at the General Store to pick up some homey novelty item, someone who wanted to explore caves or do some camping, but mostly Bald Eagle Falls didn't attract outsiders. Even though Erin had been there for a year, she was still considered a newbie. In some neighborhoods, she would be considered part of the old guard after a year. But in Bald Eagle Falls, anyone who hadn't been born there was considered an outsider. And even some of those who had been, if they moved away for a significant length of time.

Bella had seen two strangers arguing with Don Inglethorpe. Erin had seen two people arguing in the middle of the street, almost coming to blows over damage that was so minor Erin hadn't even been able to see it.

It couldn't be a coincidence. And if one of those arguing strangers was a drug dealer, then how had he been connected to Don Inglethorpe? Was Inglethorpe a drug user? Was he a dealer? Someone who was just curious? And what about the woman?

∼

Jeremy was there when Erin got home. In spite of her talk with him, she wasn't sure if he would be, or if he would again take off without letting her know where he was. He hadn't taken it upon himself to make supper, and Vic was likely out with Willie, so that left it up to Erin. Ordinarily, she would probably visit one of the local eateries on a Saturday night when she was by herself. Or she and Terry would go out somewhere. But with Jeremy there, she didn't feel comfortable just abandoning him to go eat on her own.

"You want to help with supper?" she suggested to Jeremy. "I'm not planning on doing anything big, but I wouldn't mind a hand."

"Sure, of course," Jeremy agreed. He went ahead of her into the kitchen and checked the supply of frozen dinners in the freezer. "I should have thought of it before. I could have had something waiting for you."

"No, you're my guest, you don't need to do that. I just thought that since you're here…"

He was competent enough in the kitchen, even if he was slow and seemed to always be consulting his mental record for how to do things. Like he'd been trained, but didn't have much experience. Erin suspected that his mother had given him instruction to make sure that he could get around the kitchen in a pinch, but that he hadn't had a lot of opportunity for building up his skills. He would have spent more time on the farm equipment than in the kitchen.

Erin was still thinking through the day's events and puzzling through what it might all mean.

"What reason would a drug dealer—or any criminal—have to be seeing a lawyer?" she asked Jeremy. "Not a lawyer representing him in court, but like a corporate lawyer."

Jeremy looked at her, frowning. "Why?"

"Just something I'm thinking of. Say a drug dealer. He's in town to see a lawyer. Why?"

"Just like anyone else, I guess," Jeremy said, still looking puzzled and slightly disapproving of the subject. "Maybe he needs a will or needs a company created."

"Would a drug dealer need a corporation? Like an LLC?"

Jeremy was chopping vegetables for a salad. He diced them small, frowning. "Not a small-time street dealer, no. But a bigger operation… they're sometimes built up to look like legitimate businesses."

"The lawyer could be helping him launder money. Taking it from his illegal business and running it through a company that does something else."

"Right."

"Like a bakery?"

"What are you getting at, Erin? Is this hypothetical?"

"Yes, of course. I wouldn't know anything about any actual criminal enterprise."

He looked at her, eyes narrow. "Where is this all coming from? You think there's something going on in Bald Eagle Falls?"

"Oh, there is definitely something going on in Bald Eagle Falls," Erin said with a laugh. "I just don't know what it is."

"What?"

Erin explained to him about the drug dealer and the collision in the middle of town.

"What makes you think this had anything to do with the lawyer who died?"

"I don't know that it did, I'm just thinking about possibilities. We don't get a lot of tourists through Bald Eagle Falls. What are the odds that a couple of strangers would be having an argument with Inglethorpe before he died and then a couple other strangers would be having an argument in the middle of town today?"

"It's possible. It could all be unrelated."

"You're right. I could be putting together two things that had nothing to do with each other. I just find it difficult to believe that they don't have something to do with each other. And if this drug dealer did have some argument with Don Inglethorpe, then maybe he had something to do with his death too."

"But why would this guy stay around? If you killed someone and you didn't have a legitimate reason to be in town, you wouldn't stay on the scene."

"Maybe..." Erin tried to puzzle it through. "Maybe Inglethorpe wouldn't agree to do what he wanted, so he had to get someone else to do it instead? Maybe he's here to see another lawyer."

"He's here now?" Jeremy looked toward the door.

"Well, not now. He looked like he left town after Terry talked to him. But that doesn't mean he's really gone. Or if he is, there's nothing to say that he can't come back or send someone else."

Jeremy nodded slowly. At a tug on his pant leg, he looked down and saw Marshmallow sitting up on his haunches expectantly. Erin laughed.

"You can give him a few veggies."

The tension in Jeremy's manner melted away, and he talked to Marshmallow and gave him the ends of the vegetables he'd been cutting up. Orange Blossom *mrrowed* and hurried over to see if he was going to get a treat as well, but when he discovered that all Jeremy had were vegetables, he hunched back and swished his tail crossly.

"Come here, Blossom," Erin called to him. He looked at her and didn't move out of his sulky pose.

"If you want a treat, you should listen," Erin told him. "If you're just going to pout, you're not going to get anything."

He looked at her for a moment, then got up and approached her. "That's a good boy. You don't think I'm going to forget to feed you, do you?" She opened the fridge and got out some leftover chicken. Orange Blossom immediately perked up, rubbing against her legs and purring loudly, letting out the occasional excited yip.

CHAPTER 18

*E*rin was happy when she heard the familiar knock at her door, but was also nervous about the fact that Jeremy was still there, shut away in Clementine's room. She had advised him that if he wanted to stay under the radar, he'd better stay quiet and behind closed doors while Terry was there. It would be pretty hard to keep his presence a secret if he decided to shower or use the commode in the middle of Terry's visit. Trained to be observant, the police officer might just notice.

"Hi, Terry." Erin accepted a kiss from Terry and gave his partner an ear scratch. "Hi, fur face."

K9 panted and sat back with a happy doggie grin.

"Long day today?" Erin asked Terry.

"Things do seem to heat up when there's a murder in town," he admitted. "Even stuff that's totally unrelated to the murder. It seems like everyone just gets a little crazy."

They sat down together, cuddling up with each other and then waiting while the animals made themselves comfortable.

"I know I saw you today," Terry said, "but I feel like it was ages ago. And I didn't find out how you are doing. I mean, if you're okay after finding the body."

Erin nodded. "I guess. I'm trying not to think about it, mostly. I didn't really know Mr. Inglethorpe and if I keep thinking about it, I'll make myself sick. So I'm just trying pretend nothing happened."

"Good." He stroked her hair. "I don't want you to be traumatized by it."

Erin tried to lighten the mood. "It isn't like it's the first body I've come across."

"No, but the violence of this one… the others were not so gory."

"But still violent. And when I think of poor Bertie…" Tears stung Erin's eyes all of a sudden. "Oh, I'm sorry. I thought I was over that…"

Terry hugged her to him. "Don't be surprised that this stirs up old feelings. That's normal. And out of everyone who has died, Bertie was the only one who was really your friend."

"Well…" Erin sniffled and reached for a tissue from the side table. "There was my father, too."

"I didn't mean *he's* not important. But it was such a long time since you had seen him, and the memories are pretty dim. With Bertie, though… that was very tragic, and right in front of you."

Erin dabbed at her eyes, trying not to cry in earnest. If he'd just stop talking about it, she'd have a much easier time staying calm.

"Have you talked to a therapist?" Terry asked. "It could be very helpful, after some of the things you've had to deal with lately."

"No. I'm fine. I don't need any therapy."

"It's not a bad thing, you know. It's not a show of weakness. It just means that you know you could use a bit of help to get through something traumatic or troubling."

Erin shook her head adamantly. "I dealt with enough therapists in the system. Now that I'm adult, you can bet that I'm never doing that again."

Terry didn't say anything, just stroking her hair. She had been expecting a fight, but not getting one, wasn't sure how to react.

"It's up to you. I'm not going to force you into anything."

Erin let her breath out. "Good."

"Just remember that everybody needs help sometimes, there's no shame in getting it when you need it. Whether it's counseling or something else. You don't have to do everything on your own."

She knew that she tended to do just that, insisting that she could handle anything that came her way all by herself. But it had been good for her to get Vic to help her at the bakery, and then Bella to help out part time. She had found that she could delegate and get others to do some of the work and not have to do it all herself.

"I know. Thanks."

They were both quiet.

"So how is the case going?" Erin asked tentatively.

"You know I can't talk much about it, especially when you are... a person of interest... but so far, we don't have a lot of leads. There are not a lot of people who had motive to kill Don Inglethorpe. Unfortunately, you are one of the few, with your livelihood possibly being threatened by him changing his vote to allow Charley to open The Bake Shoppe."

"There must have been others. Or something to do with his business. Bella saw him arguing..."

Terry raised an eyebrow. "I thought you were not investigating this one."

"I'm not... I just... people tell me things, because they know I have an interest in the outcome."

"I'll bet they do. Yes, it's possible that it was something to do with his business. An irate client or somebody he did wrong in setting up a deal or settling a lawsuit. People sometimes get riled up over the strangest things."

"Maybe he was laundering money."

Terry's eyes narrowed. Erin hated that look of suspicion and kicked herself whenever she saw it come into his eyes.

"I don't *know* anything," she told him. "It's just speculation."

"Money laundering is always a possibility. But we would need to show a connection with criminal enterprise. Organized crime. So far, we don't have anything pointing in that direction."

"And you don't think he's involved with this drug dealer?"

"What drug dealer?"

"The one today, that got into the fight. I thought that he might be one of the people that Inglethorpe was fighting with the other day. He obviously has a temper."

"It's quite a jump to the idea that he was somehow involved in something with Don Inglethorpe. You don't even know that he was a drug dealer. Because I certainly didn't tell you that."

"Well... not exactly, no."

"I didn't."

"Okay. You didn't say he was a drug dealer. But he sure looked like one."

"Things aren't always as they appear." Terry's gaze was steady. Then the dimple appeared in his cheek. "And sometimes they are," he admitted, eyes twinkling.

Erin laughed. She snuggled against him. "I just want it to be solved. I don't want to have to worry about it, and I don't want you to have to worry about it. I just want things to go back to normal."

"Normal for Bald Eagle Falls hasn't been normal since you arrived here, I'm sorry to say."

"That's just… an anomaly. I didn't have anything to do with any of the… increased crime. I'm just minding my own business."

Terry nodded. "I know you didn't do anything… except maybe ask questions when nobody wanted you poking your nose into their business. And that's not going to happen anymore, is it?"

"Do you hear me asking questions about anything?"

"Well, *I* do."

"But that's you and me, not anyone else. And you're not going to try to kill me for asking you how the case is going, are you?"

Terry nuzzled her hair. "No. You've got me bewitched."

"You'd better not say *that* too loudly. They'll burn me at the stake."

"I'm not on shift in the morning."

"That's good. You can take a Sunday off for once."

"And you're not at the bakery in the morning."

"Nope. Vic and Bella have it covered."

Terry didn't say anything. Erin turned her head to look him in the face. "What?"

"I was just thinking, neither of us has anywhere to be tonight, and neither of us has anywhere we have to be in the morning. That doesn't happen very often."

Erin started to grow warm. She searched his eyes for his intent, and then dropped her gaze. She'd been waiting for some time for him to make the next move and give her some sign he was ready to go beyond spending a few stolen minutes together or exchanging a kiss.

She wanted badly to pursue his suggestion to its natural conclusion, but all she could think about was Jeremy in Clementine's bedroom. If Terry stayed the night, Jeremy would be forced to reveal himself. Erin didn't know what Jeremy was involved in, but she had promised him and Vic to keep his presence there a secret. Especially from Terry.

"Erin?" Terry's voice was uncertain, clearly worried that he had misjudged the situation.

"Uh… yeah. You're right. We should go out for dinner."

"Haven't you already had dinner? You don't usually want to stay up much later than this."

"Well, yes. I did. I just thought you wanted to go out and do something, since we're both off tomorrow. We could… go into the city. Catch a movie."

Terry's eyebrows lifted, bewildered. Erin hated to do it to him. She wanted to be able to tell him about Jeremy being there so that he wouldn't think he had done something wrong or was on a completely different page from Erin.

"Sure, if you wanted to," he agreed slowly.

"I hear that new Marvel is really good." Guys liked action films. He'd be delighted that she wanted to watch one with him.

"Sure. Or something more… romantic, if you like." He tried once more to clue her in.

"You know what?" Erin rubbed the ticklish spot on Terry's knee. "After the movie, we could go back to *your* place."

Terry brightened a little, though he still looked thoroughly baffled. They never did anything at his place, Erin always preferred the space and comfort of Clementine's home, and since they never knew whether Terry would be able to get away to see her, she always let him come to her. She could see him trying to compute why Erin would want to go back to his house, on top of the already-mind-boggling suggestion that she wanted to go all the way into the city to watch an action movie instead of just staying in and going to bed at the usual hour. Erin was a creature of habit. He knew she didn't like unexpected changes to her schedule.

"Just stay here for a minute," she told him. "I just need to grab my purse, and a couple of things…"

If she didn't get up right away, she was just going to have to keep explaining herself, and that wasn't getting any easier. Erin hurried into her room. She pulled out her phone and texted Jeremy to fill him in on the developments. She would have to give him the code to disarm the burglar alarm, because Terry would insist she armed it before they left. If Jeremy didn't want to be stuck in the house until she returned, he'd have to disarm it.

Erin wondered if Orange Blossom would behave himself, or whether he'd start yowling when she left. He had been okay during the day, but he was used to her usual routine. If she left him alone at night with Jeremy, she didn't want to think of what might happen.

She threw a couple of overnight items in a large handbag and returned to Terry within a couple of minutes. Not long enough to be suspicious of anything.

"Uh, I guess I'd better feed the animals their bedtime treats before we go."

Terry stood up and watched her, not offering any objection or demanding an explanation, but she knew he had to be wondering what the heck she was thinking. She could give him a story about feeling funny about having him overnight at Clementine's house, but then she'd have to come up with an explanation for her change of heart when Jeremy was no longer there. It was better to just let Terry come up with his own explanation for her strange behavior.

CHAPTER 19

*E*rin stretched languidly. She knew that it was much later in the day than she would normally get up, but it had been a very late night too, and she knew she didn't have to be at the bakery, so she just let her body curl into Terry's.

There was a buzzing that seemed far away. She thought she should know what it was, but wasn't quite awake enough to connect her thoughts and be sure. Terry groaned and rolled over away from her. Erin made a disappointed sound, and in a few seconds, he rolled back into the warm pocket of blankets.

"What does your sister want?"

Erin squinted, opening her eyes just the barest crack to get more information. The room was too bright with morning sunshine and she didn't want to have to wake up the rest of the way. Terry held a phone out toward Erin.

"Reg?" Erin asked. She took her phone from him and looked down at it. "Oh, Charley. Right."

She hesitated, not really wanting to talk to Charley. She didn't want to let anything else break into their little paradise. The phone stopped buzzing and was still and silent in her hand.

"Oh, well," Terry said, cheek dimpling. "If it's important, she can leave a message, right?"

Erin nodded. Terry hugged her closer to him, his eyes suggesting that he was not quite as interested in going back to sleep as she was. Erin yawned. She knew she shouldn't be so lazy. They had the whole day together, something that almost never happened. Or it hadn't before. She might be insisting that they manage to coordinate their schedules better in the future.

Erin's phone started buzzing in her hand. She looked down at it. Charley again. She really wanted Erin. Maybe something was wrong at the bakery. But then it would be Vic or Bella who would be calling her, not Charley. Maybe the trustees had told Charley that she wouldn't be able to open The Bake Shoppe after all and she needed someone to talk to about it.

"Go ahead," Terry said, leaning back, putting a few inches between the two of them.

"I'm sorry. I'll be right back. Promise." She swiped the phone and put it to her ear. "Hi, Charley. What's up?"

There was a long blast of sound from the phone. Erin pulled it away from her ear and frowned, trying to interpret it. It didn't sound like a pocket dial. It sounded like someone's mouth was too close to the microphone and they were yelling or crying or making some other caterwauling noise.

"Charley? Is that you? What's going on?"

This time, she was pretty sure she could detect a few hitching sobs in the middle of the noise. She looked at Terry, frowning, and then back at the phone.

"Do you need help, Charley? Is someone else there? Do you need the police or a doctor?"

"No…" This time, at least, she was sure there was actually a person on the end trying to talk to her, and pretty sure that it was Charley.

Terry sat up, looking concerned about at least Erin's side of the conversation. Erin wasn't sure if he could hear or understand any of the other noises.

"Are you sick, Charley?"

"No."

"Hurt?"

"No." Charley burst into bubbling, noisy tears again. Erin was really starting to get concerned.

"Where are you? Are you at home?"

Erin thought—or imagined—she could hear a 'yes' in Charley's answer.

"Okay. I'm going to come over there. Is that okay? Is that what you want?"

More noise from the other end of the phone. Erin shook her head at Terry, unable to make any sense of it.

"I'll be right over. Hang in there," she told Charley, and hung up the call.

"What's going on?"

"I don't know. It sounds like she's crying. I think. It's really hard to tell. But I think she said she's at home, so I'm going to go over there and see if I can help her."

"I'll come with you."

"I really don't think she's going to want you there. She's got a real thing about police."

"I don't have to stay if she doesn't want me there. But I think I should at least check and make sure she's safe and hasn't been the victim of violence."

Erin nodded. "Uh… okay. That makes sense. Just don't be insulted if she acts like you're an intruder. She did call me, and I'm telling you, she doesn't like dealing with police after everything that's happened to her."

"Understood," Terry agreed. "No problem."

He got out of bed and started pulling on his uniform. Erin followed suit, grabbing her own clothes and ducking into the bathroom to change.

"You don't have to hide," Terry called to her through the door, chuckling.

Erin's face burned. "I know. It's just… faster this way…" she explained, telling herself that she could take off her nightie, get dressed, use the commode, and brush her teeth all more efficiently if she were already in the bathroom.

"I'll make some coffee. Do you want anything else? I have a few muffins in the freezer."

"Yeah, maybe you'd better thaw some out. I'm not ready to eat yet, but I don't know what kind of a state Charley is in. She might need something, or I might end up being there for a long time."

"See you in a minute, then."

Erin quickly got herself together and was in the kitchen before Terry could finish thawing the muffins. She let K9 out of his kennel, and he ran excited circles around her, his big tail making wide sweeps back and forth.

"Settle down, partner," Terry told him. "We've got work to do."

At the word *work*, K9 stopped playing and was still, waiting for a command from Terry.

"I'm going to leave you to get breakfast together," Terry said. "Throw the coffee in a thermos and find a container for the muffins. Juice or jam if you want them. I'm going to take him outside, then we'll be right back."

"You got it," Erin agreed.

Terry went outside and Erin familiarized herself with the kitchen. In ten minutes, they were both ready to go, and Terry drove over in the squad car.

"She's at her house, not at the bakery?"

"That's what she said. She wouldn't be able to get into the bakery, would she? Isn't it still a crime scene?"

"It's been processed. She can access it if she wants to. Depending on what the trustees of the estate have to say."

"She must really hate having to check with them on everything she does. She's so independent."

Terry nodded. "I suspect you're right."

"But that doesn't mean she would kill one of them just because he wouldn't do what she wanted." Erin didn't want anyone saying she was trying to throw suspicion on Charley.

"Particularly when he was letting her do what she wanted to," Terry agreed.

They pulled up to the house and Erin jumped out of the car first. She hurried up the sidewalk to Charley's door and knocked. Terry was right on her heels.

"Don't you think I should go in first?"

"No. She's just upset. It isn't a crime."

Terry acquiesced. Erin knocked on the door again, harder. "Charley, it's Erin. Open up."

It took a couple more times, then the door finally opened. Erin stepped in and gasped.

CHAPTER 20

*C*harley's apartment in Moose River had been neat and well-maintained. Charley had been embarrassed at having left a pair of socks and other everyday things out where they didn't belong. But her house looked like someone had turned it upside-down and shaken it. Erin looked around, gaping.

"What happened? Did someone break in?"

"No," Charley blubbered. Her face was red and sweaty, wet with tears and snot. And it was no wonder. It was obvious someone had broken into the house and ransacked the place. Erin would have been in tears too. "No, it's just me," Charley said, voice thick and choked. "I've been busy with the bakery... I haven't had time to take care of anything around here... and I just... can't... deal..."

Erin could smell the alcohol oozing from Charley's pores.

She looked back at Terry, who was trailing them into the house. If the house was in that state just because Charley was busy and hadn't been able to look after herself, then she clearly needed help. Maybe a maid and maybe a psychiatrist.

"Why don't we sit down, and you can tell me what happened?" Erin suggested.

Charley made gulping noises, attempting to stop the tears, but it appeared to be useless.

"Shh. It's going to be okay," Erin soothed. "Just tell me."

"It's all too much," Charley bawled. "Trying to open the bakery, and people stealing things, and Don Inglethorpe getting himself killed on my property, and Bobby! I miss Bobby!"

Erin was doubly shocked. Charley had barely mentioned her late boyfriend in the months since she had been falsely accused of his murder. Erin had decided that Charley hadn't really had any feelings toward him at all, but had just been attracted to someone who was powerful in the organized crime syndicate she had been working for. He might have been handsome, but she hadn't actually loved him.

"Bobby? What does any of this have to do with Bobby?"

Charley scrubbed at her eyes. "Nothing!"

"Nothing, but...?"

"I just miss him. Nothing has been the same since he died. I thought that if I came here and opened the bakery, everything would be fine. I'm not with the clan anymore, but I could start something new and it would turn out okay."

"But things haven't worked out the way you were hoping," Erin surmised.

"Why did that idiot have to get killed in my bakery? Do you know what a pain it is having someone killed in your place of business?"

Erin looked at Terry and couldn't help smiling. "Well, actually, yes. It sucks."

"Who's going to come to a bakery where someone was killed? Two people, if you want to count Trenton Plaint, but that happened before I ever came to town, so that's not my fault!"

"None of it is your fault." Erin cleared a place on the sofa for Charley to sit down and guided her into it. She sat beside Charley, giving her a sisterly hug around the shoulders. "None of this is your fault. It's just the way things go sometimes."

"I'm never going to be able to open the bakery now. So where does that leave me? I've got nothing! I was hanging on to this, thinking that if I could make it work, I could be independent of my family and the clan and just be a... a businesswoman like you. How come everything works out for you, and it just turns to crap for me?"

"Charley..." Erin rubbed Charley's shoulder and shook her head. "Everything doesn't work out for me. My mom and dad died, and I went into foster care. I had nothing. I was out on my butt at eighteen and had to find a way to survive. The only reason I've got the bakery is because my Aunt Clementine died and left it to me. And starting it out hasn't been all roses. Angela Plaint dying of an allergic reaction on opening day wasn't exactly the thing to convince everyone how well I could handle baking for people with special diets."

"But it worked out," Charley sobbed.

"Yes, eventually. But not all in a day. I had to work through the same things that you are."

"Not all of them," Charley snapped.

Erin shrugged. "Maybe not."

"You don't even know all the stuff that's going on with the clans in Bald Eagle Falls right now."

Erin broke out in goosebumps. She shivered. *All of the stuff going on with the clans?* She looked at Terry, but he gave her wide eyes and a shrug. He didn't know what Charley was talking about either.

"What?" Erin pushed a lock of Charley's hair back behind her ear. "What's been going on with the clans?"

Charley sniffled. She wiped her sweaty red face with the back of her arm. "Nobody cared about Bald Eagle Falls before. It's such a little place, no one bothered to add it to their territory."

"And that has changed…?"

"They're fighting over it. Dysons and Jacksons. Maybe some of the smaller players too, I don't know. Someone is going to get it. And there's going to be more blood shed before they do."

"But why would anyone want Bald Eagle Falls?" Erin was shocked. It was such a safe little community, despite the rash of murders, she couldn't imagine that there was any benefit to a crime family claiming ownership over the community.

"Why do gangs fight over inner-city blocks?" Charley countered. "It isn't because they've valuable. It's just to prove who is more powerful."

"How do you know all this? How do you know they're fighting over Bald Eagle Falls?"

"I might not be in the Dyson clan anymore, but I still hear things." Charley snorted, sucking back the mucousy tears. "This sleepy little town isn't as sleepy as you might think."

Erin looked at Terry. His expression was stony. This was not good news for him or anyone in town.

Erin rubbed Charley's back soothingly. "It will work out in the end," she repeated, though of course she had no way of knowing if that were true. Charley had been through some pretty rough times recently, and if the clans were stirring things up, who knew what else they all might be facing.

Images from old black and white movies about prohibition times and The Godfather series flashed through her brain. They might not be strictly factual, but she had met with a couple members of the Dyson clan in Moose River, and they weren't just paper-pushing figureheads.

Charley rubbed her eyes. "If you had any sense, you'd get out of Bald Eagle Falls," she said. "All of you."

~

Terry was quiet as they got into the squad car. They had only taken as long as was needed for Erin to get Charley calmed down, knowing that Terry needed to get in and report the rumors of a possible clan war in Bald Eagle Falls to the sheriff and to consider how to address it.

"Do you think it's true?" Erin asked.

He glanced sideways at her, not answering immediately.

"I think she spent a long, hard night drinking," he said eventually. "That's obviously going to affect her perceptions. She has been through a lot of challenges and big changes lately. That may be all it is."

"But you don't think it is."

"No," he admitted. "I've seen some signs... people hanging around town that shouldn't be. Increased chatter. I was hoping it was just people who were attracted by news of a murder. You do get people who want to be where it all happened, whenever something sensational happens. I was hoping that it would just die down naturally."

"But if it's some kind of gang war, then it's not going to, is it?"

He stared off into the distance before starting the car. "It depends how much they really want Bald Eagle Falls. It could just be a flash in the pan, and then they get bored with it. There's not that much to attract big criminals here. But if they really do decide to have a showdown..."

"I sure hope not."

"Me too. I'll talk to the sheriff, but chances are, we're going to need to get the feds in here. Our little force is just not equipped to deal with something of that scale."

They were both quiet as Terry started the car and pulled out.

"Do you mind coming by the police department with me? Or do you want me to drop you at home?"

"I don't mind coming in, if you don't mind having me around. Are you going to have to clock in?"

"No. Just because this came up today, that doesn't mean that the clans are closing in and I'll be needed for one last stand. It's highly unlikely anything will happen today. I'll just talk to Sheriff Wilmot, let him know the rumor, and we can deal with it next week."

"Sounds good. I'll hang around, then."

"He might want to talk to you anyway, get your opinion on whether Charley is telling the truth or exaggerating."

"She could be doing both."

Terry gave a small smile. "Yes, she could be doing both."

"I couldn't believe her house. Her apartment in Moose River was so neat and organized."

He nodded, but didn't have any comment about Charley's housekeeping.

"Do you think she really loved Bobby?" Erin asked, as they pulled into the reserved parking space behind the civic center.

Terry's brows went up. "Hard to say. I'm no expert on matters of the heart…"

"Just your gut feeling. As a cop."

"People get emotional when they are tired or when they're drinking. She was obviously overwrought. But does that mean she didn't love him and is just dramatizing? I don't think so. I'm sure she had feelings for him… I'm just not sure how deep they really were. You just can't tell by the way people react to a death."

"She seemed so together when it happened. Perfectly calm. She hardly gave any sign that she cared about what had happened to him. Now this…"

"The truth is probably somewhere in between. In the aftershock of a violent death, people are often less emotional than you would expect. It isn't until everything should be back to normal—after the funeral ends and everyone goes home—that it really hits them, and they begin to grieve."

"And then to be hit with Don Inglethorpe's death right in her bakery, and the possibility that she'll never be able to reopen the bakery again…"

"She could probably use a hand," Terry said, "some counseling, maybe."

He was obviously hearkening back to their earlier conversation that Erin might need some therapy in the wake of her traumatic experiences. Erin just rolled her eyes and didn't take the bait.

"I'm sure Charley will be fine. And she does have family she can go back to. They can help her get over this and figure out what to do with her life."

"You're not including yourself in that?"

"Well… no," Erin admitted. They might be blood, but they weren't much of a family. Charley was young enough that she could go home, and her parents would help her. Erin hadn't ever had a safety net like that.

She probably should have enough compassion for Charley to offer to take her in hand and help her to straighten her life out, but Erin couldn't bring herself to take on that project.

CHAPTER 21

Sheriff Wilmot seemed unimpressed by Charley's report that the clans were descending on Bald Eagle Falls to have it out. He shook his head slowly.

"No, I don't see it. Bald Eagle Falls has never been the type of place the criminal element were interested in. Sure, we've had our share of moonshiners and pot-smoking high school students, but we're not an epicenter for drug activity. There's no market here. Why would they waste their time and energy on staking out a claim?"

Terry shrugged. "I couldn't tell you. I don't know the inner workings of these organizations. Maybe Charley Campbell could fill you in a little more about that. I just thought you should know."

Wilmot nodded. "Appreciated. But I haven't seen too much to bear the rumor out."

"We have had a few bad characters around the last few days who aren't normally part of the picture here."

"Not unusual after a murder. People want to see where it happened. It will quiet down again."

Terry had expressed the same possibility himself, so he just nodded. Only time would tell.

"Erin," Sheriff Wilmot hadn't acknowledged her up until this point, but having dealt with the possibility of organized crime invading Bald Eagle

Falls, he noticed her waiting for the handsome Officer Piper and took advantage of the opportunity.

"Morning, Sheriff."

"Can you tell me of any reason Charley's fingerprints would be on your rolling pin?"

"Oh… well, I assume she's the one who took it from my kitchen, so she would have gotten her prints on it then."

"She didn't cook with you at any point?"

"No. She'd hardly ever even been in my kitchen. We didn't bake together."

"And when you loaned her the rolling pin—"

"I never loaned it to her," Erin cut him off. "I never would have given it to anyone to use on gluten doughs. It would be contaminated, and I wouldn't be able to use it for my gluten-free doughs. I wouldn't want to take the chance, however slim, of ever poisoning someone."

"I see. She had led me to believe that you had let her use it. But in fact…"

"I told her several times that she couldn't borrow any of my pans or equipment. Again… it wouldn't have been safe for my customers. She seemed to really have difficulty understanding that. She didn't just ask once, and she kept insisting that I would just have to wash them afterward."

"Couldn't you?"

"I couldn't wash them and be one hundred percent sure that there wasn't a single particle of flour in it. And for some people, one particle would be enough to make them sick."

"I see." He nodded slowly. "So, when you went over to The Bake Shoppe to get the rolling pin back, you were prepared for there to be trouble."

"I was ready for an argument," Erin admitted. "But I wasn't planning on beating anyone to death."

"Of course not." But Sheriff Wilmot pursed his lips and seemed to be considering the idea.

Erin hesitated. "Charley said she never took the rolling pin. She said that she wasn't the one who took it. She had never touched it."

"Well, obviously she had touched it. Fingerprints don't lie. If she hadn't ever had the opportunity to use it while it was at your bakery, then she was the one who took it."

Erin didn't know what else to say. The next question was a logical one—had Charley been the one wielding the rolling pin when Don Inglethorpe had met his demise? Erin wasn't sure she wanted to know the answer.

∾

In spite of the way the day had started and being short on sleep, Erin ended up having a pretty good day with Terry. She was able to forget about the heavy pall hanging over her and just to enjoy herself and spend time in the moment. It was almost like being on vacation. What little spare time she had was usually filled up with running errands, making lists, cleaning the house, and planning out advertising campaigns. Doing nothing was a rare treat, especially if she could do it with Terry Piper.

Erin was feeling tired, but relaxed and satisfied when Terry dropped her off at home at the end of the day. She let herself into the house and reached over to disarm the burglar alarm, then saw that it was already off. She checked to make sure that the door was shut.

"Jeremy? You home?"

He didn't answer. Erin walked by his bedroom to put her purse in her own, and saw that he was sitting on the bed, phone to his ear. He gave Erin a little wave of greeting. Erin put her things away and went into the kitchen to feed the animals and take a look across the back yard to see if Vic was home.

Reality started to reassert itself. Erin frowned and the knot began to tighten in her stomach again. Was it only a matter of time until organized crime made it to Bald Eagle Falls? Or had it already?

Vic was just arriving home, saying goodbye to Willie before retiring. Erin drew back from the window to give them their privacy. She looked in the fridge for anything good to eat, even though she wasn't actually hungry. In a couple of minutes, she heard Willie's truck engine roar to life and Vic came in the back door, smiling and relaxed.

"You look like you had a good time," Erin observed.

"We did. I think…" Vic hesitated before finishing, "I think we're finally over all of the bumps and can just move steadily forward." She gave Erin a grin. "And you and Officer Piper? I got my fill of gossip at the ladies' tea this morning. It would seem that you have been seen together around town."

"Well, of course. Where else would we be seen?" Erin asked, trying to mask her self-consciousness. "We have been seeing each other for quite some time now. You already knew that."

"But you haven't slept over at his house before." Vic's voice was full of teasing innuendo. Erin had always been very careful not to poke her nose into Vic's business or to tease her about her relationship with Willie, but she was starting to regret that fact. She would feel better if she knew that she had given as good as she was getting.

"We couldn't very well sleep here, could we?" she asked archly.

Vic's eyes got wider. "Why couldn't—oh, because of Jeremy! Where is Jeremy?"

Jeremy joined them in the kitchen a minute later, having pulled himself away from his phone call. "Is that my sister's voice I hear?"

"Jeremy, didn't you know you were supposed to be chaperoning these young people?" Vic demanded, gesturing to Erin.

"Chaperoning them?" Jeremy repeated. He looked quickly at Erin, and then back at Vic. "You're pulling my leg, right?"

"Of course I am. But you could have been a gentleman and spent the night in my apartment so that Erin could have *her* gentleman over."

"I… well, I suppose… but I didn't want to be in your way in case you brought *your* guy back…" He was turning quite red. "I mean, it's one thing to have an older couple that you don't really know around, it's a little different when it's your little sister, who used to be… and I don't really know…" he broke off, scratching the back of his neck and looking incredibly uncomfortable.

Vic was laughing so hard Erin was worried she was going to pop a blood vessel.

Erin raised an eyebrow at Jeremy. "An older couple? Are you serious?"

"Well… you're older than me," Jeremy protested, turning from the hazard of thinking about what his sister might be doing to repair the damage his words had done. "I just meant—older than me," he protested. "You're older than I am. Not by that much, but…"

"I'm not much older than you and neither is Terry," Erin agreed. "Now Willie, he's older than either of us."

They both looked back at Vic, who was standing with her hands on her hips.

"You just go there," she challenged Jeremy.

"Uh, no. I wasn't going to go there. You can do whatever you want with whoever you want." It was going to be a long time before all of the blood suffusing his face faded. He clearly did not want to be imagining his younger sibling with Willie.

"I clearly need to find a place of my own soon," Jeremy said. "I had no idea that it was such a hotbed over here. You guys need your privacy, and *someday* I'm going to need mine."

"Not too soon, I hope," Vic said in a parental tone.

"You're younger than I am," Jeremy repeated. "If you're old enough, then I certainly am."

"You make sure you wait until you're ready and have someone really special that you plan to spend a long time with."

Jeremy chuckled. "You're going to make a good mom, Vic."

She grinned at him, pleased. Then Vic turned her attention back to Erin. "Things went well with Officer Piper? The two of you... enjoyed each other's company?"

"We always do," Erin said evenly. "And that's all I'm going to say on the matter." She looked at Jeremy seriously and then back at Vic. "We need to talk."

"Okay." Vic nodded. She would know that they needed to discuss the living arrangements before too much more time passed, but she didn't know there was more to it than Erin's need for privacy or the difficulty in keeping Jeremy's presence a secret from Terry Piper.

CHAPTER 22

hey all withdrew a little reluctantly to the living room and sat down. Erin sighed.

"Jeremy… we're going to need to know what's going on. We can't just keep hiding you here. You really need to fill us in."

He chewed the inside of his cheek. "It's not that easy."

"A lot of things are hard. But you still have to deal with them. You need to tell us what it is you're running away from. What you're hiding from. Don't try to tell me that you just need to find yourself. You could have found yourself a home without hiding from the police."

"I really can't talk about it," Jeremy protested. "I don't want to get anyone else in trouble."

"Well, if you're in trouble, you're already getting us in trouble, because we've been aiding and abetting you. You'd better tell us just what it is that you've gotten us into."

"Erin," Vic protested, "we don't need to know everything. Jeremy is entitled to his privacy…"

"Is the Jackson clan trying to take over Bald Eagle Falls?" Erin asked flatly.

Vic stared at her, mouth open. Then when neither Erin nor Jeremy laughed, she looked at Jeremy, who was no longer red with embarrassment, but as white as a ghost.

"The Jackson clan doesn't want anything to do with Bald Eagle Falls," Vic asserted.

"They didn't," Jeremy agreed. "But because of everything that's been going on lately, they might just have changed their minds."

Vic shook her head. "That doesn't make any kind of sense. What would they want to do with Bald Eagle Falls? There's nothing here. The biggest criminal enterprise is jaywalking, and there's only one street you can even cross against the lights. There's no reason for the clan to bring any of their crap here."

Jeremy was looking at Erin. "How did you know?"

"I have my sources. So explain to me how you're involved here. Were you sent to scout it out? To keep an eye on things? Are you supposed to do something, or just sit back and report on everything that happens?"

"I was supposed to be involved," Jeremy said with difficulty. He gave Vic an apologetic look. "They wanted me to... to do things that I couldn't."

"Who wanted you to?" Vic demanded.

"They said... it was time for me to prove myself. That I've just been living off the clan and getting all of the benefits, and I hadn't paid my dues. So, it was time to join an operation and show that I was really Jackson material."

Erin shook her head.

"So, you were supposed to do what?" Vic demanded. "Kill Don Inglethorpe?"

He cut his eyes toward her and his expression didn't change. He swallowed and kept his eyes down, lips tight.

"Is that it?" Erin asked. She had assumed that he would be involved in some lower-level activity. Reporting back to his organization on numbers. Maybe testing out some drug distribution or trying to spot the soldiers from the opposing clans. She hadn't expected it to be anything big.

"I don't know who killed Inglethorpe," Jeremy said cautiously. "It wasn't me. It wasn't anything to do with me."

"But if you had stayed home, it would have been," Vic suggested.

"I don't know. It might have been clan. They had more than one thing going on. I'm sure there were lots of ways I could have cemented my position with the clan."

"I don't understand," Erin said, shaking her head. "I get that these organizations run along family lines... but... you're saying you don't have a choice whether to be involved or not? If you're a Jackson, you're expected to be a criminal, doing whatever it is they want you to?"

Jeremy chewed on his lip. It was Vic who tried to put it into words.

"You're raised that the Jacksons are on the side of the angels. Anyone who opposes them is obviously on the devil's side. So that makes it right to protect your family's safety and freedom. It's okay to do things that you've been taught were wrong, because that's part of being a Jackson and protecting our way of life."

"Did they expect you to be like that too?" Erin demanded. "I mean, you were just a kid before you left home. A minor. They didn't ask you to break the law for them, did they?"

"It's small things when you're younger," Vic said. "Little things are easier, and then it doesn't bother you as much when they ask you to do the big things."

"Like killing someone?"

Vic looked at Jeremy. "I was never told to kill someone. I was told to get rid of problems, yes, but no one ever told me anything like that."

"Soldiers aren't really told ahead of time what they're going to be asked to do," Jeremy said quietly. "I guess they figure that you'll do what you're told in the heat of the moment. You don't have time to think about it, you just do what the boss tells you to do, and if you feel bad about it after, you have a drink and you laugh about it with the others, and then you're one of them, and you can try to forget about the details."

Was that how it had been for Charley too? Just acting and reacting in the heat of the moment, until she wasn't a living, breathing individual anymore, but a robot, programmed to do what the mob wanted her to do? Was it any wonder that she hadn't shown any emotion after Bobby had died? That she hadn't known what she felt like at the time, not until weeks later when she was faced with another death and the potential loss of her business?

"Then what are you doing here?" Erin challenged Jeremy. "It seems to me that if you wanted to avoid the clan and start life fresh, you wouldn't come to the one place that they're concentrating on at the time."

"I didn't know what to do. I wanted to protect Vic. I thought it would be easier if I was closer." Jeremy looked at Vic and swallowed. "I knew I wouldn't ever be able to talk her into leaving Willie and the bakery and running away somewhere else. So I thought I would stay here... keep an eye on things… make sure that if there was violence, she would be out of the way."

"But you couldn't guarantee that, could you?" Erin pointed out. "You haven't stayed with us. You don't know what might happen while we're out. Who else might get killed. Maybe someone like Inglethorpe, a pillar of the community. Or maybe someone's wife or child. Or someone's sister."

"I didn't want anything to happen to either one of you," Jeremy reiterated. "I came here to protect you."

CHAPTER 23

*T*hey had gone to bed without anything being resolved. Jeremy didn't want to leave, but likewise didn't want to talk to Terry to tell him what he knew. Vic didn't want to kick him out and was worried about their security. It had failed before, and they couldn't be sure that it would keep them safe in the future.

Vic ended up calling Willie to come back to the house. She had Jeremy go back to the spare room and didn't tell Willie their specific concerns, she simply told him she needed him there and asked him to stay. Maybe Willie already knew there was clan activity going on around Bald Eagle Falls. He had, after all, been part of the Dyson organization at one point, and still had occasional contact with them to help with computers or one of Willie's other specialties.

"Should we all stay in the house?" Vic asked Erin. "Would you feel better if Willie was there?"

"No, you can stay in your apartment." They couldn't all be in the main house without Willie figuring out pretty quickly that there was someone else there who shouldn't have been. It would look pretty suspicious if Erin wouldn't allow them to sleep in the empty bedroom. "I'll be just fine here with the burglar alarm and Orange Blossom. You know he'll attack anyone who tries to break in during the night." Erin laughed. It was Orange

Blossom who had fended off the previous intruder, until Vic had been able to get there with her gun.

"You should have some protection," Vic encouraged. "I can leave you with this."

She patted her concealed weapon. She had a permit for it and knew how to use it properly, but Erin did not. At some point, she might have to break down and do as they were all telling her to and take a firearms course and practice shooting at the range. Then she might feel confident enough to have a gun and to use it if she needed to.

But it was Erin's opinion that if she weren't armed, there would be less opportunity for anyone to shoot her. They would see that she was just an inexperienced, unarmed civilian, without any ties to organized crime or any kind of crime at all, and they would leave her alone. They would let her go.

"No. No guns. I'll be just fine."

"You should call Terry," Willie said, a twinkle in his eye, "I'm sure he wouldn't mind acting as your bodyguard."

In spite of herself, Erin felt herself blushing again. She glared at Willie, then made a shooing motion with her hands.

"I'm going to sleep now. No need for extra people or guns. Everybody out."

Willie obeyed, chuckling. Vic gave Erin a quick hug and whispered in her ear that Jeremy would look out for her.

Erin was too tired to do anything but go to bed. She'd been up too late the night before and had early bakery hours in the morning.

But sleep eluded her as she thought about Don Inglethorpe and the pool of blood and about Jeremy and Vic's other brothers.

They were all expected to be soldiers for the clan. What if they refused?

What if they accepted?

~

"Somebody didn't get enough sleep over the weekend," Adele observed, when she caught Erin yawning. Erin tried to cut the yawn short, but it was no use. She smothered it with the back of her hand.

"I had a hard time sleeping last night," Erin explained.

"And maybe you didn't get to bed until late Saturday night."

Erin looked at her. "You live in the woods, isolated from everyone else. How do you know about that?"

"I have my sources."

"Well, that's freaky. Have you got Skye spying on me?"

Skye was Adele's crow. Or a crow that sometimes spent time with Adele; she didn't claim any ownership over him. Adele didn't answer. She just looked mysterious, not filling Erin in on who her source might be.

Adele had come in the afternoon, when the bakery was usually quiet before school let out and people started rushing in to pick up something to go with dinner. She was the only one there.

"I had a run-in with a trespasser a couple of days ago," Adele said, as she waited for Vic to ring up her total.

"Who? A kid?" Erin asked.

"No. A young woman. I'm still not sure what she was out there for. She said she was just out for a walk, but…"

"You didn't know her?" Vic asked. "I think you know pretty much everyone in town now, don't you?"

Adele nodded. "She wasn't from around here. I would say she was native to Tennessee, but not to Bald Eagle Falls."

"What did she look like?"

"Army fatigues. Long, blond hair. Little or no makeup."

Erin thought she recognized the woman who had rear-ended the drug dealer's car in the description. She wished she had taken a picture so she could show it to Adele.

"Long nose and a big mouth?" she asked Adele, a bit embarrassed to be pointing out anyone's flawed features.

Adele nodded. "Sounds like you know her."

"No. Just saw her once. A couple of days ago. She rear-ended a guy on Main Street."

"That was not very bright. It isn't like we have heavy traffic."

"It might have been intentional… I don't know. I couldn't say for sure. But she certainly didn't seem upset about it. And she basically got away with it, because the guy she hit didn't want to open his glove box for Terry."

"You don't know who she was?"

"No. Terry would know her name. You didn't find out anything? Just that she was out for a walk?"

"That's as far as it went. I told her she was on private property and where the boundaries were, and she eventually went on her way. But I don't like people with guns hanging around on the property."

"Back up a minute!" Vic interjected. "This woman had a gun?"

Adele looked surprised at the question. "A hunting rifle. I mentioned that, didn't I?"

"No, you sort of missed that part!"

Erin tried to reconcile the picture with a drug dealer. But army fatigues and a hunting rifle didn't sound like a drug dealer or anyone else from the clans. It sounded like someone who was out hunting or participating in some war games.

"Did you ask her name? Or for some ID?" she asked Adele.

Adele's eyes were surprised. "I've never done that before."

"If we've got trouble coming into Bald Eagle Falls, then maybe we should start. If you don't know who it is, I mean."

"What trouble?"

Erin looked at Vic. "Well, we can't say for sure, but rumor has it... that the Dyson and Jackson clans are battling for possession of Bald Eagle Falls. No verification that it's true, of course, but here have been more strangers in town lately."

Adele considered this seriously. She took her bag of baked goods and her change. "I'll keep my eyes open. But I don't know why they would be interested in Bald Eagle Falls."

She turned and took a step toward the door, then froze.

CHAPTER 24

*E*rin looked to see what had caught Adele's attention.

"Speaking of unsavory strangers," Adele murmured.

There was a man getting out of a shiny red convertible outside the bakery. He was middle-aged, but had an irresponsible playboy look about him. His hair was artfully mussed, and he had laugh lines around his eyes and mouth. Adele turned and looked at Erin.

"Do you think I could sneak out through the kitchen?"

Erin was floored. Adele was always so calm and serene. She never seemed to hesitate over anything. She avoided crowds and preferred to be on her own, but she had never gone so far as to avoid contact so obviously.

Erin didn't want to set the precedent of allowing a customer to walk through off-limits areas, but Adele was different. There was no one around to see the breach, and she was sure that Adele wouldn't take advantage of the situation, assuming that letting her into the kitchen once meant she was allowed to use it any time she liked. Adele had always gone to great lengths not to take advantage of Erin's hospitality.

"Okay," she said quickly, as it became apparent the stranger was headed straight for Auntie Clem's, "go, go!"

Adele scurried around the counter, past Erin and Vic, and into the kitchen. Vic looked at Erin in surprise.

"What was that all about? I was sure you were going to say no."

"I know. I would have, but…" Erin looked toward the door.

The man walked in through the door, making the bells jangle. He was wearing a simple white t-shirt and cargo pants, but somehow made them look as if he'd just stepped off a yacht. He gave Erin and Vic a smug smile.

"Hello, ladies. How are you this fine afternoon?"

Erin had not been expecting the New England accent. She had opened her mouth to greet him and ended up just staring at him, mouth open.

"Good afternoon," Vic greeted cheerfully. "I don't think I've seen you in these parts before."

"No ma'am," he agreed. "First time I ever set foot in town. My name is Rudolph Windsor."

Even Vic was speechless for a beat. Then she smiled.

"Welcome to Bald Eagle Falls, Mr. Windsor. I'm Vic and this is Erin. What can we help you with?" She gestured to the bakery display case.

Windsor barely looked at the baked goods. He clearly wasn't there to buy a turnover.

"I wonder if you fine ladies would be able to help me. I am here looking for my wife." He looked at each of them expectantly. "That would be Adele Windsor."

There was a long pause while they considered what to tell him. Adele clearly did not want to meet up with him. She had never spoken of her husband; they had only recently discovered she was even married.

"Your wife," Vic repeated. "Adele has never mentioned you."

"Well, I'm hurt." His smile suggested that he was not. He didn't give the impression of being a family man. "To tell you the truth, Adele and I have been estranged. But she is still my wife, and I'd appreciate it if you could point me in the right direction?"

"She lives backwoods," Erin finally found her voice. "You'll need someone to show you the way. She doesn't have an address you can put in the GPS."

"I'm sure I could find it if you just point me in the right direction. I am pretty good at finding things."

Something about the way he said it gave Erin the willies. She rubbed her arms, not sure why she would be getting goosebumps in the Tennessee heat.

"Maybe Terry could help," Vic suggested.

Erin nodded, relieved to find a solution. She didn't get a good feeling about Rudolph Windsor and didn't want to give him directions to Adele's cottage. "I'll text him."

She did so, giving him a heads-up that Rudolph Windsor was not someone that Adele wanted to see. He acknowledged the message.

"Should just be a couple of minutes," Erin told Windsor.

He smiled and nodded, pleased with the way the matter was progressing.

"Could we get you a cookie and an iced tea while you're waiting? First cookie is always on the house."

Windsor looked down his nose at the display case, shaking his head. "I eat low carb," he advised. "This stuff is pure poison to the body. Worse than cocaine."

Vic bristled at that and Erin held up a hand to stop her from going off on Windsor. Best if he were still in one piece when Officer Terry Piper got there. "Different strokes for different folks," she murmured.

"But your baking—"

"Shh."

Vic subsided. "I'd better go check on those cookies," she muttered, and retreated to the kitchen.

Windsor gave Erin another sardonic smile. He turned and looked out the front window, waiting for his escort to show up. When he saw the uniformed police officer and his K9 partner approaching, he did not look pleased. Erin saw him take a quick look back and forth, looking for a way to avoid meeting him.

Terry opened the door and walked in. He nodded to Erin, and turned his polite, no-nonsense, public-service smile on Windsor.

"Good afternoon, sir. Something I could help you with?"

Windsor took another look at the door. "I think it's all taken care of, officer." He cast a glance over to Erin for confirmation.

"This is Terry."

Windsor didn't seem to know what to do about that. "I don't think we need to put the police force out. I can find the way on my own."

"What was your name?" Terry asked, flipping his notebook open and holding his pen at the ready.

"Rudolph Windsor."

"And where are you from?"

"I don't see why you would need to know that."

"Are you refusing to answer?"

The superior smile was gone from Rudolph's face. He licked his lips. "No need to be that way... Massachusetts."

"Boston?"

"Thereabouts."

Erin wouldn't have pegged his accent as Bostonian, but she kept her peace.

"Little bit different coming to a small town like Bald Eagle Falls," Terry commented.

"Yes... it certainly is."

"So, Miss Windsor knows you were coming to see her?"

"*Mrs.* Windsor," the man retorted. "I should know. I married her."

"And she knows you're coming?"

"Is there some kind of law out here that I'm not aware of? That a man isn't allowed to visit his own wife without some kind of appointment?"

"If we actually knew you, that would be a different story. But we like to look after our own. I don't know you from Adam, and even if you are who you say, that's no guarantee Miss Windsor didn't come here with the express purpose of leaving you behind. The fact that you're avoiding my question suggests that she doesn't know you're here."

"Look, Officer," Windsor attempted to turn on the charm, smiling in a way that made Erin's flesh crawl. "There's no bad blood between my wife and I. I appreciate your desire to protect your citizenry, but you don't have the right to keep me from visiting her or to detain me. So rather than making a big thing of this... I'm just going to leave."

He held up his hands like he was fending off an attack and retreated from the bakery. Terry swiveled, watching him go.

"Where's Adele?" he asked Erin, without turning back around to look at her.

"I'm right here, Officer Piper."

Erin startled at the voice behind her. She hadn't expected Adele to still be in the kitchen, but well on her way home. Adele appeared in the doorway with Vic.

"I'm sorry to cause all of this trouble. I just lost my head when I saw him. It's okay, really. There's nothing to be concerned about."

Adele wasn't the type to lose her head. Erin studied her for a minute, wondering what the story was. But Adele was a very private person and she wasn't about to tell them about her personal life.

"Have you ever had a restraining order against him?" Terry asked.

Adele walked past the counter into the front area of the bakery. "No. No restraining orders."

"Does he have a criminal record?"

"He might... I don't know."

"You don't know if your husband has a criminal record."

"People often don't know everything about the people they live with. Rudolph has a past that I was not involved in. It's been some time since I left him. Even while we were together... I wasn't with him every minute of the day, and there were nights he didn't come home... Could he have a record? Of course. Does he?" She shook her head. "I have no idea."

Terry scratched his chin, considering this. Erin figured that since Adele hadn't immediately jumped in to say that there was no way her husband could have a record, that she was aware of criminal activities that he might be involved in. The way she answered suggested that it was entirely possible that he'd been caught breaking the law at some point.

"How do you want this to be handled?" Terry asked. "Do you want him to stay away from you and your house? Do you have reason to get a restraining order?"

"No... I shouldn't have run away. I could have just stuck around here and dealt with him face-to-face out in public. I just hate having my dirty laundry spread out for everyone to see."

"Do you feel safe seeing him? If you don't want this guy showing up on your doorstep, we should set up a meeting away from the cottage. Do you know what he wants?"

"What Rudolph always wants. To get back together. But that's not going to happen."

"You're not worried about any violence?"

"No. We had... different lifestyles. But he never hit me."

"Still, you make sure you meet with him in public, a restaurant or some-where people won't overhear your conversation but are around if he does get angry."

Adele nodded. "Okay. I will. Sorry for the trouble, Officer Piper. I didn't mean to cause any concern."

"No problem. I'd rather be here when I wasn't needed than not be here when I am. He knows I'm around and that people are keeping an eye on things. He'll think twice before doing something stupid."

"Oh, you don't know my husband," Adele said, her mouth curling into a slight smile. "He's never in his life thought twice before doing something stupid."

CHAPTER 25

*A*fter hearing that Adele had made arrangements to have supper with her husband at the family restaurant, Erin and Vic decided they needed a night out as well. They booked a table of their own and were pretending not to watch Adele and Rudolph as they ate their dinner. Erin and Vic were just there in case Adele needed them, like Terry had said. They both had Terry on speed dial, so he could be there in a few minutes if it looked like things were getting heated between the two.

But so far, things seemed perfectly calm. More than that, Adele and Rudolph seemed positively friendly with each other. Adele wasn't smiling, but she wasn't scowling, either. That blanched, worried expression she'd had when she had first spotted Rudolph was nowhere to be seen.

Rudolph himself was in fine form. He was practically gushing over Adele. He beamed at her and frequently slid his fingers through his hair as he flirted with her. He sat across the table and held her hand for several minutes at a time. Erin couldn't hear the conversation between them, but there didn't seem to be any harsh words. No argument.

"Well, this isn't as exciting as I expected," Vic grumbled.

"We don't actually want it to be exciting," Erin countered. "We don't want Adele to be in any danger."

"I don't mean I want her to be in danger, just not to be sitting there smiling at him and pretending she likes him. If she doesn't want to be with him, then why can't she look like it? She can't be that afraid of making a scene. She's just letting him walk all over her."

"Nobody's walking over anybody. She's just having dinner. And I assume he's paying, so she gets something out of it. She said that she's not getting back together with him. She's just humoring him by having dinner and a discussion. She'll let him down easy and he'll go back to Mass, and that will be that. No need for any fuss or bother."

"I know." Vic sighed. "I shouldn't be wanting them to argue. I just feel like it would be healthier if they did. They should get their problems all out in the open."

Erin smothered a smile. "I think that's the whole point of eating here. They want to lay it all out on the table, discuss things civilly, and then come to some kind of settlement. Which would preferably be Adele going home and Romeo leaving town."

They were both quiet for a minute, watching Rudolph talk earnestly with Adele, his cheeks slightly flushed, leaning toward her as he caught her up on his life or asked her for a favor or whatever he was there for.

"Don't look now," Vic murmured, "but I think it's your favorite blond accident victim."

Erin looked around. "Accident victim?" She spotted the woman in army fatigues. "Oh, her. She wasn't the victim, she was the one who caused the accident."

They gazed at her, trying to glean anything they could by looking at her. She stood by the hostess podium, waiting to be seated. She looked just as Adele had described her, with the camouflage shirt and pants. Just no gun. What exactly had she been up to in Erin's woods with a gun? Out hunting? But hunting what? There were still plenty of people around Bald Eagle Falls who hunted for their own food, but they didn't do it right in town. They would go out farther into the wilds and look for deer or other big game.

The woman looked like a hunter, so maybe she had just been in the wrong place, thinking she was on public land and would be able to bag something.

The woman looked over and saw the two of them staring at her. She raised her brows and gave them a questioning smile. Erin didn't know what to do; should they acknowledge that they had been looking at her, or pretend that they had just happened to be looking in that direction? She looked at Vic to see what she thought.

"Oh, sheesh," Vic murmured. "She's coming over here."

"Well, you're the one who wanted some excitement."

"I wanted to watch someone else get into an argument, not me!"

The woman had a slow, rolling gait that brought her efficiently to Erin's and Vic's table without even a whisper of sound.

"Hi. I'm eating alone today; would you mind if I joined you?"

Erin looked at Vic, who looked back at her, and neither of them was sure what the proper protocol for such a situation was. It would be rude to turn the woman away without a good reason, but they were there to spy on Adele, not just to eat and visit.

The woman waited for a few moments, then pulled out a chair and sat down.

"Rohilda Beaven," she introduced herself. "Folks call me Beaver."

"Beaver?" Erin repeated. She looked around to see if someone was secretly filming them. It had to be some kind of joke. People didn't just invite themselves to join you at your meal. And women did not go by nicknames like Beaver. Even if they did have strange Christian names like Rohilda. What kind of a name was that? Danish?

"Beaver," the woman agreed. She crossed one ankle over a knee, spreading out to take up plenty of space. Like a cat puffing out its fur to make itself look bigger. She seemed to be taking up as much real estate as possible. "And you are...?"

"I'm Vic, and this is Erin."

"Vic and Erin. Nice to meet you. I hope you don't mine me horning in on your dinner too much? I'm usually a loner, but the way you were watching me when I came in... I thought maybe you wouldn't mind."

"No, of course not, we wouldn't want you to have to eat alone," Vic assured her. "Erin and I spend so much time together, it's probably a good thing to have someone else join in to spice up the conversation."

Beaver nodded. "Are you two a couple?" she asked, making a gesture to include them both.

Erin was taking a drink of her RC and just about sprayed it across the table. She was used to hearing comments made to Vic about her gender identity, but it had been some time since anyone had accused the two of them of being an item.

"No, no," Vic tried to cover Erin's spit-take. "We work together. And I rent an apartment from Erin. We don't live in the same house and we're both… We're both straight."

"Oh, okay." Beaver shrugged. "Sorry. I just thought maybe you were out on a date. You said you spent a lot of time together, so I figured…"

"No. We both have boyfriends," Vic said firmly.

Erin nodded in agreement. She wondered whether Beaver was gay herself or had just made a wrong assumption. There were stereotypes about a woman in army fatigues or with a brush cut. Not that Beaver had a brush cut. She had a beautiful long ponytail which would have had to be done up in a tight bun if she were actually in the army. And then there was the name Beaver. What kind of a name was that for a woman?

"I don't. No boyfriend or girlfriend. So, no judgments here." Beaver looked around for the waitress. It was a few minutes before she managed to get someone's attention to order a drink and get a menu. Then she flipped through it in a slow, relaxed pace. "What's good here? There anything special?"

"It's all good," Vic said. "All done from scratch, even the mashed potatoes. I don't think there's anything bad on the menu, do you, Erin?"

"No, I haven't ever been disappointed."

"The two of you work together? Where do you work?" Beaver asked.

"I own the bakery," Erin offered. "Auntie Clem's Bakery. That's me."

"You're Auntie Clem?"

"No, I'm Erin. My aunt was the real Auntie Clem. I named it after her, because I inherited from her, so I had enough money that I could take a run at opening a place of my own. It was really a great break for me."

"Sounds like it," Beaver agreed. "I wouldn't mind if someone would die and leave me a business. That seems like a pretty sweet deal."

"You wouldn't want someone you loved to die, though," Vic pointed out.

Beaver considered this seriously before finally nodding agreement. "No, you're probably right there. I wouldn't want someone I loved to die. But someone else could, that would be okay."

Vic shook her head, bemused. Erin decided to try to steer the conversation to something a little less morbid.

"So, what about you? Are you a hunter?"

"I'm a *sort* of a hunter," Beaver said with a mysterious smile. "You could say that."

"I hear you were over on my property earlier and Adele sent you on your way."

Beaver looked around and saw Adele talking with her husband at their table. "That one, you mean? Yeah, she told me it was private land and I couldn't be wandering around on it. You pay her too?"

"Uh, well, she's my groundskeeper. She makes sure that no one is messing around with anything out there, and she gets free rent of the summer house. It works out for both of us."

"You might want to suggest she start carrying a gun. Anything could happen out there, and she wasn't even armed. You don't know what kind of people you're going to run into."

"What's that supposed to mean?" Vic challenged. She looked Beaver over, her brows drawing down in anger. "Is that a threat of some kind?"

Beaver's eyes widened, either surprised or pretending to be. "A threat? Me? Heavens, no. What reason would I have to threaten anyone?"

Vic dialed back her tone. "Okay, then. I just wanted to... We've had some things going on in town. There are some shady people hanging around, and we're a little worried about them causing trouble. So I just... I wanted to make sure you weren't with them and weren't making some kind of threat..."

"I'm not with any one." Beaver slurped an ice cube out of her glass of water and chewed it. "I have seen some characters around town, though... I think I know what you're talking about."

"That man that you rear-ended," Erin said. "He's one of them."

Beaver laughed. "Oh, you heard about that, did you? I guess word does get around, even if you're not from these parts. Yeah, I hit the idiot."

"You know him?"

"I know his kind," Beaver said, her mouth twisting into a sneer of distaste. "And I figured I'd give him a hard time."

"You really shouldn't do things like that! If you'd made him mad enough..."

"Nah. He wouldn't have done anything. What's he going to do, shoot me there on Main Street? He couldn't do anything that might attract the attention of the police. When that cop came afterward..."

"Then he made a break for it," Erin agreed. "But if you provoke someone like that enough..."

"He'd have to get permission from whoever his boss is. And then he'd have to find me. And he'd have to get the drop on me. Because I'm always armed and I'm no shrinking violent about using my weapons."

"His *boss*," Vic repeated. "What do you know about him, then? I just knew he was from out of town..."

"That guy? He had drug dealer written all over him. But not a kingpin. Just the guy at the bottom of the totem pole, finding new clients and doing the street-level sales. Not the kind that climbs to the top. They always die before they get that far."

Erin's stomach turned over at Beaver's casual tone. Bragging that she always carried a gun and then talking about how soldiers like that drug dealer were just going to die... she didn't like the cold, greasy feeling the conversation left her with.

Glancing over at Vic, she saw her own feelings etched on Vic's face.

CHAPTER 26

*T*he waitress brought Erin's and Vic's meals and took Beaver's order. Erin looked down at her food, no longer hungry.

"Don't wait for me," Beaver said. "I'll probably catch up to you. My parents always did say that I eat way too fast. I never slow down and enjoy the meal."

Erin didn't believe it. Everything about Beaver was thought out and deliberate.

"Where did you say you're from?" Erin asked, though she knew very well that Beaver hadn't said anything about where she hailed from.

"Here and there," Beaver said. She creased her napkin and unfolded it again several times. "I've been all over."

"Like Erin," Vic offered. "I think she's been everywhere. Me, I just grew up on a farm here in Tennessee, and I've hardly even been out of the state. Redneck girl if you ever saw one."

"I haven't lived *everywhere*," Erin countered. "Mostly northeast. I spent my first few years around here, but after that... Maine, New York, eastern seaboard... other places. I haven't lived west coast or anywhere past the Midwest."

Beaver nodded. "I've been everywhere."

"Army?" Vic suggested.

"Army brat," Beaver admitted. "Never got the knack for staying in one place after growing up like that. I stick around too long, and my feet start to itch. My mom said she always knew when she got to the bottom of the moving boxes… then it was time to start packing again. Didn't matter whether it took her two weeks or two years to get everything unpacked, as soon as she emptied that last box, Dad would get new orders and they'd be on the road again. So I'm more comfortable living out of a suitcase than confined to one place."

"That's hard for me to believe," Erin said. "I was always being moved from one place to another. There was nothing I wanted more than to just have one family and stay in one place. I love having a house of my own, knowing that I don't have to ever give it up to go somewhere else. It's mine for good."

"Never say never," Beaver warned. "Fate is always listening, and just like my mom unpacking those last boxes… as soon as you say you're safe and secure and no one can take anything away from you… that's for sure when you start to tempt fate."

"I don't believe in fate." But Erin couldn't deny the foreboding Beaver's words stirred up in her. Had she become too complacent? What if something did happen? What if she did lose everything, like she always had before?

"I think Erin's been through enough in life," Vic said. "She's burned through all of her obstacles. Leave some for the rest of us."

Erin chuckled and shook her head.

She was trying to eat her ribs daintily, but it was no use. She couldn't help getting sauce on her fingers and on her face, and eventually, she just had to give up trying to keep them clean. "Just don't look at me," she said. "This is way worse than it should be. You'd think I would have learned how to eat by now."

"You just look like you're enjoying it," Beaver said. "If I was you, I'd make as big a mess as I could. If you're going to get dirty, you might as well get really dirty!"

The waitress eventually brought over Beaver's steak and potatoes, and Beaver proceeded to cut everything up efficiently. She didn't exactly stuff her face, but she was making her way through her meal a lot more quickly than Erin had expected. Beaver looked at Erin.

"I did warn you. I'm going to be done before you are."

"You probably are," Erin admitted, looking at the couple of bones she had cleaned off. She still had a long way to go.

"It's not a race," Vic said primly. But she was eyeing Beaver's plate, looking at her own and calculating how long it was going to take her to finish.

Beaver looked over at Adele and Rudolph. She studied them for a few minutes.

"You said that *she* rents from you. Not her and her husband."

"That's right," Erin admitted. "He doesn't live here. He just showed up today. She's supposed to be turning him down, but it doesn't look as if she is. They are looking pretty friendly."

"She'll turn him down," Beaver said certainly. "She's got a good head on her shoulders."

"What makes you think that?" Vic asked. "You only just met her today for two minutes. How did you even know that they're married? We didn't know until this afternoon."

"I know his kind."

"I hope she's not going to take him in," Erin said.

Beaver continued to watch the interplay between Adele and her husband.

"What is it you do?" Erin asked. "You know that we are bakers and you said you're sort of a hunter, but that just leaves me wondering what it is you actually do?"

Vic cocked an eyebrow at Erin. Erin was normally reluctant to pry into people's personal lives. Too much experience with foster care, where the social workers and foster parents weren't supposed to share information about their kids' backgrounds even with the other kids, and asking was taboo. She usually just sat back and let other people do the asking, or watched and waited until people revealed themselves.

But there were too many people with unknown pasts showing up in town lately. Erin was too anxious not to ask. It was obvious Beaver was holding back, giving only general answers and focusing the conversation on things other than herself. Normally, people loved to talk about themselves.

Beaver didn't answer at first. She was intent on eating her steak and potatoes, and was putting them away at a surprising rate. After a few minutes of silence, she wiped her mouth with her napkin and looked at Erin.

"Okay," she said, "why not? I'm not the kind of hunter you might think I am. I don't hunt animals."

Erin waited, but a more full explanation was not forthcoming. Erin ran through the possibilities. Maybe Beaver was a bounty hunter or a private investigator. Maybe she was like Alton Summers, someone skilled at tracking down heirs or other people who had dropped off the radar.

But if she wasn't hunting animals, what was she doing with a gun?

CHAPTER 27

*B*eaver had remained coy about what exactly it was she hunted, just grinning at Erin's and Vic's questions and giving nothing away. But they had her name, assuming that she hadn't made up Rohilda Beaven, and that at least gave them some leverage to figure out more.

"We should give her name to Terry," Erin said as they discussed Beaver, sitting in the living room making their plans for the next day. "He can run background on her."

"He already has her name from the accident forms," Vic pointed out. "He's the one who isn't sharing information."

"Oh, yeah. Well... he can't, really."

"But we've got her name, so at least let's do an internet search. She's bound to have social media accounts that say something about who she is and what she does."

"You think if she's involved with one of the clans she's going to say that on Facebook?"

"Well, maybe not that," Vic said, "but she said she's a hunter, which would make me think she isn't with the clans."

"That could have been misdirection. Or she might be... hunting people." Erin remembered Beaver chewing her gum, clearly enjoying winding up the drug dealer, and then later grinning away as Erin and Vic

130

tried to figure out what she meant by saying she was a hunter. She shuddered.

"A hit man?" Vic said skeptically, "I wouldn't think so. Those kind of people don't generally go around announcing what they are. Let's just look."

Erin couldn't see any harm in looking the woman up, especially if Terry already knew who she was. "Okay, fine. Let's see who she is."

Vic eagerly pulled out her tablet and tapped in a search. "I'm going to assume that Rohilda is spelled just the way it sounds…"

"I don't have any idea. It should give a suggestion if not." Erin waited for the results.

"There are some news articles," Vic announced. She tapped on one, and her eyes skimmed back and forth as she read the page. She started to laugh.

Erin relaxed. Not a hit man, then. At least they didn't have to worry about that.

"She's a treasure hunter. She's not hunting animals or people. She's hunting for treasure or artifacts."

"The little scamp. Why didn't she just tell us that?"

"Because it was more fun to keep us guessing, obviously."

Erin shook her head. "What a brat!"

Vic was chuckling. "Well, it made our evening more entertaining." She scrolled down the article, her eyes wandering over it. "So… what do you think she's doing in Bald Eagle Falls?"

Erin considered. "Good question… but you get them in this area sometimes, don't you? With all of the mines and the possibility of Confederate gold. I remember talking about that when I first opened up the bakery. Remember the map of Clementine's that we found in the recycling?"

Vic nodded. "Yeah, that's right. That's one of the fun things about spelunking around here, the idea that one day you might run across a treasure that no one else has seen in a hundred years. That there is still a big haul just sitting out there somewhere, untouched. I guess that must be what Beaver is here looking for." Vic grimaced. "I really don't like calling her that. It seems disrespectful."

"It's what she wanted to be called. You've had experience with people who won't call *you* by the name you want to be called."

"I do at that," Vic admitted.

"I think she enjoys making people uncomfortable, don't you? The way she was acting when she rear-ended that drug dealer. Making us try to figure out what kind of a hunter she is. She likes stirring the pot and then sitting back to see how people react."

"Do you think she *did* rear-end him on purpose?" Vic asked.

"I don't know. It certainly makes me wonder."

"That's crazy." Vic grinned. "She's quite the woman."

"I don't think she's as crazy as she would like us to think."

"No. I agree with you there. It seems very calculated."

"With all of these new people around town, I thought she was one of the clans. I really did. It's a relief that she's just a regular person. Or however much of a regular person she can be as a treasure hunter. I think all of those people are a little bit crazy."

"Maybe you have to be in order to believe there's some wonderful treasure buried around here, that if you can just find it, you'll be set for the rest of your life. It's exciting if you believe it. If you don't believe it, then it's just a dream and there's really no point. Unless you really just like crawling around in caves."

Erin's goosebumps returned. She shivered from deep down in her stomach and tried to force her mind away from her cave experiences and pretend that she was only thinking about Beaver.

"Sorry," Vic said.

"I'm fine," Erin brushed off her concern. "That's all in the past. I don't ever have to go into another cave again if I don't want to."

"No. I just wish… you hadn't been through all of that and you were interested in going spelunking with me. I think it's really interesting."

"That's fine. You can go with Willie to any cave you want. I'm just not interested."

"When he took us together, you did okay at that."

Erin had gone with Vic, with Willie as her guide, back when she was trying to prove to herself that she could and wanting to impress Willie. Now that Willie and Vic were together… she didn't have anything to prove to him. He couldn't care less whether she wanted to crawl around in the caves. He could take Vic into his mine or exploring other caves and it didn't bother her one bit. In fact, she enjoyed it.

"I guess we'd better be getting to bed," Erin looked at the time on her phone. "In spite of all of the potential excitement tonight, nothing actually happened, and we need to be up as usual tomorrow morning."

"I'll just go say goodnight to Jeremy, then I'll head out."

Erin nodded. Vic knocked softly on Jeremy's door and then poked her head in.

"Hey, Jeremy. I'm just knocking off."

Erin couldn't make out his murmured reply. She looked over her lists for the next day and carefully layered them into a pile. Whatever was going on in Bald Eagle Falls, she certainly wasn't going to solve all of its problems. She would leave the detecting to Terry and the police department.

Melissa was at the bakery at opening the next morning, her curls practically bristling as she waited to gossip with Erin and Vic. She looked like she'd been waiting all night and could barely contain herself.

"You were at the restaurant last night," she said. "What do you think?"

"Um... about what?"

"About Adele and Rudolph, obviously," Melissa said irritably. "They were together at the restaurant. You were there, so dish."

"There's nothing to dish," Erin said, raising her hands in a shrug. "We weren't sitting with her. We couldn't hear anything they discussed."

"They're still married," Melissa pointed out, as if Erin might have missed this point. "If they have been apart since before she moved into town, then why are they not divorced? Why isn't he her ex-husband instead of her husband?"

"Not everybody wants to rush right into divorce," Erin said uncomfortably. "Some people do a trial separation... decide whether it's really what they want, or whether they might want to get back together instead."

"And he does, doesn't he? He wants to get back together, and Adele said she didn't, but she was sitting with him at the restaurant. Just the two of them, holding hands. You don't hold hands with your ex."

"He isn't her ex, you just said that."

"I know that!" Melissa nodded emphatically, her dark curls bouncing all over. "That's what I'm saying! They're still married and they're still holding hands. What have they been doing since they separated? It's like... what if he's been undercover and it was all just a hoax, being apart. What if he's finished whatever he was doing, and now he wants to get back together again, because they didn't *really* break up, it was just because of his job."

Erin tried to follow the convoluted logic. "You think… he's an under-cover cop? Is that what Terry said?"

"No, no!" Melissa flushed red. "He didn't tell me anything. I know he looked Rudolph up, but he wouldn't tell me anything about it and didn't leave any reports to be filed. But why didn't he? Is he trying to keep something from me?"

Terry knew he had a couple of leaks in the department, and Erin figured he knew exactly who they were. He probably just didn't want Melissa spreading the results of whatever searches he had done far and wide.

"Well, if he didn't tell you what the results were, you can't assume that Rudolph is undercover. Maybe he's just what he appears to be. Some bored playboy who thought he'd try to get back together with his wife."

"I don't think so. I think he's up to something. He must have been undercover. Otherwise, why would she just accept him back? I sure wouldn't take my husband back if I thought he'd been fooling around on me. I'd want him out of my life for good."

"But we don't know that's what happened."

"Have you seen the guy? Of course that's what happened. He's fooling around, cheating on her, and then he expects her to take him back again. And instead of telling him to hit the road and not bother her, she's holding hands with him!"

"So, which do you think? That he's a playboy or an undercover cop?"

Melissa spread her hands wide, exasperated. "How am I supposed to know? Terry should have told me something."

Not if he wanted it kept quiet.

"How about the other guy?" Erin asked, on a whim. "You know, the one that Rohilda Beaven rear-ended. Did you find anything out about him?"

"Bo Biggles?" Melissa asked, then laughed. "I can't believe that's actually his name. Can you imagine walking around with a moniker like that?"

"Bo Biggles?" Erin repeated. "Yeah, I would think he would have changed it!"

"Well, Rohilda goes by Beaver, so what are you going to do with that?" Vic said.

"Beaver?" Melissa apparently hadn't heard this tidbit. "For a woman? I can't imagine being taken seriously with a name like Beaver. She doesn't use it for real life, right? Just for a silly nickname. I mean, you couldn't rent a house with a name like Beaver. You'd be a laughingstock."

"This Bo Biggles," Erin tried to redirect Melissa, "he's a drug dealer?"

"Terry told you that?" Melissa asked.

Erin evaded the question. "It was pretty obvious."

"Is he with one of the clans?" Vic asked. "Is he with Dysons? It gives me the creeps, thinking that they're in town."

Melissa shook her head. "No, I think he's with your clan. Jacksons."

"Not *my* clan," Vic countered. "I'm not part of that family anymore. Remember, they disowned me. I couldn't be part of it if I wanted to."

"But it's still your clan. They're still your family, whether you stay with them or not."

Vic shook her head. "I got away from all of that when I left home."

Melissa sighed loudly. "Fine then, Bo is with the clan you used to belong to. The Jacksons. But really, you can never leave the clan," Melissa said ominously. "It doesn't matter if you want out, they'll follow you and they'll make sure—"

"Melissa," Erin interrupted. "What did you say you wanted to order? Are you looking for something for the department or for yourself?"

Melissa looked at the display case, her mouth open. She looked at Vic as if she were going to continue the conversation, then apparently caught Erin's warning look and decided she didn't want to be thrown out with no one to gossip with and no baking.

"Maybe a muffin for lunch," Melissa said. "No turnovers today?"

Erin had pulled a couple of batches of turnovers out of the freezer, but she couldn't quite bring herself to make any more since Inglethorpe's death. She remembered him asking her about turnovers, and then the shock of walking into the crime scene and thinking the blood was cherry pie filling. She wasn't sure she'd ever be able to make cherry turnovers again. Hopefully, she'd be able to bring herself to make blueberry or apple.

"Sorry, nothing right now. They're time intensive, so I have to find the time to make them. Not like muffins, where you can just mix up the batter and pour it into the cups."

"They sure were good. I hope you make some more soon."

Vic looked in Erin's direction. "We'll have to see."

They managed to keep Melissa focused on choosing the baking she wanted to buy, and then hustled her toward the door as other customers arrived. Melissa went, knowing that she wouldn't be able to speak freely in front of others. Melissa wouldn't gossip about police files with just *anyone*.

Erin was the one who solved mysteries and had some influence over Terry. Erin was practically family.

Erin sighed as she and Vic dealt with the next few customers, until it was quiet and they were left alone together again for a few moments.

"So," Vic drawled, lengthening her words. "Just what *do* we think about Adele and Rudolph?"

CHAPTER 28

*E*rin dreamed she was back at the bakery. At first, she thought she was in her own kitchen and she looked around, trying to orient herself, but nothing was in the place it was supposed to be. Then she realized she could not be in Auntie Clem's kitchen, but rather was in The Bake Shoppe.

"I don't know where you put anything," Erin muttered, turning around again and trying to decide where to begin.

She went to the fridge and opened it to see what had been prepped. She and Vic always made some batters and doughs ahead so that it would be quick to get started in the morning and the flours would have had a chance to soak and soften. But there was nothing in the fridge.

Except... maybe there was. When Erin looked more closely, she realized that her rolling pin had been left in the fridge. She reached in and grabbed it. The marble was as cold as ice, and when she turned it and examined it more closely, she realized that it was sticky with cherry sauce. But the smell was not the smell of cherries. Erin gagged at the cloying, coppery smell. It wasn't cherry sauce at all.

She turned around and saw the body lying on the floor. It wasn't Mr. Inglethorpe this time, but someone else who was vaguely familiar.

Even though she was starting to realize that it was a dream, she tried to identify the shape on the floor. Who was it? Who had Erin hurt this time?

She stepped closer, her shoes sticking to the floor like they did in a movie theater.

"Mr. Inglethorpe...?"

There was white powder everywhere. Erin tried to avoid getting any of it on her. Had someone opened a bag of flour? Everything was going to be contaminated and she wouldn't be able to serve anything safe.

"It's not flour," Vic laughed. "It was never flour."

"Okay. I think... it's time to go back to Auntie Clem's. I don't want to be here anymore."

Erin tried to leave, but her eyes were drawn again to the figure on the floor. She should have recognized that uniform. It was as familiar to her as the dimple in his cheek. Erin crouched down beside him. "Terry? No! Terry, what happened? Who did this? Who could have done this?"

She couldn't rouse herself from the dream. She tried to pull herself from its grip, but she couldn't escape.

"Help me! I need help! It's Terry!"

"What's wrong? Erin? Erin, are you okay?"

Erin tried to pull away from the grip on her arm. Then she jumped, feeling the sensation of falling. And then her eyes were open, and she was lying on her bed, awake, staring up at Jeremy's face. He looked anxious, his mouth turned down and his eyes squinted at her in concern.

"Are you awake? Erin, are you okay?"

"What happened?"

"Nothing happened. You were just calling out. I thought... I didn't know whether I should wake you or not."

Erin gripped Jeremy's hand. "Yes. Yes, I couldn't get out of it."

She didn't let go of Jeremy's hand. He looked at her for a minute, then sat down on the edge of the bed.

"It must have been pretty nasty."

"Yes..." Erin was breathing as evenly as she could, but couldn't seem to quite catch her breath and calm herself down. Her heart was thumping wildly. "It was Terry..." She gulped. "I guess it's normal to have nightmares after something like that."

"Like that? You mean the murder?"

Erin nodded. "Yeah. It was... kind of a gruesome scene."

"That would be tough," Jeremy admitted. "Sometimes... things stick with you. Even when you think it should just be a minor thing. When it's something bigger like that, it must be worse."

Erin nodded. She could feel Orange Blossom sleeping curled up next to her leg, and she reached out and patted him and scratched his ears. Orange Blossom awoke and started purring loudly.

"But Terry's okay," Jeremy said. "Nothing is going to happen to him. Everybody is safe. You can just take a breath and relax. Go back to sleep."

"Right," Erin agreed. "I'll just close my eyes and go back to sleep."

No problem. She could do that. She did that every night. It was simple as pie.

Cherry pie?

Erin shuddered. She looked at Jeremy. She was still holding on to his hand. Probably harder than was comfortable for him. But it was comforting to her and she wasn't ready to let go.

"It will be okay, Erin," Jeremy said. "Really. Your friend is okay. There's nothing wrong with him. If you just go back to sleep, in the morning everything will be fine, and you'll feel much better. Okay?"

"You're just a kid, what do you know?" Erin laughed.

Jeremy looked at her for a minute, not answering.

"I'm just joking," Erin said uncomfortably.

"Just close your eyes. Go back to sleep."

Erin took in a long breath and blew it out very slowly. She was just starting to relax and to quiet her mind when the phone rang.

Both she and Jeremy jumped.

"Oh, no." Erin looked at the phone, afraid of what she was going to see. Terry calling her to tell her that something was wrong? Vic? Somebody calling to tell her that something had happened to Terry?

Jeremy looked over at it, reading the screen. "Unknown caller."

"I hate those… I don't answer them, but I always wonder. Late at night like this, no one should be calling. It has to be important, right? It's not just a curious client hoping I'll make cupcakes for a birthday party."

"You don't need to answer it. If the person won't let you see their caller ID, that's their problem."

Erin pressed her lips together anxiously. She wanted to do the right thing, and she was too worried to let the call go to voicemail in case it was something important and she was really needed. If it was just a spam call, she could hang up.

She took a breath and picked up the phone. She swiped it to answer the call.

"Hello?"

"Send your friend Jeremy out and no one will get hurt."

Erin stopped breathing. She looked at Jeremy. "What?" she squeaked.

"You heard me. We want to see the traitor. Face-to-face. You shouldn't be protecting him."

"I'm… I'm not doing anything wrong…"

"Tell Jeremy we want to talk to him."

Erin shook her head emphatically. "No."

Jeremy was staring at her, his brows drawn down, unable to hear the voice on the other end.

Erin tried to analyze the voice. Terry was going to ask her to describe it. But she knew by the robotic quality of the voice that it had been altered. It didn't matter whether it sounded like a man or a woman, it could be totally different in real life.

"Who is it?" Jeremy asked urgently.

Erin pulled the phone away from her face and deliberately pressed her finger over the smooth glass of the screen, ending the call. If the caller thought that she was going to listen to them threaten Jeremy, they were wrong. He was her guest and she wasn't turning him over to some psychopath to do whatever they wanted with him.

"Erin. What was all that about?" Jeremy demanded.

"Wrong number," Erin said tersely. She tapped until she found Terry's speed dial, and tapped it.

"Wrong number? You don't talk like that with someone who calls a wrong number."

"No," Erin admitted, "you don't."

"Then who…?"

Terry answered his phone as soon as it rang on his end. "Erin? What's wrong?"

"I just got a threatening phone call. On my cell phone. Could somebody trace it? Could you come here? You'll need backup. At least, I think you will. He said 'we' like there was more than one of them…"

"More than one of who, Erin? What exactly was this call about? Was it something to do with Don Inglethorpe's death?"

"I don't think so. I don't know. Can you come?"

"I'm on my way. I'll get the others dispatched. But you need to tell me what you can about what we're walking into. Do you have some reason to believe that this person is going to hurt you? Did they utter threats? Do you know who it is?"

He gave a quiet command to K9, and Erin heard him start the engine of his car. He called the dispatcher on his police radio. He'd stay on the phone all the way over to her house to make sure she stayed calm and was safe.

"It's… they're threatening someone else. I'll explain better to you when you get here. But they said they wanted me to send out… this other person and to turn him over to them. But I'm not going to do that."

"Of course not. I wouldn't expect you to."

His engine raced in the background. Erin waited to hear the sound of his siren or engine approaching the house. She really wanted to know that he was there and would protect her. He and the others in the police department. She tried to shake loose any fear that they wouldn't be able to handle it. Of course they could handle it. There probably wasn't even more than one person involved. The caller was just saying 'we' to scare her. To make himself sound stronger and more threatening.

"Who is there with you, Erin?" Terry asked quietly.

"It's… Jeremy, Vic's brother."

"Jeremy?" Terry's voice was surprised. "When did he get there?"

Erin didn't bother trying to answer that one. Jeremy was looking at her, shocked that she had revealed his identity to the police. Now what was going to happen to him? She didn't know what kind of trouble he was in, but with murder and drug running and maybe all-out drug war going on, Erin wasn't about to keep quiet. They needed to know everything in order to act. They had to know everything there was about the situation.

Jeremy didn't run away. Maybe he was worried about what was going to happen the minute he walked out the door. Maybe he wanted to stay and make sure that she was okay. Or maybe he just didn't know what to do.

"Sorry," Erin breathed. She shook her head. "I really… don't know what else to do."

"You're doing the right thing," Terry said firmly in her ear. He didn't ask her what Jeremy was doing there. Would he assume that Jeremy had just gotten there? Or as soon as Erin had said it, did he understand that Jeremy had been there for several days and Erin had been lying about it or avoiding telling him what was going on?

"Almost there, Erin," Terry said calmly. "Can you tell me if the burglar alarm is set?"

"Yes… I set it."

"So, no one is going to get into the house?"

"No. I mean… I don't think so, but last time they did. There's no one inside yet." She looked at Jeremy for confirmation. She needed to know that there was no one else there. That the two of them were alone.

"No one," Jeremy confirmed. He walked to the doorway of the bedroom and looked toward the living room. "We would know it if someone had broken in."

"Okay. No one else here," Erin told Terry.

She could hear his car then. No siren, but she could hear the roar of his engine and then he skidded to a stop outside the house. She waited. He said he would call the others as well. She didn't want him to get hurt. He had been dead in her dream. Had she just put him in the crosshairs of someone who was willing to kill for what he wanted?

"I'm here, Erin. I don't see anyone. But I might have spooked them pulling up."

"Wait for backup. Don't get out yet," Erin begged him. "I don't want you to get hurt."

"I won't. It's okay. There's no immediate danger that I can see. As soon as it's clear, I'll come inside, and we'll talk about what happened and how to protect you."

"I'm more worried about you."

Terry chuckled. "No need to worry about me. I'm just fine."

Erin looked at Jeremy. He knew about Erin's dream. Was it a premonition? Precognition? Had she known what was going to happen before it did?

But she tried not to read anything into it. After all, in her dream, the body had been in The Bake Shoppe's kitchen, not in her bedroom or somewhere else in the house. And he'd been beaten with the rolling pin. While she did have a rolling pin in the house, it wasn't a big heavy one like the marble rolling pin she had lost and that had been in the dream. Whoever wielded it as a weapon would need a lot of strength to do the kind of damage that Don Inglethorpe had suffered.

"Here come the others," Terry advised.

It was a moment before Erin could hear the other vehicles, but then she heard them pull up to the house, one of them behind and another one in front. Terry coordinated the approach and they cleared the front and back yards and checked the doors to the garage and Vic's apartment before Terry knocked on the front door. Vic hadn't come out of her apartment, so Erin assumed that she had been told to wait there.

Erin went to the door and opened it. She fell into Terry's arms.

"Thank you so much for coming. I was so scared." She felt his arms go around her and hold her tight. Everything on his utility belt was jabbing into her stomach and body, but Erin didn't care. For the first few minutes, she just wanted to be held and to know that he was safe and so was she.

"I had a dream," she murmured into his chest. "I dreamed that you were hurt…"

"I'm fine, Erin. You didn't call me because of a dream, did you? You said that someone was outside? Someone called you?"

"I don't know who it was. They used a voice changer. You can try to trace the caller, right? It said unknown, though, so it was blocked. I just don't know if you'll be able to find out who it was."

"Well, let's get all of the facts established first. Can I come in?"

Erin gave a little laugh and stepped back. "Yes, of course, come in."

They entered and sat down on the couch. Erin cuddled up to Terry's warm, strong body, looking for comfort. Jeremy reluctantly joined them, ducking his head low at Terry's questioning look. Terry looked at Erin, kissing the top of her head. "I suppose we should also get Vic in here? Does she know what's going on?"

"She doesn't know what happened. I just called you."

"But she knows that Jeremy is here?"

Erin swallowed and nodded.

"Am I the only one who didn't know about this?"

"No," Erin protested. "Vic and I are the only ones who know. Not anyone else."

"How long?"

"Wednesday."

"He's been staying with you since last Wednesday?"

"Yes. Wednesday night."

Erin felt like a child caught with her hand in the cookie jar. And one that she knew very well she wasn't supposed to be sticking her hand into. But she had gone and done it anyway.

She had lied to him and hidden things from him. How would he be able to trust her again?

CHAPTER 29

*T*erry clicked his radio. "Bring Vic into the house."

There was a brief acknowledgment from Tom, and in a few minutes, he was leading Vic into the house in her nightgown and housecoat. Vic's eyes were wide and worried. "What happened? Is everybody okay?" Her eyes went to Jeremy, but she didn't know what to expect.

"Everyone is okay," Terry confirmed. "There was a threatening phone call, and Erin called me. Exactly what I would expect her to do. Unlike lying to me about Jeremy living at the house. How long did you think you were going to be able to keep that charade going?"

"I've been looking for a place of my own," Jeremy said. "I wasn't planning on staying here forever. Just for a few days. The lies are my fault. I asked them to please not let anyone know that I was staying here. I was worried… I wanted to keep it a secret."

"They had their own free will. They didn't have to agree to any terms or conditions they didn't want to."

"I wouldn't turn my own brother out," Vic protested.

"If he dictated terms that you were weren't willing to comply with, you would not have let him stay."

Vic looked for a way around that argument, her face getting red. "It's my fault too," she told him. "Erin wouldn't have agreed to keep it a secret if I hadn't asked her to."

"I think Erin is fully capable of making her own choices," Terry said slowly. "She's a big girl. She has a mind of her own—as we all know."

Erin felt her own face getting hot. The way that he said it, it was hard not to automatically fight back. But he had every right to be bitter and disappointed in her. She had chosen someone else's wishes over telling him the full truth.

"So this is why…" Terry started out. He looked at Erin. She felt tears springing up to her eyes and wanted to tell him that what he was thinking was not true. She hadn't just suggested that they go out to a movie and then to his house because she was trying to distract him and lead him away from Jeremy.

"This is… why I didn't want you staying over," she admitted. "Why I said we should go to your place instead. Because I wanted privacy."

"Jeremy would have given us privacy," Terry said. "It was more than that."

He was obviously hurt. Erin couldn't think of what to say to make it better. Terry's face was frozen like a mask. He looked at Jeremy. "I think you're the one we need to hear from. You're the one who knows what's going on here. Why exactly did you want to stay here and why didn't you want anyone to know about it?"

"I'm trying to find my own way," Jeremy said, sticking to the story he had told Vic and Erin. "I just needed somewhere to crash while I figured out what to do with my life. I need to get my own place… and a job… There's a lot to do before you can really get established independently."

Terry rolled his eyes. "What a load of crap. No one has to hide out because they're looking for a new job. Try again."

Erin had been feeling much the same way. She was pleased that she was finally going to hear the real story. She was proud of Terry for also recognizing that the story Jeremy was telling them didn't make sense. There had to be more to it.

Jeremy sat there, his hands folded, staring down at them.

"I do want to get out. I do want to get out on my own and be my own person."

Terry nodded and waited. The silence grew out uncomfortably long. Vic did her best to coax Jeremy on. "Come on, Jer. We're your friends. Tell us what's going on."

"Things at home..." he darted a glance at Vic. "Things haven't been good."

"Why? What happened?"

"It's just that... now that we're all getting older, we're supposed to be getting more responsible... taking more on... being better contributors."

Erin nodded. "That makes sense."

"Only... that didn't mean just taking on more chores at the farm. The farm hasn't been operating at full potential for a long time."

"What?"

"We still farm some," Jeremy explained. "But the money that we make from the farm... That's mostly just for show. You know: 'This is how we make a living. Nothing suspicious about that, is there?'"

"Who would you say that to? The police?"

Jeremy hesitated, then nodded. "Yeah. It was all for show... for the cops... any authorities who came around to make sure that everything was kosher. And Dad still loves the farm and likes taking care of the horses and other animals, and planting crops, and all of that stuff that..." Jeremy shrugged uncomfortably, "all the other stuff that we all really hate doing, because it's so dang boring."

Vic nodded slowly. "I know it can be boring... but I thought you still did it. Daniel and Joseph... they aren't running the farm? They aren't taking over from Pa?"

"They'll take it over, but the farm isn't ever going to be what it used to be. It's just an excuse now. A front."

"A front for what?" Terry asked.

"I guess you probably got that figured out already. A front for the Jackson clan."

"You're going to have to be more clear about that," Terry said slowly. "Tell me what kind of operations they're running that your farm is covering for?"

"The farm isn't covering everything, It's just a little part of the picture."

"Which is?"

Jeremy swallowed and looked at Vic. "I'm not really ready to start talking about everything the clan is doing. I'm not sure I'll ever be ready for that. Not unless I want to get myself killed."

"What were you expected to do? If you were not running the farm anymore, but were expected to take on more responsibility, then what are we talking about?"

"Uh… whatever they asked… whatever they thought we could handle…" Jeremy gave an uncomfortable shrug. "I used to think that it was all a pretty good deal. We didn't have to do anything much, but we got all of these perks from the clan. Money. Admiration. Whatever we wanted, really. We could go out and party and pretend for the girls that we were gangsters, and the clan would cover the drinks and the venue and whatever else… we could be the big fish. It was all a pretty good deal."

"Until they actually expected you to start paying dues. You were in debt to them and you had to do what they wanted."

"Yeah… pretty much."

"You were expected to do what you were told and not to argue about it."

Jeremy nodded. "Suddenly everything went from not doing anything, and getting whatever we wanted to… 'you owe us big after all we've done for you.' And without the farm to support us, how are we going to take care of Mom… what are they going to do to survive, now that all of that income from the farm has disappeared? If we even wanted to keep the farm, then we had to do some jobs… you need to hurt someone or make something right… take care of any little problems… and I don't…" Jeremy's voice choked up and he had difficulty going on. Erin felt tears in her own eyes. Jeremy was just a kid. Barely older than Vic. Barely an adult. But they had a tight grip on him, and they weren't letting go.

"So I thought… I'd come out here and stay with Vic. Make sure she was okay. She's the only other family I've got… or the only family that I feel like I can trust who isn't under the clan's thumb… and so Vic and Erin said I could stay here in the house or with Vic. There was more space here, so that's what I did. I didn't think anyone would really care. No one would follow me."

"But it sounds like tonight, they did." Terry looked down at Erin. "What did they say to you on the phone? Did they say it was about Jeremy? Did they threaten you or him?"

"They said I should send him outside to talk to them. That he was a traitor and I should just send him out and they would take care of it."

"Did they threaten you?"

"I…" Erin was having trouble recalling exactly what had been said. "I really don't know. They wanted me to send Jeremy out. They knew him by name. They knew he was here."

"And you told them no? Did you ask them who they were? Why they wanted Jeremy?"

"No, I don't think so. I'd just woken up from a nightmare and I was kind of freaked out. I was trying to calm myself down when the phone rang. I just didn't know what to do, except to call you."

"It was the right thing to do," Terry said. "I'm glad you didn't hesitate to bring me into it once you knew there was danger." His mouth was a long, thin line, completely serious with no hint of dimple or good humor. "I wish you had trusted me before this, but..."

"I trusted you. Jeremy asked us to keep you out of it, not to tell anyone that he was here, so... I agreed to do that. I'm sorry. I didn't want to keep anything from you, and I didn't want to mislead you about anything, I just did what Jeremy asked me to. I thought it would just be for a day or two, and then everything would go back to normal again."

"Do you think there *was* someone outside the house, or do you think it was just a threat? Was it to flush him out?"

"I... I didn't doubt that there was someone outside waiting for him."

"Did you hear any vehicles leaving? Did anyone pass by your windows in either direction?"

"I... I didn't hear anything," Erin said uncertainly. She looked at Jeremy. "Did you?"

"No, I didn't hear any engine... if they had a vehicle, it must have been a block away, out of earshot, and they didn't gun it out of here. I suspect that when Erin hung up on them, they knew what was happening and quietly left."

"You hung up on them?" Terry asked, his mouth quirking up slightly.

Erin nodded. "Well... I guess I did. I didn't see any point in letting them threaten me. They had their say and I wanted you to come and... take care of it. And I wanted to make sure that you were okay, and my dream wasn't real."

His look had softened a little. "What exactly was it that you dreamt?"

Erin thought for a moment about whether she could tell him about it, and then shook her head. "Just a dream," she said. "I guess I must have been thinking about Don Inglethorpe when I went to bed, and my brain changed that into thinking it was about you." She swallowed. He could figure it out from there.

"I'm sorry, Erin. You know… you might want to reconsider seeing someone… I know you said you don't want to, but sometimes it's for the best. We all need help sometimes. If you were on the police force, there would be mandatory counseling. It's not weak to need help working through something."

"I'm working through it my own way."

"I think your brain is trying to work through it… but you could maybe speed the process along if you were willing to take it a step further."

"Weren't we talking about Jeremy?"

Terry conceded and turned his attention back to Jeremy. "So what made you decide to come to Bald Eagle Falls?"

"I told you. I wanted to be with Vic. I knew she'd put me up for a few days while I figured out what to do."

"Except that meant that you could be traced. If you had just left town and gone for parts unknown, you would be a lot less traceable than if you stay here with your sister. Anyone could follow your trail here. And with all of the new activity in town… the timing seems just a little suspicious. If you wanted to get away from the clans, then why would you put yourself right into the middle of the playing field?"

"I just… wanted to get away, and to make sure Vic was okay."

"We've got all kinds of out-of-town representatives hanging around, causing trouble." Terry leaned back, looking at Jeremy as if he were one of them. "We've got drug dealers and enforcers and we've got other people who seem totally unconnected, but I sure wouldn't bet the farm that they aren't clan… It's all connected, somehow."

"I wouldn't have come here if I thought it would put Vic in danger. Or Erin. I'm sorry. I didn't think I was important enough for anyone to care about."

Terry let it go. "Who do you think came for you tonight?"

CHAPTER 30

$\mathcal{J}$eremy's face was an unreadable mask. In an instant, all of the caring and animation was gone from his face and he was like stone. "I don't know."

"You must have some idea. Who would they send after you?"

"I hardly know anyone that active in the organization. Everybody my age was just like me... taking part in the benefits without really doing anything to earn it. So, I don't know who they'd send."

Vic bit her lip and looked at Jeremy. "Did the others know where you were going?"

"No. I just told you that. No one else knew where I was going."

"I don't mean the bosses in the clan, I mean... the family. Joseph and Daniel. Did they know? Did Pa?"

Jeremy shook his head. "No. I didn't tell them where I was going. I just got on a bus and left. There wasn't anyone to say goodbye to. I just packed my bag."

"But your family knows about Vic living here. So they could probably figure out that if you needed a place to stay, this is where you would come."

Vic and Jeremy looked at each other. Vic nodded slowly. Jeremy still denied it, but Erin could see it was more out of fear than belief. Had he been betrayed by his own brothers? Had they just told someone where

Jeremy might have gone, or had one of them actually been waiting outside the house for Jeremy? Or could it be their pa? Erin hated to even consider the possibility.

"Regardless of why Jeremy came or who else might be in Bald Eagle Falls, what are we going to do now?" Erin asked. "How are we going to keep Jeremy safe? People are after him. It doesn't matter if it's somebody in the family or someone more distant. What do we do next?"

Vic looked at Terry. Terry sat there, saying nothing, considering the question.

"You're not responsible for me," Jeremy said quietly. "I got myself into this mess, I'm the one who is responsible for getting out of it. Not you. There's no need for anyone else to jump in and help me."

"Of course there is. You're here. You're family and you need somewhere safe," Erin told him.

"I'll leave town. I can't stay here and make you or Vic a target."

"I don't want you leaving town," Terry said. "Not before I can establish whether you're involved in anything that's going on. If I have to, I'll take you into custody."

"You can't do that!"

"Not forever, but maybe a couple of days will give me time to sort things out and figure out what to do with you. Do you have any outstanding warrants for the work you've been doing for the clan?"

Jeremy's face tightened. "No."

"You're sure?"

"Go ahead and check."

"I will."

"There has to be somewhere Jeremy could stay that no one would think to find him," Vic said. "What about with Adele?"

Erin grimaced. "I don't think that would be a good place for him. The summer house only has one bed and an open plan, so neither of them would have any privacy. We don't know whether Rudolph is staying with Adele…"

Terry frowned. "Why would her ex be staying with her?"

"He's not an ex," Erin reminded him. "They're still married."

"Doesn't mean he has to stay with her. After all of the dramatics earlier, why would she allow him to stay with her? In a one-room home with no privacy?"

Erin and Vic exchanged glances. "They met at the restaurant. Like you suggested, a public meeting…" Erin started.

Terry nodded, encouraging her to go on.

"We happened to be there for supper too…"

"Happened to be."

"We wanted to make sure everything was okay, that he didn't get abusive with her."

His eyes were narrow. "And how did he behave?"

"They seemed to get along together really well. Holding hands, eye contact, deep conversation… that's why I say, he could be staying there. I know she said she wouldn't take him back, but a lot of women say that, and then they do. Even when it's a really bad relationship. She said he came to get back together with her, and it looked like he was getting on pretty well."

Terry shook his head. "I didn't get a good vibe from the guy."

"Did you run a police check on him? Does he have any police history?"

"Fraud and theft. Nothing violent, no drugs."

"And he doesn't have any connection to the clans?"

"None immediately apparent."

"What about treasure hunting?"

Terry frowned. K9 shifted his position and let out a loud sigh, expressing his displeasure with having to lie in one place for so long. Terry patted his side.

"Why are you asking about treasure hunters?"

"Just because of Beaver… Rohilda…"

"I thought you said you were staying out of trouble."

"I am. I haven't done anything. We just met her at the restaurant. She was evasive about what it was that she did, so we looked her up."

"You need to stay out of it!"

Erin was surprised and hurt at the snap in Terry's voice. She swallowed and turned away from him, looking for Orange Blossom. The cat was watching her from the hallways, ears pricked forward while he watched K9. Erin smacked her lips to call him, but he paid her no attention.

"It's not Erin's fault," Vic said. "Beaver really did just walk up to us and invite herself to our table. And I was the one who said we should look her up. I didn't think it could hurt anything to look her up on the internet to see what it really was that she did. I figured she was just winding us up."

"And you think that people who want to hide who they are put it on the internet?"

"No," Vic's voice took on a belligerence Erin had rarely heard in her. "I figured if she was really someone dangerous, we wouldn't find anything online. How does us looking her up damage your investigation? We haven't interfered with anything!"

"You need to stay away from these strangers and just keep your head down. You shouldn't be doing anything that will attract attention to you. You made yourselves obvious at the restaurant. That will make people ask questions about you. When they find out who you are and your histories…"

Erin did have a reputation for having put more than one person in jail for crimes committed in Bald Eagle Falls. And Vic had, under her previous identity, been part of the Jackson family. Someone who, like Jeremy, might have benefited from clan activities and be expected to prove her loyalty and do something in return. If Beaver or someone else who had seen them at the restaurant had thought they were acting suspiciously and started asking questions, they might decide that Erin and Vic were getting too close to their secrets and had to be eliminated.

"I'm sorry," Erin said. "I didn't realize…"

"You know it's dangerous in Bald Eagle Falls right now. You were the one Charley told about it. If *she's* scared, don't you think you should be too? Don't you think maybe you'd better stay out of the way?"

Erin looked over at Vic. "Why *did* she come over to us? People don't just invite themselves to other people's dinners."

Vic frowned. Her arms were folded across her chest and she had adopted a very aggressive posture. Having her brother threatened and Erin called out by Terry brought out her protective mama-bear streak.

"It wasn't anything we did. She just looked around while she was waiting to be seated and saw us. So she came over and asked if she could join us."

"But why?" Terry asked. "How obvious was it that you were there to watch Adele and Rudolph?"

"Well… it might have been obvious."

Terry looked at his watch. "I'm going to check out the summer house as soon as we're sure everything is secure here."

"Aren't you already sure of that?" Erin asked, the anxiety that had waned since his arrival already building back up in her chest at his words.

"The sheriff was just going to check out the garage and the loft to make sure everything is safe."

"The loft?" Vic demanded. "I didn't give you permission to search my apartment."

"We don't need your permission to search the loft," Terry said evenly. "We have reason to believe that there may be a dangerous person on the property. Criminal threats have been made. We need to assure ourselves that there is no further threat. It's our duty to protect the citizenry."

"But there wasn't anyone in my apartment. I was there, so I know it's clear. You don't need to search it."

"It's procedure. It won't take long. Then you can go back to bed if you like."

"I don't want anyone searching my apartment."

Erin looked at Vic, not understanding the irritation in her voice. "They're not going to mess with anything. They're just making sure it's safe."

"I don't like having my privacy interrupted. And I don't like my civil rights being violated."

Terry's voice was calm and even. "No one is violating your civil rights. Yes, you have a right to privacy, but you give up some portion of that right in a case like this."

"It won't be long," Erin repeated, wishing she could say something else to make Vic feel better. But she couldn't understand why Vic wouldn't want her apartment to be cleared just like the rest of the property.

"You're going to stay here for the rest of the night?" Erin asked Jeremy. "You won't be able to find anywhere else tonight."

"I don't know if that's a good idea," Terry said with a frown. "Whoever called is going to know that he hasn't left. They could come right back, and with no warning this time."

"I'd rather someone else was here with me. And Jeremy shouldn't have to find somewhere else in the middle of the night."

"We can provide Jeremy with somewhere for the rest of the night."

"What, sleeping at the police department?"

"I'm not sleeping in a cell," Jeremy interrupted. "I didn't do anything wrong. I might have done something stupid, but I didn't do anything wrong."

"You can sleep on Sheriff Wilmot's couch with a blanket and pillow," Terry said. "We don't even have a holding cell. So just cool it."

"Okay," Jeremy gave a little shrug. "Sorry, but I'm a little sensitive…"

Erin still didn't want Jeremy to have to leave the house in the middle of the night. And she'd sat on that couch; she remembered how uncomfortable it was. He'd be better off sleeping on the floor.

om stuck his head in the door. He nodded to Terry. "Sheriff said to let you know it's all clear."

"Great. Vic, if you want to go back to your apartment, you can. Or if you'd like to stay here with Erin, I'm sure she wouldn't mind. Jeremy, I think, should come with me. I don't want him drawing unwanted attention to you girls."

"I can handle it," Vic said, patting her side.

Erin frowned, studying her. "You have a holster on under that housecoat?"

"You really should too. Especially when stuff like this keeps happening!"

"It doesn't *keep* happening, this is the only time..." Erin trailed off. It wasn't the first time she'd had to call Terry to the house to take care of an intruder. And it wasn't the first time someone had threatened her or someone in her home. She didn't like Vic sounding like it was something that happened all the time, but she also couldn't deny that it wasn't the first time they'd had to make an emergency call in the middle of the night.

"If it makes you feel better, I'll call Willie," Vic suggested to Terry.

"Well, yes, I'd feel better if I knew he was here."

"You think the poor women can't look after themselves?"

"Let's just call it a southern gentleman looking after the ladies," Terry said, and he gave Erin a little squeeze. "I'm just old-fashioned that way."

Vic snorted. "Good way to hide your chauvinism."

"Give him a call. I want to head over to Adele's to make sure everything is good over there."

"Go ahead. You heard what the sheriff said, it's all clear, and he and Tom are still here to defend the helpless ladies. You don't have to wait until Willie gets here."

"And *I'm* still here," Jeremy pointed out, gesturing to himself.

"No offense," Terry said, "but I know Vic, and I suspect she handles a gun just as well, if not better than you do. What I'd like is someone with a bit more muscle and experience, and that's what Willie's got."

"I can shoot—" Jeremy started to protest. Then he met Vic's eyes and faltered. "Okay, she can shoot better than I can. But two guns are still better than one."

"Are you armed?" Terry hadn't done a pat-down of Jeremy or Erin when he had come in. They had been completely focused on the outside threat.

Jeremy's hand dropped and Terry went stiff. He was off the couch and onto his feet before Erin realized what was happening.

"Hands up!" he ordered Jeremy. "Keep them away from any weapon!"

"I'm the one who told you—" Jeremy raised his hands in the air slowly, moving with caution.

"Just be still. What have you got?"

"Handgun in a back holster."

Terry lifted Jeremy's shirt to reveal it and then removed it carefully from the holster.

"What else?"

"That's all."

"What else, Jeremy?"

"I just got out of bed. What makes you think I'm sleeping with my guns on?"

"Hands on the wall."

Jeremy obeyed, grumbling to himself. Terry put his hand on Jeremy's back, holding him still.

"Now, are you going to tell me, or you want to get it automatically confiscated because you're lying to an officer?"

"I'm not."

Terry started to pat Jeremy down, his fingers firm and deliberate.

"Ankle," Jeremy admitted, before Terry got down past his waist.

Terry continued his careful pat-down, until he reached Jeremy's ankles. He lifted Jeremy's pajama pant leg to see the other holster, holding a second small gun. Terry removed that one too.

"And is that it?"

"You know that's all there is. You would have found anything else." Jeremy's voice was sullen, almost a pout.

Terry looked at Vic. "You know he was carrying concealed weapons?"

Vic licked her lips and shook her head, looking at her brother. "No. I didn't know."

"You have a concealed carry permit?" Terry asked Jeremy.

"Not exactly."

"Then you're not supposed to be walking around like this, are you?"

"I'm in my own home. Sort of. Not out in public. You can't arrest me for having a gun in my own house."

"You'd be surprised what I can do. I'm going to go over to Adele's to make sure everything is okay over there, and then I'm going to be back here. I'll take you to the police station for the rest of the night, however long that ends up being, and the girls can go back to sleep." He looked at his watch. "For a couple of hours, anyway. You might want to open the bakery late today. Give your bodies long enough to rest and recover."

Erin nodded her agreement, but she knew she wouldn't. She would still get up at the regular time and open the bakery on time, even if it meant that she only got two hours of sleep all night. She wasn't going to let the bad stuff going on around Bald Eagle Falls be a detriment to her business.

"I'll see you in a while then," Terry told them all. Hearing the finality in his master's voice, K9 got up and stood at the ready. Terry kept both of Jeremy's guns.

"You can't take those," Jeremy protested.

"We'll see about that. I'm not leaving them with you right now, anyway." He walked out the door. Erin could see him hand the guns to Tom and saw him make a motion toward the house, leaving him with instructions.

Erin waited until Terry was in his car and on his way before pulling out her phone and dialing.

∽

It took a few rings for Adele to answer the phone. She didn't sound tired when she answered, but then, she was usually up late and slept later in the morning than Erin.

"Erin? Is something wrong?"

"We had a bit of trouble over here. I wanted to call and give you a heads-up that Terry's on his way over. Just to make sure that everything is okay with you. He got it into his head that somebody might make trouble for you, so he's going to head over there and have a look around."

"Right now?"

"He's on his way." Erin expected Adele to hang up, but Adele stayed on the phone.

"You are all okay?"

"We're fine. There was a threat, but nothing came of it. I think we'll be just fine for the rest of the night. Terry just wants to make sure everything is kosher."

Erin could hear the smile in Adele's voice. "If he's looking for kosher, then he maybe shouldn't be looking for it with a Wiccan."

"Ha. Right. Well, he'll come make sure it's... whatever you would say."

"I think that's him now," Adele said. Erin couldn't hear the noise of the car approaching. She waited. Adele spoke to someone else. "We've got a visit from the police."

"Police?" Rudolph's voice was thick with sleep or maybe with drink. "What are the police doing here?"

"Just doing a check. Don't be a pain. Don't cause trouble."

There was a knock at the door. Adele answered it. "Officer Piper. Come in."

"Mrs. Windsor." Erin kept waiting for Adele to hang up the phone, but she kept the line open and Erin could hear most of what was going on. "And Mr. Windsor."

"What are you doing here?"

"There's been some trouble at your landlord's house. I'm just checking to make sure that no one ended up out here. People will be trying to get out of town, and I wouldn't want them thinking they could hijack your ride or steal your money."

"No one is going to do anything to me," Rudolph growled. "I can take care of myself, thank you."

"Never hurts to have the police around to make sure everything is peaceful. I'm sure you'd rather not have any trouble."

"Well," Rudolph's voice was still belligerent, "you can see that everything is fine here. So you can get on your way."

"Can I talk to you for a moment, Mrs. Windsor?" Terry asked, ignoring her husband's rancor.

There was a pause, Adele considering the request. Then she made a murmur of acknowledgment and Erin could hear them both moving, then heard the bang of the door and the gentle whistle of the night breeze across the phone mic.

"What else can I do for you, Officer Piper?"

"I just wanted to talk to you about your husband. I was surprised to find him out here. Are you... is he here with your permission? No coercion? You don't mind him being here?"

"Yes, Officer. No need for concern."

"Okay. I just wondered because earlier... you were trying to avoid him."

"And I told you I shouldn't have done that. These things are better dealt with face-to-face than trying to avoid contact. It's fine. Don't worry about it."

"You haven't seen anyone out here tonight?"

"No sign of anyone."

"I'm going to take a look around. Just make sure there's no unusual activity."

"I'm not sure how you're going to find anyone in the dark."

"I have a flashlight."

Erin looked out her own window. She didn't know how much difference it was going to make. Anyone would be able to see the beam of the flashlight before it reached them, and move out of its way if they didn't want to be seen.

Erin heard the rustle of footsteps. Adele brought the phone back up to her face. "Everything is fine. Your officer will take a few minutes to look around and then he'll be back to you. Alright?"

"Thanks," Erin said. "I'm glad everything is okay."

Before Adele hung up, Erin heard Rudolph growl at Adele one more time.

∾

Before Terry could get back from Adele's, Erin heard another approaching engine. A big engine, like a truck. It approached at a fairly high speed and screeched to a stop close by. Erin tensed up, unsure what she was going to be facing. Someone who had decided they could take on the last two cops in the police department and didn't have to wait for anyone or anything? The bad guy, come back to take Jeremy this time without any hesitation or negotiation?

But then she heard a voice greet the sheriff and she settled down, recognizing the familiar rumble. Willie was in the door a few minutes later.

"What's going on?" he demanded. "What happened?"

Vic hurried over to him to give him a big hug. "Not much time for talk," she said. "Everybody's okay, but people know Jeremy is here and we need to protect him. Terry wants to take him into custody and make him sleep at the police department."

"That doesn't sound like a whole lot of fun," Willie said. "I can tell you from experience that their facilities are not exactly the Ritz."

Erin wondered when Willie had had the opportunity to enjoy the police department's hospitality.

Willie looked at Jeremy. "Jeremy. How long have you been here?"

"A few days."

"I should have guessed that something was up. So, what do you need?"

"We need to put him somewhere no one is going to find him," Vic said. She looked Willie in the eye. "We can do that, right?"

Willie nodded. "Sure. I know of places."

Vic made a hurrying motion to Jeremy. "Go with him. Before Terry gets back."

Jeremy and Willie looked at each other, then left together. Vic looked at Erin. "You don't know where they went," she said firmly.

"Well... no, I don't."

Vic nodded. She gave a big sigh and rolled her eyes. "What a night." Erin was sitting alone on the couch, so Vic sat down beside her and gave her a sisterly hug. "How about you, are you okay?"

"I am right now... whether I'm going to fall apart in another hour when the adrenaline wears off, I don't know."

"I hear you," Vic agreed.

Erin looked at her young assistant. Despite the fact that Vic claimed to understand, Erin didn't know if she really did. She wasn't the one who had seen Inglethorpe dead and bloody. She wasn't the one getting crazy calls in the middle of the night.

"Are you going to be able to get back to sleep after all of this?"

"I don't know," Vic looked at the wall. "A little too late to be taking sleeping pills. What about you?"

"I don't think so."

"Then after everyone is gone, why don't we just throw a movie on, and we'll veg and watch it. It will be more relaxing than tossing and turning or having nightmares all night. How does that sound to you?"

Erin nodded. "Yeah. That sounds good." It would help her to relax just knowing that she didn't have to try to sleep. And if either or both of them did fall asleep, that would be just fine.

CHAPTER 32

They both had bloodshot eyes at the bakery the next morning. Erin took a break from the baking to hold an ice pack over her eyes to try to disguise them. It was best if the customers didn't know that they had been up all night.

It soon became obvious that even though the incident had taken place late at night and the police had not used any sirens, everyone knew something had happened at Clementine's house. Again.

Even Charley, when she stopped by in the afternoon, was up on the gossip. She wasn't a fully accepted member of the Bald Eagle Falls community, but she was still attached to the grapevine.

"Are you going to tell me what happened last night?" she demanded from Erin, as if Erin had been trying to keep a big secret from her.

"Not much to tell," Erin said with a shrug. "We just got a phone call, I was a little worried about it, so I called Terry… everything ended up being okay. Nothing happened."

Charley learned in. "Come on, give me the real scoop!" she insisted. "That's just what you tell everyone else. I want to know the sister's inside scoop."

"The only scoops we have are ice cream," Erin pointed to the cold case. "You pick out your flavor, and I'll give you a scoop. Two, even."

"Erin! Come on, don't be a tease. I'm worried about you."

Erin had a pretty good idea that Charley wasn't asking because of her deep concern over her half-sister, but due to her own curiosity and wanting to know what was going on with the clans in Bald Eagle Falls.

"We got a threat," Erin said. "Sort of a threat." Because she couldn't remember exactly what the voice had said to her. Had he threatened her at all? "So I called Terry. When he got there, whoever had made the threat was gone. End of story. Terry spent a bunch of time looking around, and Vic and I sat up watching movies because we were too hyped up to go back to sleep after the visit from the police."

"You don't look like you slept."

"Well, that would be why.'" Erin studied Charley critically. "You're actually not looking like you got a whole lot of sleep yourself. Are you okay?"

For a moment, Charley gave her a deer-in-the-headlights look, and then she managed to mask it. "I sleep just fine in this Podunk little town. Why wouldn't I?"

Erin wasn't so sure of that. "You weren't feeling too well the other day."

"I'd just had a bit much to drink. I'm sorry I bothered you. Sometimes… a story needs to be told. That one kind of got away from me. I didn't mean to bother you and your sweetheart with my tales of woe."

"You *can* talk to me about Bobby," Erin said. "It sounds like you're really missing him."

"What's to tell? If he was still alive, we'd be together. But we're not. I don't have what it takes to do a memorial or something for him. I just wish… that I could have the chance to mourn him. But that's not the way things work in this life, is it? We all have to keep on living, even if someone we love dies. Life goes on. There's no point in making a tragedy out of it."

"It was tragic. You loved him and you must really miss him."

"You know what else I miss?" Charley asked.

"What?"

"Being in the know. It used to be, I pretty much knew everything that was going on. Top level stuff. Anything important, I knew about it. I knew where Bobby was and what his plans were, even if they were just to go out on the town and have drinks with his buddies. I knew what the Dysons were doing and what my place was and what I was supposed to be doing."

"Did you know they were interested in Bald Eagle Falls and were planning on coming over here?"

"No. No one had hardly even heard of Bald Eagle Falls. Nothing ever happened here, so why would anyone care about it?"

"But they do now."

"Yeah, my wonderful sister attracted their attention. And I moved here, and I guess they caught up with everything else. Now, it's the place to be. Everyone wants a piece of the pie."

Erin saw cherry pie in her mind's eye. When was she going to stop conjuring it up out of thin air?

"What pie?" she asked. "What exactly is it they're trying to do? Cook and sell drugs? I can't imagine there's that much of a market out here."

"If there's a big enough market to support you on baking, then there's enough for a drug trade."

"But I'm sure... not that many people would buy drugs."

"No. But they'll pay a lot more for dope than they will for sugar. Sugar may be a gateway drug, but it's not going to put a lot of cold hard cash in your hands. Drugs, on the other hand..."

Erin remembered her dream. The part of the dream where she had seen the flour on the floor of the bakery, and Vic had told her it wasn't flour. Or maybe it had been Charley. Had Charley been in that dream as the other baker?

"But you didn't... I mean you don't... You're not looking to get in on the drug trade, right? You wanted to run the bakery, not a front for the drug trade."

"My plan was to have a legitimate business," Charley agreed. "But it looks like that's a dream, now. No one is going to let me open the bakery, which means I'm just going to go further and further in debt until I can get a job that pays more than the grocery store does. And where am I going to get that, other than going back to crime? Man, Erin. You're so lucky. You just fell into this whole thing. I feel like it's all just such a mess. Everything I touch turns to dust. I might as well not even try."

"I wish you wouldn't give up. Isn't there any way to talk the trustees into letting you open it up? Just even on a trial basis?" Even as she encouraged Charley, she felt a stab of anxiety. She wanted her sister to succeed, but not at the expense of Auntie Clem's.

"No. They're not going to do it. They're too afraid of the negative press about people dying there. Pretty soon, everybody will think that just setting foot inside the door could be enough to get someone killed."

"That's ridiculous."

"Yeah, but we're talking about people who still practically believe in fairy tales. These aren't rational human beings. They're superstitious. They believe all of it. They might say that they don't, but they totally do."

"I know they're superstitious, but believe me, they all want The Bake Shoppe to open again." Erin let out a sigh. It was true; she could see it whenever she looked at her church ladies. They told her how much they wanted Erin to succeed and how good her baking was, but they made no secret of the fact that they missed The Bake Shoppe and that if they could, they would just buy regular food at the regular bakery. They didn't want gluten-free baking and other specialty baking. No one except for Erin and the few who need gluten-free or other special diets.

"You and me," Charley sighed. "It seems like one of us has to fail while the other succeeds."

"Yeah."

"I always hoped that we could be like the brothers in that story."

"What?"

Charley grinned. "There's this story about these two brothers, and they ran competing businesses. I forget what they were supposed to be, but their shops were right next to each other, and they had this vicious rivalry going on for their whole lives."

"Okay."

"Well, after they both died, when people went in to take care of all of their personal effects and to sell the stores, they found out that there was a tunnel between the two stores. The two brothers had really been devoted to each other and had spent all of their time together in the evenings. The rivalry had all been for show."

"Why would they do that?"

"I guess people thought they were getting a good deal, because the rivalry kept the prices honest. Or they liked the drama or liked to gossip about them. Whatever it was… it was the magic ingredient in their businesses…"

Erin shook her head. "Funny story. I think I might have heard it before. It *would* be fun if our stores were side by side and connected by a tunnel." But then, Charley drove Erin crazy, too. If Charley had been back and forth to Erin's house and business twenty-four hours a day, Erin might just do something she'd regret.

"There are supposed to be tunnels between some of these buildings," Charley offered.

"What? In Bald Eagle Falls?"

"Yeah, you know, dating back to civil war, or something. People who needed to hide or to escape. They could slip through the underground tunnels and stay safe. Or maybe it was just a way to get around without having to face the Tennessee heat!"

"Which buildings were supposed to have tunnels?"

"I don't know. Most of them, I think. So people had somewhere to go that was safe. It's kind of fun to imagine."

"There isn't any tunnel in my basement."

Charley shook her head. "Mine either. I checked! If there is any tunnel down there, it's been bricked over so no one can access it."

Erin thought of the bricks that lined a couple of the walls of her basement. Not the whole basement, just a couple of walls. Had those walls been made differently because they were built at a different time? Was there something to hide or had they just shored up a crumbling wall?

Like Charley had said, it was fun to imagine. But that's all it was, just make-believe.

Charley looked over the baked goods and picked out a hand-shaped loaf of multigrain bread and a couple of cookies. When she left and Erin looked around to see the rest of her customers, she saw Rohilda Beaven standing nearby, her expression thoughtful.

Mary Lou approached the counter. She seemed like she was in better spirits than she had been lately. Maybe things were going better for her little family. Erin didn't want to inquire too closely, in case it made Mary Lou uncomfortable, but she was glad to see her friend in better spirits.

"I think maybe we'll have a pizza night," Mary Lou pronounced, looking into the display case. "I don't know when the last time was that Josh and I just had a fun, mother-son time together. Things have been so stressful the last couple of years..." A shadow passed over her face. "I don't want to lose him. He's only going to be home a couple more years and I want to make sure we maintain a good relationship."

Erin nodded. She pointed at the pizza shells. "You want the herbed crust? Or the one with cheese baked in?"

"The herbed looks very nice. And I don't think it's too… uh, highbrow for a teenager, is it? I don't want to look like I think we can't let down our guards and enjoy ourselves."

"I don't think it's too high-brow," Erin said. "Pizza is pizza. You're just going to cover it up anyway. He'll like it."

Mary Lou nodded. "It's a deal, then." She looked over at Vic as Erin packaged the pizza shells up for her. "And how are you, Victoria? Enjoying your brother being in town?"

Vic froze, mouth open, hand hovering over the cash register as she moved to enter Mary Lou's purchases.

"Uh… what?" she eventually managed.

"I saw your brother the other day. Tall boy, long blond hair?"

Vic nodded slowly. "I didn't think he'd been out at all. Where did you see him?"

Mary Lou frowned. "Oh, you would ask me that, wouldn't you? It was just casual, I didn't stop to talk to him, so I'm not sure even what day it was… I think I saw him over at the business center? I assumed he was seeing a lawyer, maybe for your folks. But I really don't know who he was visiting over there. There are a lot of different offices he could have been at."

"Yes, that must be it," Vic agreed. If she had continued to question Mary Lou about the meeting, she would draw attention to it, and that was not what she wanted to do. Why would Jeremy tell them that they had to keep his visit under the radar, and then go out during the day where anyone could see and recognize him? "It's been nice to have a little visit with him. I don't see my family often enough."

"No," Mary Lou agreed. "I imagine you'd see them more if you lived the values that you had been raised with."

Erin gave Mary Lou a warning look. If she were going to go any further along that vein, she was going to get herself thrown out of Auntie Clem's. Erin didn't allow any harassment of her employees.

"Anything for dessert?" Erin prompted.

"No, with just the two of us, I have plenty in the freezer still."

Vic rang up the purchase and completed the transaction. Mary Lou smiled politely and wished them both a good day before leaving the store. Vic looked over at Erin, her eyes wide.

"Why would he have been where people could see him?" Erin demanded. "I thought he didn't want anyone to know he was here!"

"I don't know. It's bizarre. Maybe he did have to see a lawyer or do some business over there."

"But if it were me… and I wanted to stay unseen… I'd ask them to come to my house. Or to see them after hours. I wouldn't just go out in the middle of the day when anyone could have seen me."

"Maybe she saw someone else and just thought it was Jeremy."

"No… who else is she going to see that she could mistake for him? How many young men do you know of in Bald Eagle Falls who wear their hair long like Jeremy's?"

"Well… I don't know about at the high school. Some of the teenagers have less conservative styles."

"But who is going to mistake Jeremy for a teenager?"

"I just don't know." Vic shook her head anxiously. "They might. I don't understand what's going on here."

"Where did Willie hide him?"

Vic looked quickly at her. "Don't talk about it. I don't want anyone to overhear and figure it out."

Erin thought of how Beaver had been standing so close, listening to everything that was being said when Charley was there earlier. She had been very stealthy. Erin hadn't even seen her come in. She had just been lurking there, listening in on the gossip. A treasure hunter? Was that all she was? Someone who thought she could line her pockets with a quick job? Read some old blueprints, poke around, and find the secret lost treasure of…

"Erin."

Erin snapped to attention, looking at Vic. "Sorry! Lost in thought."

"I said I don't actually know where Willie hid the you-know-what." It took Erin an extra second to remember that Vic was talking about Jeremy, not some buried Confederate gold. "I figured the fewer people who know, the better. I can hardly slip up and give it away if I don't really even know."

"Yeah, good plan. I'm sure he knows lots of good hiding places."

Willie was a kind of a treasure hunter himself, at least as one of his lives. He was the type who could never have his finger in just one pie. His mining was a kind of treasure-hunting, and he knew a lot of the natural caves and tunnels that went through the mountain.

"Terry was not too pleased that Jeremy took off," Erin commented.

"Uh, no. I don't think pleased is the word I would use." Vic gave an impish grin. "Holy cow. You would have thought that Tom had let the crown jewels walk out the door while he was on watch. Tom did the right thing. He didn't have any reason to stop Jeremy. He wasn't under arrest. He could come and go as he liked."

"Terry would have found some reason to take him in, I think."

"Probably. But luckily, Tom is not Terry."

Erin wiped down the top of the counter and then went around the display case with her cloth to wipe away children's fingerprints and nose prints from the other side of the glass. "You don't think there are really any tunnels between the old buildings, do you? Or lost treasures?"

"I would say no, that it was just a silly fairy tale… except that every few years, something like that turns up. Someone actually does find a treasure or a secret tunnel that was used for smuggling during the war. Just when you think you know what's real and what's not, something like that will come and knock you off your feet, and then for weeks after, you're second-guessing everything you've ever heard."

"Hmm." Erin buffed the surface of the glass lightly to bring out the shine. "So, you think that's really why Beaver is here? She really is looking for old gold? Some Confederate payroll or pirate booty? It just doesn't seem like she's the type of person who would be hunting that kind of thing. She seems to be so… I don't know…"

"I still don't know just what Beaver is and what she's up to. I do know that I don't like her hanging around here eavesdropping on conversations."

CHAPTER 33

*E*rin descended the back stairs to grab another bag of buckwheat flour. There was a noise ahead of her that made her freeze for a moment on the stairs, listening for more and trying to identify what she had heard. Maybe she had just been hearing something from the bakery overhead. Vic had put something down on the floor, and the sound had carried through the joists, echoing to make it sound like it had originated downstairs instead of upstairs. Erin resumed her descent, holding on to the handrail for balance as she strained her ears for another sound. She reached the bottom of the stairs.

"Anyone down here?"

She listened, but there was no response.

Going down to the basement still gave her a twinge of anxiety now and then, since that was where Angela had expired, and Erin had been the one to discover her body. Even though she knew it wasn't her fault and that nothing like that would ever happen again, she couldn't help feeling a pall every time she went downstairs. Not something she would *ever* tell Bella.

The basement consisted of both the tiny public restroom for customers and the storeroom stocked with dry goods. She hadn't ever had any problem with customers going into the "employee only" area, but maybe she should put a locking door on the storeroom just to be sure. Especially with so many undesirables in town.

The door to the commode was slightly open, but the room was dark, the light switch turned off. Erin turned the other direction and looked around the storeroom, watching and listening for movement. There was no one there. It had to have been a noise from upstairs. Erin took one more look for anything that was out of place. She couldn't see anything wrong, but had an unsettling feeling that things had been moved.

She hefted the large bag of buckwheat flour and took one more look around.

"It's fine," she murmured. "Everything looks just the same as always."

As she went by one of the brick-faced walls, she couldn't resist thumping it, listening for a hollow echo or feeling for some give indicating that it was a false wall, maybe on a swivel so it opened like a doorway to let her into some long-forgotten passageway like a scene out of Scooby-Doo. But it felt like a solid wall, just like she had always assumed.

She climbed the stairs back to the kitchen.

"Everything okay up here?" she asked casually before putting down the bag of flour.

Vic didn't answer. Erin let the bag land on the floor with a little thump. She looked up, but Vic wasn't there.

"Vicky?"

Erin walked out to the front of the shop, expecting to see Vic wiping out the display case or clearing the cash register. But there was no one there. Erin looked around, surprised, then returned to the kitchen. Vic had probably just taken the garbage out. She glanced toward the back door. It was not quite shut tight. Vic would return in a moment.

Erin waited. She measured out the flour for the various batters that needed to sit overnight. When Vic got back, Erin could tell her about her paranoia over something happening in the basement and they would laugh about it.

After a few minutes, Erin started to get worried. She went to the back door and called out toward the dumpsters in the alley.

"Vic? Everything okay?"

There was no answer. Erin stood there in the doorway, watching and listening. Vic was sure to come around the dumpster and see her standing there waiting any second. Maybe she had put her earbuds in and was listening to music or was on a call, so she hadn't heard Erin.

But as the seconds ticked away, she knew something was wrong.

"Vic? Vicky, are you there…?"

The night was quiet. She could hear the occasional car making its way down the nearby streets, but nothing unusual. Erin stepped out of the safety of the bakery and walked, her heart in her throat, to the dumpster. There was no one around. Erin looked around. Had someone interrupted Vic while she was emptying the garbage? Someone had called her and she'd gone to talk? But there was no one in sight.

No one at all.

CHAPTER 34

"S tay where you are, Erin, I'll be right there," Terry advised. "Did you try calling her on the phone?"

"No." Erin patted her pockets for her phone. That was a good idea. Wherever Vic was, she would have her phone on her. "I'll try that." Her pockets were empty, and frustration boiled over. "I can't find my phone! I don't know where I left it!" She scanned the counter for it. Had she left it in the basement?

"Erin."

"What?"

"You need to just calm down. You're talking to me on your phone, so stop looking for it. I'm going to hang up so you can try her. I'll be there in two minutes."

"Oh." Tears sprang unexpectedly to Erin's eyes. "Right. Okay. See you in a minute."

She ended the call and hit the shortcut for Vic's number.

"Come on, Vic. Answer the phone."

But the phone just kept ringing until it went to voicemail. Erin stared down at the phone in disbelief.

"Come on!"

"Erin?"

Erin looked up and saw Willie standing in the back door. She breathed out a sigh of relief.

"Willie! Vic must be with you!"

He shook his head. "No, I just came to pick her up."

"But…"

"We were supposed to go out tonight. Isn't she here?"

"No. She was… and I went downstairs to get some flour, and when I came up, she was gone."

"What do you mean, she was gone? Where did she say she was going?"

"She didn't say she was going anywhere. She just wasn't here anymore."

"That doesn't make any sense." Willie looked around, his eyes worried, as if she might just appear.

The front door bells jangled, making Erin jump. She whirled around and looked out through the doorway to the front to see Terry walking in with K9. She blinked at him in surprise. "Did you pick the lock? How did you get in?"

"It was unlocked."

"No, it wasn't. I'd already locked it for the night and turned the sign over."

Terry looked back at the door. "The sign is flipped over, but maybe you got interrupted before you locked it. Is that when you realized Vic was gone?"

"No. I locked it before I went downstairs. I haven't been back out to the front since then."

"Let me and K9 have a look around."

Terry walked through the main floor of the bakery and didn't appear to see anything amiss. He went down to the basement, taking the back stairs down and then the front stairs up.

"Everything is quiet. No sign of anyone else here. Just… no Vic."

"I don't understand it." Erin's voice was too high and strident. "I just went downstairs!"

"She can't have gone far. You called me right away, right?"

"Yes. It was just a few minutes… I came up and I thought she was outside for a minute… but she never came back in."

"I want you to think about what you heard while you were downstairs," Terry said calmly. "Were there any voices? Could you hear her moving anything around? Doors opening?"

"I thought I heard something downstairs. But there couldn't be anyone downstairs, so I thought Vic must have put something down or knocked something over in the kitchen, and it just sounded like it was downstairs."

"What did it sound like?"

Erin tried to replay it in her mind. "Like... somebody brushed by something in the storeroom. Like they were wearing or carrying something metal that dinged off of a shelf support. Not loud. Just... it was out of place, because I knew there couldn't be anyone down there."

"But there could have been."

"I'd already locked up, so no one could get in the front. The customers had all gone. It was just me and Vic."

"But you don't track everyone coming in and going out. You wouldn't necessarily know if someone went down to the loo and didn't come back up again."

"That couldn't happen again."

"It could. You can't watch everybody at the same time. You have your own jobs to do, and so does Vic. You trust people to go down to the restroom and come back up again without any direction or supervision."

"But I went down there, and there was no one there."

"Not that you saw," Terry agreed, "but the front door was unlocked."

Erin deflated. "If the front door was unlocked, that means someone unlocked it and went out that way after I had locked up. I was on the back stairway, so they used the other and got out. But I didn't see anyone down there."

"Would you have seen someone going up the stairs when you were going down the others?"

"No... but if the noise I heard was in the storeroom, like I thought, then they didn't have time to get to the other stairs."

"What about the restroom? Did you check inside?"

"Yes. It was empty."

"You checked? You went in?" Terry persisted.

"I... I looked in the door. It was cracked open. The bathroom was dark... so I didn't go in."

"So someone could have hidden there until you got your flour and went back up, then they just went up the stairs at the same time as you did."

"But that doesn't explain what happened to Vic. If someone was downstairs, what happened upstairs? Where did she go?"

~

Everybody was called in. Once again, the Bald Eagle Falls police force was stretched to its limit trying to help Erin. She felt guilty at having called them in yet again, but what else was she supposed to do? She couldn't just ignore Vic's disappearance.

Terry walked around the outside of the building with K9 before anyone else could get there and mess up the scent trails. When he came back, Erin raised her eyebrows hopefully, but he shook his head. "Nothing, sorry. He's not a scent dog, but I was hoping he might be interested in something that would give us a clue... but he just sniffed around a bit in the back parking lot and didn't find anything."

"If somebody was here... Vic might have gotten into a vehicle there, and K9 couldn't follow her scent any farther than that."

"Yeah, it's possible. This whole thing... it's unbelievable. For her to just disappear into thin air like that!"

"She didn't disappear into thin air. Somebody took her. Somebody else was in the bakery, and they took her."

"Whoever was in the basement went out the front door. They wouldn't take Vic out that way. People would see and would know something was wrong."

"Then there were more than one of them. Someone went out the front door, maybe to keep a lookout, and someone else came in the back while I was still downstairs, to take her away. I can't believe that she didn't scream or fight or something."

"They must have caught her off guard. Might have covered her mouth or gagged her. Or hit her over the head or even drugged her. There's no telling. But we know that she wouldn't leave without telling you where she was going or leave Willie in the lurch when they had plans. Vic's just not irresponsible like that."

"No. She'd never do that."

"What if it was Jeremy? If he came here and told her she had to go with him right away, but she had to be quiet and not say anything to anyone, would she do it?"

Erin ran the scenario through her mind. She knew how much Vic loved her family, even if most of them had disowned her. She loved Jeremy even more for being the one member of her family who supported her. If he was in trouble and needed her help and said to be quiet and not talk to anyone… she would have done it in a minute. Erin sighed.

"Yes. If it had been Jeremy… she would have done it."

"So scenario one is that she's with Jeremy. Do you know if she had any contact with him after Willie took off with him yesterday?"

"No, not as far as I know."

"She didn't even talk on the phone with him, text him?"

"No… she was working all day. We took our breaks, but she was just visiting and eating during our breaks. Not on her phone."

"Can you remember what she was wearing?"

Erin did her best to remember Vic's outfit that day, but it was a challenge. They wore aprons and hats and Erin didn't really notice what was on underneath. There had been days when she'd gone home only to find that she'd been wearing mismatched shoes all day.

"Nothing unusual happened today? You didn't… see anything when you went downstairs or out to the dumpster? You didn't smell anything out of place?"

Terry knew Erin's sensitive nose. She closed her eyes and breathed in and tried to remember. Any soap or cologne? Body odor? Some other smell that shouldn't be there?

"No. I can't think of anything downstairs. Just… dust. Concrete. Nothing really out of place."

"Okay. That's fine. There isn't always anything to smell."

"Are we going to call people in to do a search? Like when Roger disappeared?"

"No. When Roger disappeared, we knew he was wandering, and the best bet was to get a lot of people out looking for him. But this… it's different. She probably didn't go under her own power. She isn't just wandering around somewhere. She's locked away somewhere, and we don't know where."

It was an impossible task. Erin didn't even know where to start. She didn't even know what to put at the top of her list.

"Let's talk to Willie," Terry said. "He could have the key."

Erin knew that Terry had already tried to talk to Willie about it once. But Willie was stubborn. He wanted to find Vic, but he wasn't about to break any confidences to do it.

"Vic wouldn't want me to tell anyone where Jeremy is," he told Terry bullishly.

"What if Jeremy came here to get her? She would have gone with him. Where would they have gone?"

"He isn't the one who took her away."

"You don't know that."

"I do. It wasn't Jeremy. It was someone else."

Erin rubbed her forehead. "Who would take her? You've got to help, Willie, you have to have some idea. Didn't she tell you… something that was bothering her? Something she was thinking of doing? An idea she had about things that were going on in Bald Eagle Falls?"

"You girls talk way more than Vickie and I do. You know her every thought. I'm just the guy she hangs out with occasionally when her mean old boss gives her a few minutes off."

Erin gave him a wan smile. "I should give her more time off. She should have more time to spend with her friends and family."

"No" Willie put a warm hand on Erin's arm. "It was a joke. That's not what I'm saying at all. Vic loves her job. She loves working here and earning her own paycheck. It's the best thing for her."

"Who would take her? I don't understand why anyone would take Vic."

Willie shook his head. "I don't know… it could be to get to one of us, or to get to Jeremy. We don't know until they tell us."

"But what if they don't tell us? What if they just did it… to keep Vic quiet about something? Or to punish someone? Or because… I don't know, a random attack? Then what good is sitting around here waiting for someone to tell us going to do? They might have already… done something to her. I can't stand to think of it."

It wasn't like Erin needed much imagination to think about what Vic might be going through. She had been taken before, and so had Bella. It was like Erin had a curse. Everyone around her was attacked or kidnapped. But she hadn't done anything! She hadn't been asking questions and getting people upset. She had just been in the bakery, doing her job. It wasn't fair. Especially not to Vic.

"We're not just sitting around waiting," Willie promised. "I'm not going to sit around, and Terry and the police department are not just sitting around. We're going to figure out what happened. We're going to dig down to the heart of it and we're going to find Vic."

Erin nodded, a tear running out of the corner of her eye and down her nose, to dangle precariously at the end. Erin wiped impatiently at it. Crying wasn't going to do any good. It was time for actions. Or at least for lists.

"All the stuff that's been going on in town... is it all connected? It has to be, right? But I can't make it all fit together."

"All of what things?" Terry asked. "Which things in particular are you trying to connect?"

"Well..." Erin sniffled, "first of all, all the new people hanging around town. Are they all related to each other? To the clan war over Bald Eagle Falls?"

Terry grimaced. "I wish I could answer that one. There have been representatives from both the Jacksons and the Dysons, as well as some hoods that we can only assume are from smaller organizations. Drug dealers and other lowlifes trying to ply their trade..."

"Like Bo Biggles," Erin contributed.

Terry's eyes narrowed at her. "Yes. Like him. He's not the only one hanging around, but he's been one of the most visible. I've done my best to run them out of town, but they're all digging in their heels. It isn't easy. I've been talking to the feds about getting a task force in here to deal with things before they get too bad, but they're not inclined to actually do anything until there have been more deaths, or at least some blood on the ground."

Erin remembered the red pool of blood around Inglethorpe and felt nauseated. Terry must have seen a change in her pallor. He gripped her by the elbow. "Whoa, now. Hang in there."

"I'm okay."

He didn't let go. "You sure?"

Erin swayed slightly. Maybe it was a good thing if he continued to hold on to her, just for a few minutes. "Go on. Inglethorpe's death isn't enough? Why do they have to wait?"

"Because they want proof that we really do have a situation here. Something that needs their intervention. It has to warrant the amount they have to spend on it, which is a pretty penny. So I get where they're coming from... but on the other hand, I think we've given them some pretty convincing evidence of what's going on here and they could just take it at face value and come."

Erin nodded. "So... Don Inglethorpe... you do think he was part of the clan war?"

"I'm convinced he was… I'm not entirely sure how, but it's just too much of a coincidence that he died right at the onset of a gang war over Bald Eagle Falls. I don't think that it was Charley or anyone who was jealous or angry about a court case he had screwed up. He was seen arguing with a man and a woman the day before he died. Outsiders, not Bald Eagle Falls residents. I can only assume that they were clan and he was either arguing that he didn't want to be involved in whatever they were doing… or asking for a bigger cut."

"What do you think they wanted him to do?"

"He's a lawyer, so your guess is as good as mine. Set up some fraudulent corporate structure? Money laundering? Some other kind of fraud? I have no idea."

"He was killed at the bakery."

Terry's eyes stopped moving around and he looked at her for a moment. "Yes. He was killed at the bakery. If he wasn't there to meet Charley, and she wasn't the one who killed him, then why was he there?"

"Were the people who were arguing with Inglethorpe Bo Biggles and Rohilda Beaven?"

"What makes you think that?"

"I don't know. Just the way that they had that accident on Main Street… I'm sure they knew each other. I don't think it was any accident. So if they were both from out of town, and knew each other, I thought maybe they were the man and woman who were arguing with Inglethorpe."

Terry nodded. "I can't really get into that investigation in any detail. But if it were Biggles and Beaver, what would that tell you? How would that help us to find Vic?"

"If we know who it is, then we know better where to look. Right now… I have no idea where to look. I don't know why she was taken or where they would have taken her."

"I've called in the Staties to put up some road blocks, in case they're not out of town yet. There are too many backwoods roads to stop everyone leaving Bald Eagle Falls, but we can at least put roadblocks on the main highways. We could get lucky if someone tries to smuggle her out of town."

At least he was doing something. With every second that ticked by, Erin grew more anxious.

"But they're not the only ones who are new in town. There's also Adele's husband…"

Terry nodded. Willie looked at him. "You think he could be involved somehow?"

"It's hard to nail the guy down, he's a pretty slippery fish. He's been involved in a lot of fraudulent activity in the past... He's mostly a loner, or works a scam with one or two other people. Does that mean that he's not involved with any of the locals? Not necessarily. It's a small world, especially when you're looking at criminals. They all meet each other sooner or later. So, he could be related. He says he's just here to see Adele, and she confirms that, but you know you can't trust the guy."

"So probably a weasel," Willie said, "just not our weasel."

Terry laughed. "Exactly."

"And what about... Jeremy?" Erin was afraid to voice the question. She wouldn't have said it in front of Vic. She wouldn't have ever gossiped about him with Willie or anyone else. But she knew that he was involved in the clans and it seemed highly unlikely that he hadn't known something was going down in Bald Eagle Falls before arriving. He knew what was going on, or he had been sent and had been conducting business the whole time he'd been there.

Willie and Terry both looked at her, then exchanged glances with each other. All of them knew that Jeremy had to be a suspect, but none of them wanted to admit it. Erin had put it into words. Could he be at the center of the trouble? The person who had killed Don Inglethorpe?

"Mary Lou said that she'd seen him around town. But he was supposed to be staying in Clementine's room and keeping his head down. So that's another thing that doesn't add up."

"Do you believe that he just came to see Vic and stay with her?"

Erin shook her head. "Why would he say he didn't want the police around if he was just there to be with us? He was hiding from someone. And that someone tried to get him out of there last night. He eludes them, and then Vic is taken..."

"Jeremy has to be mixed up in this."

Terry looked at Willie, but Willie again shook his head. "Jeremy is right where I left him. And I'm not going to lead the bad guys right to his doorstep. We need to hang back and look around, see who is left."

"The one guy that we know for sure is involved from the Jackson clan is Bo Biggles. So I guess I go haul his butt in and lean on him until he talks."

Erin couldn't restrain a nervous giggle. "I've never heard you talk like that before."

"I don't normally have to get all Kojak in a case, but this one is getting on my nerves. Every time I turn around, there are clan connections, but nothing to arrest them for. That's what they're counting on. That we won't be able to get them on anything until they are thoroughly entrenched. Then it will be like picking burs out of a dog's fur."

"What should I do?" Erin asked. Terry was going to lean on Bo Biggles, but that left her alone. No Vic, no Jeremy, no Terry. She wouldn't have anything to do while she sat around waiting to see if Terry's interrogations produced any fruit.

"Go home and wait there. I don't want you in the way. That means you're not asking questions and not trying to track down Vic, you're just waiting for the police to do their job. Understand?"

"I'm not going to mess it up. I just... don't know what to do with myself while I'm waiting."

He gave her a brief hug. "You'll find something. Bake a cake. Make a list. Call your sister."

"Okay."

~

Willie followed Erin home in his truck to make sure that she got home safely and there was no one lying in wait there. He took a look around the outside of the house before letting her approach, then once she opened the door and disarmed the alarm, walked through the house, just to be sure.

"Last thing we need is you disappearing too. You call if you're worried about anything. If you get a call or you think there's someone around, anything at all, okay?"

Erin nodded.

"You should call someone. Don't sit here by yourself going crazy. You need someone to help hold things together."

Erin considered the advice. He was probably right. She was feeling very vulnerable about not being with Terry and not having Vic's support. With everything else that had happened in Bald Eagle Falls, she'd always had a friend to rely on. But with Vic gone, Erin had no one to fill that void. She wasn't going to pick her sister, in spite of Terry's advice. Charley just wasn't on the same wavelength as Erin, and would wind her up instead of helping to calm her down.

Adele, though… Erin had always found the tall, slim redhead to be a stabilizing influence. Even when everyone else was in a panic, Adele would stay calm and not get hysterical or blame Erin for being afraid.

"Okay. I'll give Adele a call."

"Good. Make sure it's her before you open the door. I don't want you disappearing too."

"Where are you going?"

It was strange that he wasn't helping Terry, but if all Terry was doing was interrogating a suspect, Willie couldn't very well help with that. And staying home waiting for a phone call wasn't going to get him any closer to the answers.

"I'm going to drive around… I've lived in Bald Eagle Falls for a lot of years, and I'm hoping I'll be able to get a feeling for what's out of place or who is not behaving the way they should…"

"You don't think it's Bo Biggles?"

"I know who the guy is. I'm sure he is wrapped up in it all somehow. But is he the one who took Vic?" Willie waited a few beats, and Erin wasn't sure whether he was expecting her to fill something in or was just thinking about it. Finally, he shook his head. "If he took her, then it was under orders. I can't see him doing something like that on his own. If he's involved, then maybe Terry can get something out of him. If we're lucky."

Willie took one more look around the house to make sure that everything was okay, then said goodbye and headed out. Erin wanted to stay at the door and see him off, but he wanted her to be inside with the door locked to be sure she was safe. So she locked it as soon as he was out and watched the truck drive away.

"Good luck, Willie. Please find some sign of her."

After the truck was gone, Erin sat down on the couch, scooping Orange Blossom to nestle in her arms. She juggled out her phone and dialed Adele's number.

It rang a few times, though looking at her watch, Erin wasn't sure why. Adele was usually quite active in the evening, stopping by Erin's shop if she needed something for the next few days, running any other errands, and then up throughout the evening and night for whatever it was she did.

Gathering herbs, praying, communing with nature, and any of the other things she valued.

"Hi, Erin."

"Adele! Are you busy, or could you come over? Something has happened…"

"What? What's happened?"

"It's Vic. She's… missing. I don't know what to do."

"Call the police! Don't wait around. What happened? Were you supposed to meet up? Wasn't she working today?"

"We were both working today. I went downstairs to get some flour, and when I got back upstairs, she was gone. Just like that. No sign of her."

"Willie didn't pick her up?"

"He's out looking right now. I mean, not looking for her, because if she was out there, we'd be able to find her, but looking around to see what's not right, you know?"

"You need to get the police onto it too."

"They are. Terry knows. Everyone has been brought in. They've looked around the bakery, and Terry is going to… question some people who might be involved."

"Where are you?"

"I'm at home."

"I'll be right over."

"Are you sure? I don't want to put you out if you had other plans tonight."

Adele didn't answer immediately. One thing that Adele never did was answer a question quickly. She thought about it, composed her answer, and then thought about it some more. "Do you really think that I wouldn't drop everything for you and Vic?"

Erin felt her face flush. "Well… okay. I just don't want to put you out."

"Don't be silly. I'll be exactly where I need to be."

Erin breathed a big sigh of relief after she hung up the phone. She looked around the room, trying to figure out what to do while waiting for Adele. She could change into her pajamas, but then if Terry found something and suggested they go out somewhere, she wanted to be be prepared. She could make herself a sandwich, but she really wasn't hungry. She could sit down and make a list, but she wasn't sure what to work on. Something for Vic, to help find her? Or one of her regular lists, with her plans for the next day on it? She was going to have to go into work, and what if Vic hadn't been found and couldn't be there? It was inconceivable that she would have to work with her best friend and colleague still missing.

The doorbell rang a few minutes later, and Erin went to get it, surprised that Adele had gotten there so quickly.

She went to the door and opened it, but there was no one there. Erin looked around, frowning. Why ring the doorbell and then run away? Unless it hadn't been Adele, but someone that didn't want her to see them.

Looking down, Erin saw a small cardboard box, and her heart sank. She wasn't sure what she was going to be facing, but she had a pretty good idea she wasn't going to like it.

CHAPTER 35

hen Adele did arrive, some time later, Erin just stared at her, her whole body numb, with no idea what to say.

"Erin?" Adele moved closer to her. "Erin, the door was open. Are you okay? You really do need to lock it, especially with all of this stuff going on."

Erin just stared back at her.

"Erin, what's the matter?" Adele looked at Erin's face, then looked down at the package in her lap. "What's that?"

"That's... the end."

"The end of what?"

"The end of everything," Erin said flatly.

She should have known, when she had first come to town, that it would happen. It was too good to be true. Sooner or later, it was all going to come crashing down, she was going to lose what she had, and she would be out on the street again, on her own, with no way to support herself or place to sleep at night.

Because that's how it was for Erin. Anything else was just a pleasant interlude. It had been nice to live in Bald Eagle Falls, to bake at Auntie Clem's Bakery and think that she had a chance to make something of herself. But it had all been superficial. When the time came, it was just all over.

Adele sat down next to Erin and touched the box. "Can I see?"

Erin didn't stop her. She didn't offer the box to Adele. Adele tentatively slid it out of Erin's hands. Erin didn't look down at it. She already knew what it said. She already knew her life at Bald Eagle Falls was over.

Adele opened the box and teased out the piece of paper, holding it by the very corner in case it was evidence.

If you ever want to see James Jackson again, leave Bald Eagle Falls for good. Take nothing with you, just get out of town.

Adele frowned, looking down at it. "James Jackson?"

"Vic."

"Oh. I see. So you think this person has her?"

Erin nodded.

"Have you called Officer Piper to show it to him?"

Erin shook her head.

"You should. He can help you sort it out."

"There's nothing to sort out. I have to leave."

"You can't just leave Bald Eagle Falls."

Erin lifted her shoulders in a hopeless shrug. "How could I do anything else? Vic needs me. They'll kill her."

Adele looked down at the paper. There was no threat to kill Vic, but they did use 'ever again' which suggested that they might do something drastic if Erin didn't follow their instructions.

"What am I going to do with the animals?" Erin asked.

Her chest hurt. She could hardly think, but she knew that she needed to leave, and if she wasn't allowed to take anything with her, then that included the animals. She couldn't take her adored furry friends with her. She couldn't just turn them over to Doc to try to find homes for them. There just weren't enough families in Bald Eagle Falls who would take in a couple of stray animals and keep them safe as indoor pets. If he found anyone, she was sure they would just be turned loose in someone's back yard to come and go, and it wouldn't be long before they disappeared. That was the way it was with outdoor animals in a small rural community.

"Don't worry about the animals," Adele said, putting her hand over Erin's. "If you had to leave, I could take them."

"They'd drive you crazy in that little tiny cottage."

"We'd work it out."

"Then I should go. The longer I think about it, the harder it's going to be."

"Erin. Call Officer Piper."

Erin stared at Adele for a long time before finally nodding. "Alright. I will." She patted her pockets until she found her phone, and looked at it for a minute before she could remember how to turn it on and call Terry.

"Erin?" He answered almost right away. "Any word?"

His question cut Erin to the heart. It told her immediately that he wasn't making any headway. Her only hope was to do as the note said, and to hope that the note-writer did as he said he would and let her see Vic again.

"No... I... I got a note."

"What kind of a note? From Vic?"

"No. From someone else. I guess whoever has her. It says if I want to see her again, I have to leave Bald Eagle Falls. I have to leave forever."

"What? What are you talking about?"

"The note says that I need to leave and not take anything with me."

"And then what?"

"I guess... they'll let Vic live."

"Erin! Who delivered the note? Where did it come from? Are you home?"

"Yes, I'm home. I called Adele to come sit with me, because I didn't want to be alone. I thought it was her when the doorbell rang. But it wasn't. It was... someone else. Someone who left a package, with a note."

"A package? What's in the package?"

Erin looked at the box that Adele was holding. "I don't think there's anything else in it. Just the note that I have to leave town." Erin let out a long breath. Her heart rate was starting to return to normal. "Adele said that I should call you."

"Of course you should call me. You know that. I don't know what to do, Erin. We're still looking for Biggles. I don't have a clue where he's gone to ground. We're not getting anything from our usual sources. I don't know whether to stay here, or..." He made a decision, his voice changing. "I'll come to you. It's evidence. I need to see it with my own eyes and take it into evidence. Maybe the note will sound like someone and I'll know who wrote it."

"You don't think it's Bo Biggles?"

"I don't like to say, but... I don't think he has what it would take to pull off a kidnapping like this. And dropping off the note with you while we were looking for him... I just don't see him doing this."

"How well do you know him?"

"Not well. Not well enough to say no for certain... but I'll come over there. We'll get it sorted out. Once I look at the note... we'll know what it is that we're supposed to do next."

"Okay."

"Hang in there. I'll be right there. Have Adele make you some tea."

"I don't want tea."

But Terry had hung up and was no longer on the line. Erin lowered her phone to her lap.

"Tea?" Adele repeated.

"Terry said to get you to make some tea. But... I don't really want anything. I should get going."

"Not before he gets here. Just wait."

Erin reached over and picked up Orange Blossom, who was snoozing on the couch nearby. He startled and made a sleepy noise, looked to see who had picked him up, and started purring his loud, thrumming purr. Erin scratched his ears and patted him. She'd rescued him when he was just a starving, homeless kitten, and she was going to have to let him go to someone else. Someone else who wouldn't have nearly the same ideas about how to care for a cat as she did.

"Just stay put and let me get you something. Have you had any supper?" Adele asked.

Erin shook her head. "No."

"You need to get something in you. You can't be expected to make any kind of decision without having had something to eat."

Erin remained on the couch, staring forward, unfocused, while Adele looked through the fridge and cupboards to see what was available. By the time Terry got there, Adele was handing Erin a sandwich and a cup of tea.

"It isn't much, but you need to get something inside you. This is better than nothing."

"Terry..." Erin bumped away Adele's hands with the food offering and stood up, falling into Terry's arms just like she had done before. Was she ever going to develop any relationships that would last more than a year or two? She had thought that Bald Eagle Falls was her place. The place she would be able to make her own and live for the rest of her life. "Terry, I don't understand what's going on. Why would they take Vic? What does it have to do with me? What did I do? What do I know or have that they would care about?"

"We don't know that. There's no way for us to know." He looked at the package on the coffee table. "Is that it? Can I see it please?"

Adele nudged it toward him. "I'm sorry, both of us have handled it. I tried to only touch the edges of the note."

Terry took it out carefully, like Adele had. He read it over quickly out loud.

If you ever want to see James Jackson again, leave Bald Eagle Falls for good. Take nothing with you, just get out of town.

"Okay," Terry cracked his knuckles and considered the message. "Okay, it's not a lot to go on, but it gives us a little. First off, it calls Vic by her old name. So it's someone from her past."

"Or someone who doesn't know what she goes by now," Adele suggested.

"No, I don't think so," Erin said. "Anyone who knew she was here would know what she goes by. Much better than her dead name."

Terry looked startled. "Dead name?"

"That's what she calls it. It's a name and identity that's dead to her. That person doesn't exist anymore. Just Victoria. There is no more James."

Adele looked at Terry. "Do you think there's some significance to that?"

"To the fact that he calls her by something she calls her dead name? I certainly hope not. Just an unfortunate coincidence. It doesn't mean that she is dead or that he's threatening to kill her. There's nothing in this note that says what he will do if Erin doesn't do what she's told to. It's just an empty threat. We don't even have any evidence that the person who wrote this note has any idea where Vic is. It could just be someone who wants Erin to leave town."

"But who would want Erin to leave town? From what I've seen, she's got a lot of friends here. Even the people who might not consider her a friend... I don't see a lot of animosity toward her."

Erin thought about Charley. It would be an opportune time for Charley to get Erin out of the way. First try to frame her for murder. Then send a threatening note to try to get her to leave town. Then there would be no more competition in Bald Eagle Falls. How could the trustees turn down the opportunity to have the monopoly on baked goods in Bald Eagle Falls?

"I don't know... Everyone has been pretty good," she said, not voicing her thoughts.

"Let's keep analyzing the note," Terry said. "Probably someone who knew Vic, who shares a past with her."

"Someone who doesn't accept who she is," Erin suggested.

"Right. Could be an old friend, love interest, a family member, someone who feels betrayed by her changes and leaving town. Could that be all that it is? Someone who is jealous of Vic? It could be that it isn't even anything to do with the murder or the drug activities."

"Jealous how?" Erin demanded. "That's she's working with me? That she has a job? Because we're just friends, it's not like we're in a relationship."

"If it was *that* kind of jealousy, then I'd expect them to be targeting Willie."

"Have you talked to him? He said he was going to drive around, see if he could spot anything out of the ordinary."

"I haven't talked to him. I've been trying to track down Biggles. But he seems to have disappeared."

"Then he's got to be the one that has Vic," Erin said. "If he's the one person who we can't track down, then he must be the one who has Vic."

"There are too many people in Bald Eagle Falls for us to track them like that." Terry shook his head, scratching the back of his neck. "He's just the one person I thought might have some insight, and he happens to be out of touch. There could be a lot of other people who we can't reach right now, and a lot of different reasons for not being reachable."

"Is there anything else?" Erin bent her head to look at the words. "I don't recognize any expressions that anyone we know uses. It could be anyone."

"I'll put an APB out on Bo Biggles. If he's still around, we'll track him down. If he's left town... I'll go to the next thug on the list. We'll find Vic."

"And I should get ready to go," Erin said. "I should pack a bag and leave town."

Terry looked at Adele, then looked out the window. Erin could tell that he wanted to argue with her. He wanted to tell her, like Adele did, that everything was going to be fine and she should just stay around there until he managed to figure out where Vic was.

"I don't want you to go anywhere. But if you want to follow the instructions on the note and relocate for a couple of days until we have Vic back safe and sound, you're welcome to do that. I don't know if it will do any good. I don't know what it is these guys want. But I can have Tom watch the house and see if there's any suspicious activity after you leave."

Erin nodded. "I'm not sure where to go… but I have to try. If it can help Vic…"

"It's not going to help Vic," Adele disagreed. "Following the demands this guy or these people make just means you're caving in to the demands of a terrorist. It won't help Vic, and it won't help the next person who ends up in the same situation."

"It's up to you," Terry repeated. "But if you're going to leave… I wouldn't pack a bag. Tuck a few toiletries into your purse, but no suitcase or duffel bag."

"Why not?"

"Because he says to take nothing with you. If you want to appear to be obeying the instructions, you need to leave empty-handed. Or with no more than you would normally take out to the car."

"Right. Of course."

"Don't you think someone is going to snatch Erin as soon as she is out of sight?" Adele demanded.

"I don't know what's going to happen if she does what they tell her to. I suspect they just want her out of the way."

"But you can't know that."

"Of course not. But do you think I could stop her? Really?"

"You could put police protection on her."

"I can't put police protection on her, and watch the house and the bakery, and chase down Biggles and any witnesses or potential informants. We have a very small department. We can do more once we get some help from the feds, but until then, it's just the three of us, and we're stretched thin. Erin… if you go, you'll let me know where you're going to? And you'll let me know when you're safe?"

Erin nodded. She looked out the living room window and felt incredibly vulnerable. Who knew how many of them there were out there, and whether they had evil designs on her? She should have gotten a gun and learned how to use it, like Vic said. At least then, she would have some kind of protection going out on her own. But Vic had a gun, and that hadn't stopped her from being kidnapped and taken away. She hadn't even made a sound. She had just disappeared.

"I think you should go back to the bakery," Adele said suddenly.

Terry and Erin both turned and looked at her in surprise.

"Why?" Erin asked.

"If Vic was taken from there… there must be some kind of clue about who did it and where they took her. If someone wants Erin to leave, then they don't want her to go back to the bakery. There must be something there that she might accidentally unearth. Right?"

Erin shook her head. "We already looked all over for any sign of what happened to Vic. Me and Willie and the police, we all looked for anything… but there were no clues."

"But somebody doesn't want you to go back there."

Erin looked at Terry. "Well, should we go have a look, then? One more time? After that… I'll take off. We'll just check the bakery one more time."

He nodded. "Fine. I'll take you there on my way back to the police department. Are you coming along too, Adele?"

Adele surprised them all by saying yes. "One more set of eyes. Who knows, maybe I'll see something that both of you managed to miss."

Without a word, Erin picked up her purse and headed for the door. She couldn't let herself think about anything she was leaving behind. Only about Vic, out there somewhere, alone and vulnerable to some gangster.

CHAPTER 36

*W*hen she opened the door, she was startled to see a figure move away, trying to disappear into the shadows. But the streetlights were too bright, and the figure was too close to the house, as if she'd been sneaking close to look in the window.

"Wait!" Erin shouted. "Stop right there!"

Terry pushed past her to apprehend the subject. Erin knew who it was by the blond hair that flowed down her back.

"Stop right where you are, ma'am," Terry said warningly, holding K9's collar as he strained eagerly for release. "I'd like to talk to you."

Beaver turned her head, realizing that she'd been caught and there was no point in trying to pretend otherwise. She swung back around, her body loose and casual.

Adele came out of the house and stood beside Erin, watching.

"Officer Piper," Beaver greeted. "Fancy meeting you here. I would have thought that you had enough to investigate without stopping innocent people on the street. Don't you have a murder to investigate? And somebody said something about some kind of drug war?"

"What are you doing here?" Terry demanded. "You don't live around here."

"There's no law against me walking down the street, is there?"

"I'd like to know what you're up to. What are you doing lurking around Erin's house? Do you want to be arrested for trespass or loitering?"

"Nice try. You don't have anything on me. You'd better get on with whatever you were doing. Chasing after me is only going to slow you down."

"It seems to me that you know a little too much, Miss Beaven. Maybe you can explain that to me. What are you doing skulking around Erin's door?"

"I just thought... I was thinking I might ring the bell and chat. Erin was nice to me when we met at the restaurant and I was feeling a little lonely."

Terry got closer to her. "If you have nothing to hide, how about letting me see if you're carrying any weapons?"

"Weapons? Why would I be carrying around any weapons?"

"You want to prove that?"

Beaver eyed Terry and K9 thoughtfully. Eventually, she lifted up the edge of her jacket to reveal a gun holstered at her waist.

She continued to watch Terry with eyes narrowed like a cat's. Erin felt the knot in her stomach tighten. Was this why Beaver had approached her and Vic at the restaurant? Had they given something away when they had talked to her? Something that had gotten Vic kidnapped?

"Take it out and drop it on the ground," Terry instructed. "Do you have anything else?"

"I might have a throw-down in an ankle holster," Beaver admitted. "Would you expect me to have anything less?"

"What exactly does a treasure hunter need all of this weaponry for?"

"You'd be surprised about how emotional people can become while treasure hunting."

Terry let out a bark of laughter. "Oh, you think so, do you? After you drop that gun, I want you to take out the one in the ankle holster. Slowly, letting me see your hands at all times."

They were all quiet while Beaver obeyed Terry's instructions. Both guns were dropped on the pavement.

"Kick them away," Terry instructed.

"Here I thought you were going to forget that part."

"Any other weapons on you?"

Beaver lazily chewed on her gum, mouth wide and loose. "I guess that depends on what you'd call a weapon," she said finally.

"Any more guns?"

"No. No guns."

"What else, then? Knife? Taser? Pepper spray?"

"Yes."

"Which one?"

"All of the above."

They all stared at her. She had a hunter's jacket with all kinds of pockets on the outside, and probably the inside as well.

"Take off your coat and put it down," Terry instructed.

Beaver rolled her eyes and followed his instruction, moving slowly and keeping her hands in view as much as possible. She held the jacket at arm's length, then gave it a little toss to put some distance between it and her when it fell.

The halter-top she wore under the jacket didn't leave much to the imagination. Her body was lithe and tightly-muscled. Her movements were loose and fluid and had given the impression she was soft, but it was obvious just looking at her arms that there was nothing soft about her. Removing the jacket bared a sheath on her arm with the handle protruding. She had a tattoo on her arm, originally black, but old enough that it was starting to blue. Terry approached her, getting close enough to kick the laden jacket farther out of the way.

"Hands up."

Beaver raised her arms obediently. Terry gave K9 a command to sit and guard, and he obeyed, nose and ears pointed intently at Beaver.

Erin was anxious about the fact that Terry hadn't asked Beaver to remove the knife from the sheath. How quickly would she be able to pull it out and attack Terry if the mood struck? He seemed to care more about the tattoo than about the threat.

"You were Airborne?" he demanded.

Beaver gave a little shrug, very casual, as if it were nothing.

"Who are you with now?"

She started to smile, as if she were trying to suppress it but couldn't quite manage.

"You're investigating this? For what department?" Terry persisted.

"I'm afraid I'm not authorized to tell you anything, Officer Piper."

"But you are investigating it."

She just raised her eyebrows.

Terry looked at Beaver, considering. "What do you know about what has happened today? You know we had a kidnapping?"

"Unfortunately, I was in the wrong place when that went down... close by, but not close enough to see or hear what was happening. I was checking out... another possibility."

"And do you know about the note Erin was sent tonight?"

"Are you going to keep me standing here with my arms up all day?"

"Uh, no. Go ahead and put them down."

Beaver put her arms back down to her side, and for a moment everybody just stood there, considering the situation.

Despite Beaver not confirming that she was working for some federal department, Erin no longer felt threatened by her. While it was possible that someone ex-army would be involved in a drug war, she didn't get that feeling from Beaver, and obviously Terry didn't either.

"So?" Terry prompted. "Did you know that Erin got a delivery tonight?"

"I knew something was going on. But no, I don't know any details. What was it? What did the note say?"

Terry told her about the note. Beaver nodded, chewing her gum and considering the details thoughtfully.

"Do you know who it is?" Terry asked. "I haven't been able to track down Biggles tonight. It could be something to do with him."

"You've got people working on that? I can have mine look into it."

"Any help we can get at this point would be appreciated. I'm not getting anywhere very fast. We are a small-town police force and we haven't had any response from the federal agencies we've reached out to." Terry gave her a nod. "Except for you, I guess."

"I'll see if I can find anything out. But I haven't seen Biggles for a couple of days. I think he's pulled out."

"Then who has been sent in his place? Because the Jacksons aren't going to give in that easily. If they felt he was compromised and pulled him out, they would send someone else."

"That was my thought," Beaver agreed, giving nothing away with her casual, lazy expression.

"We were going to go back to the bakery. I don't know if we can find any clues there. I don't know how all of us could have missed anything, but we'll check, just in case."

"It's a good idea," she agreed. "Mind if I tag along? Just as an interested civilian. I wouldn't mind having a longer look around."

Terry looked at Beaver for a minute, weighing his answer, then nodded. "We'll all go together. But I expect you to behave like a civilian, and that means you do what you're told."

"Of course." Beaver looked past him to Erin. "Just like Erin always does what she's told."

Erin could feel Beaver laughing at her. Just how much did the woman know? Was she talking about the events that had occurred since Erin had moved back to Bald Eagle Falls, or did Beaver know even more than that, back into Erin's history?

Terry shook his head, obviously sensing that Beaver wasn't going to be quite as cooperative as she suggested.

"May I retrieve my gear?"

Terry hesitated, looking at the discarded guns and equipment jacket. He hadn't had Beaver's identity verified. She could be anyone. She could belong to one of the clans. But Terry had a pretty well-developed instinct.

"Yeah, go ahead," he agreed.

Beaver made quick work of gathering up the tools of her trade and shrugging back into the jacket.

At the bakery, Erin looked around, not sure what to expect. Everything looked just as she had left it, nothing out of place. It was just her bakery, feeling a little empty without Vic there to help her, even with Terry and K9, Adele, and Beaver there.

"Vic was up here, cleaning up and getting things ready for tomorrow. I went downstairs to get a bag of flour and I heard something down there."

"Your visitor bumping into something," Beaver said.

Erin looked at her searchingly. Just how much did Beaver know about the visitor?

"I told myself that it wasn't really a noise downstairs, it was just Vic putting something down upstairs. I got the flour... didn't see anyone down there and went back upstairs. Vic was gone. I looked around for her and thought she must have gone outside to the garbage bin. But she didn't come back in, so I called Terry."

Terry nodded. "We conducted a scene survey. There was no sign of her. The front door was unlocked, giving the impression that someone had been downstairs who had gone out the front, but there had to have been someone else here too, because they wouldn't have kidnapped Vic and taken her out the front door. There's too much activity on Main Street. Someone would have seen them. But no one had; they must have gone out the back."

Beaver nodded her agreement. Adele looked around thoughtfully. She wasn't familiar with the kitchen, so maybe she could spot something that Erin and Terry couldn't. Beaver too, with her sharp hunter's eyes, might see something.

Beaver walked around the kitchen area, peering into the tiny office. She looked at the back door, the one they had come in.

"No sign of forced entry."

"It would have been unlocked," Erin said. "We never lock the door during the day. We are always in and out throughout the day."

"Even after your rolling pin was stolen, you didn't start locking the back door?"

Erin started to ask how Beaver knew about that, then stopped. Of course Beaver knew about the rolling pin. That was part of the murder case, and whoever had sent her in wouldn't have done so without having first read all of the information they had about the murder. The point about the rolling pin having been stolen from Erin's bakery had been left out of the newspaper, but Erin assumed that it had been passed on to the various federal agencies that Terry had asked for help.

"I... yeah, I guess so. I just figured that Charley had taken it... She's had a pretty hard time since the murder. I really didn't think she'd be back for anything else."

Beaver's eyes were intense, despite the impression of laziness she exuded. "How is Charley doing?"

"Not good. She's been pretty upset, drinking, thinking a lot about... problems that she had."

"With the Dyson clan?"

"She was missing Bobby... but I think it was more that she was trauma-tized by everything than that she actually missed him personally. I know they were together as a couple, but... I think it was more about being kicked out of the clan than actually missing her old boyfriend."

"Do you think she was the one who killed Don Inglethorpe?"

"No. I know it looks like it, on the surface... but if you look deeper... he was the one who changed his vote to allow her to open the bakery. So he was the one she should have been the most grateful about... I can't see why she would have hurt him."

"Maybe he was threatening to change his vote again. Maybe he was blackmailing her, demanding she pay him or he would change his mind again, on the eve of the opening."

Erin shrugged. She shook her head. "I don't think that's what happened."

"Let's go downstairs," Terry suggested. "I want to have another look at what's down there that our visitor might have been messing around with."

"There isn't anything down there," Erin asserted. "Just storage and the loo."

"Let's check it out anyway. I want everyone to stay together."

They all followed after Terry, in single file down the narrow, steep stairs. There wasn't a lot of room at the bottom to mill around and take everything in. Erin moved into the storeroom where there was a little more space. She looked around. She drew in the smell of the place. Dust and concrete, just like she'd told Terry.

Terry and Beaver looked around with professional eyes. K9 sniffed around curiously, but nothing appeared to grab his attention. Adele's approach was different. Her eyes closed and she just stood in the middle of the room, listening or communing with the spirits or whatever it was she did. Maybe she was praying. Erin wouldn't discount it. Finally, she opened her eyes again.

"There's something down here," she said.

Erin was surprised. "What? We already looked..."

"It's something you can't see." Adele walked a slow circle around the outside of the room. Erin tracked Adele with her eyes. *Something they couldn't see?*

"Charley said there were secret tunnels between some of the stores. But I couldn't see anything down here. I kind of... looked earlier."

"Secret tunnels?" Terry asked. "Old wives' tale."

"Maybe," Beaver said, "maybe not."

They all turned and looked at her.

"There is a rumor circulating that a tunnel under the bakery is being used to store drugs."

Erin's stomach dropped. "Storing drugs? But there isn't even a tunnel here, you can see that. If there used to be, it would have to be behind one of the bricked walls," Erin motioned. "But I've already looked at them and they are solid. There's no way to get into a tunnel, if there ever was one."

Everyone went to the brick wall, looking over it and feeling it for some kind of mechanism to open it up. Erin looked at the floor. If someone else were using it to store drugs, then it would have been opened and closed recently, but there was no sign of the concrete beneath the wall having been scuffed or disturbed. She shook her head.

"There's no way."

The others looked at her. Erin shook her head.

"If someone had been using a tunnel down here for storage, I would know about it. You couldn't have people coming in and out of here without me knowing about it. And there would be signs. Marks on the floor, streaks in the dust. If there *is* a tunnel down here, it hasn't been accessed in years."

"People can get in and out of here without you knowing about it," Beaver pointed out. "Your intruder earlier got in and out without you seeing. Charley stole your rolling pin. You leave this room accessible so that people can use the restroom."

"But if shady characters were in and out of here, I would notice."

"I don't know if you would. And you're not here at night when people could come and go and move product without you being any the wiser."

"We're in pretty early in the morning. I've never seen any sign that anyone else has been in here while we've been gone. I don't have a bunch of extra keys floating around. You couldn't use a place this small without leaving some kind of sign of your coming and going."

Just as she said it, there was a noise over their heads. They all looked up automatically at the same time.

Erin had hung back while the others looked at the wall, so she was the closest one to the door. In a split second, she was heading up the stairs, determined to see the intruder this time.

She didn't even think about what she was doing or what she would do when she got up the stairs and confronted the burglar face-to-face. She didn't have a weapon or any kind of training.

The trespasser obviously heard her coming. There was the sound of retreating footsteps as Erin barreled up the stairs, the others calling after her. Erin heard them and put on an extra burst of speed. She needed to see who it was. Who was it that was holding Vic? She needed to find her friend and to see that she was safe. As she got up the stairs, she saw a slim figure with shaggy, long blond hair.

"Jeremy!"

CHAPTER 37

The young man turned to look back at her, and she saw that she was mistaken. It wasn't Jeremy, but an older man who looked quite similar to him. Her mind flashed through scenarios as she tried to find one that fit. It wasn't Jeremy or Vic. It was someone who shared similar features, like she and Charley did. Daniel or Joseph.

"What are you doing here?" Erin demanded. "If you're trying to help, you need to stop!"

But his look back had been fleeting and he wasn't stopping to chat. Erin watched his retreat, unable to keep up with him. She eventually stopped in the parking lot outside the bakery as the figure disappeared into the darkness.

The others caught up with Erin.

"Did you see anyone?" Terry asked, reaching for his police radio.

"I... I think one of the Jackson boys."

"One of the clan? Biggles?"

"No... I mean... one of Vic's brothers."

Terry raised his eyebrows. "Oh, is that so?"

"Not Jeremy. It wasn't Jeremy. One of the others...."

"I'll put out a bulletin. Can you describe him?"

"Just like Jeremy," Erin said. "But a bit older."

Terry called in to his dispatcher and gave them a description, as well as the possible identity of the burglar. They returned to the kitchen of Auntie Clem's.

"Did you know that any of the others were in town?" Terry demanded.

"No. I swear, I didn't. I just knew about Jeremy. I don't know why any of the others would be here."

"Well, he was here for something."

"Maybe he's just looking for Vic," Adele suggested. "Word is bound to have spread about her being missing. There's been enough time for someone to get here from Moose River."

"Then why didn't he stop when I called to him?"

"That part isn't really surprising," Terry said. "They're up to their necks in clan activity. Whether they're here on the clan's instructions or on their own, they really wouldn't want to have to stop and explain themselves."

"I suppose not." Erin sighed and looked around. She still had no clue who had come into the bakery to take Vic or where they had gone. They hadn't left any trace behind.

"I don't see any sign of him—of them here," Adele said, echoing Erin's thoughts.

There was an acrid smell starting to waft into Erin's nostrils. She looked toward the door, wondering if it were coming from outside. "Terry do you smell—wait; the tunnel is under the bakery."

Terry looked at her blankly. Everyone looked at her as if she were speaking another language.

"Not Auntie Clem's Bakery," Erin said. "What about The Bake Shoppe?"

It made perfect sense. The murder hadn't taken place at Auntie Clem's. Erin darted out the front door. If there was a tunnel under The Bake Shoppe, then all of the pieces of the puzzle fit. She could see the whole picture. She ran across the deserted street and down the block so she could access the alley behind The Bake Shoppe. It was getting to be a familiar route. Terry and K9 loped at her side, and Beaver not only kept up despite her load of paraphernalia, but passed Erin with a long, easy stride. Adele lagged somewhere behind.

Erin was focused only on getting to The Bake Shoppe. She was irritated with Beaver for passing her and going first. Wasn't there some kind of professional courtesy that the locals should be allowed in first?

When they reached the back door of The Bake Shoppe, the door was hanging open, the strike plate ripped from the splintered doorframe. Rohilda Beaven had some serious skills. Erin flashed back to entering the bakery once before when the door had been broken. She tried to focus in the present. She wasn't going to find a dead body this time. Just because it had happened before, that didn't mean it was going to happen again. Besides, Beaver was there ahead of her. Erin wouldn't be the one discovering a body this time.

Terry made a motion for Erin to stay back, and murmured to K9. K9 was totally focused, his ears forward and eyes alert, nose pointed like an arrow into the bakery.

Erin entered two steps behind Terry. She was not about to wait outside or to be the last one in the door.

The murder had been there. The drugs were being stored there. It followed logically that the bakery is where they would be holding Vic.

The kitchen was quiet and empty. There was no sign of having been a bloody murder there in the recent past. Charley had scrubbed every last spot away, hoping to be able to reopen.

And now she would be able to reopen, and it would be Erin who was out of business.

Beaver's sidearm was out, but held down at her side. "This floor is clear," she advised in a low voice. "There is only one set of stairs."

"Let me go down first with K9."

Beaver didn't look happy about the suggestion, but she nodded agreement. Terry pulled out his gun.

"Erin, I don't have to tell you to stay put until we've cleared the basement, do I?"

Erin nodded. "I will."

Beaver gave Erin a long look before nodding she was satisfied that Erin would behave herself. Terry spoke to K9 in a low voice, Erin couldn't make out all his words. K9 listened alertly, his body still. Then they started down the stairs. Beaver followed close behind, her gun held ready, close to her chin.

Erin stood by the stairs, listening intently. She heard a confirmation of "clear" from each of the professionals, then a low discussion between them.

"Can I come down?"

"You can come," Terry called back. Erin still hesitated for just a moment before descending the stairs. It wasn't her store, and she didn't exactly have permission to be there. At least she knew, with Terry calling her down, that they hadn't discovered another body or other crime scene.

The storage space was similar to Erin's. Walls lined with shelves of cans or bags of dry goods, as well as a few aisles of freestanding shelves. The walls themselves were of varying building materials. Erin looked down at the floor. It was swept clean, no dust or scuff marks to show where anyone had been.

"Don't touch anything," Terry warned as he looked around.

"I won't." Erin scanned for any sign of a door. A hole or a crack in the wall, a hinge or swivel of some sort. There was nothing obvious. If there was an old tunnel, it was well-hidden. "You're the treasure hunter," she said to Beaver. "So where do you think it is?"

The woman gave her a grin. "You might think that's just a cover story, but it's not. I actually do hunt treasure as a hobby."

"As well as working for the government?"

"No comment. Treasure hunting is fun and relaxing. Going new places and trying to solve hundred-year-old puzzles. Great way to vacation. And if you actually find something, all the better."

"So what do you think? Is there a tunnel down here?"

"I'd like to see some old blueprints, but so far I haven't been able to get them for any of these buildings. They are too old; if anything was ever filed municipally, it's long since been destroyed. Measuring out the room might help. But it's going to take some time. I don't see anything obvious, no more than in yours."

"If there is, they might have hidden Vic there. She could just be a few feet away from us and we wouldn't know it."

"You're right," Terry admitted. They were all silent, straining to hear any sound behind the walls.

"Vic?" Erin was afraid to shout; she didn't want to attract any bad guys. But she called as loudly as she dared. "Vicky? Can you hear me? We're here. Where are you?"

They again waited, but could hear no voice or other noise in response.

K9's nose was quivering as he looked around the room, looking at Terry and obviously wanting to explore, but too obedient to break away from his master's side. His ears swiveled this way and that.

"Let him go," Erin suggested. "Tell him to find Vic."

Terry looked down at K9. The dog was practically vibrating, he wanted to explore the room so badly. "Is Vic here, K9? Find Vic. Go find Vic."

K9 rocketed away from Terry and started to cast for scent along one wall of shelves. He gave a sharp bark, pushed his body partway into the shelf, and scrabbled with one paw at the seam where the wall met the floor as if trying to dig.

Erin looked at Terry. They all hurried toward the wall, surrounding K9 and looking for some sign of a door.

"Help me pull the shelf away from the wall," Terry told Beaver.

Erin didn't see how they could move it. It was piled with heavy cans and fifty-pound sacks of flour. They would have to clear it off before it could be moved. But Terry and Beaver positioned themselves on either end and gave it a heave. It didn't budge an inch. They both pushed and wiggled and shook it, looking up and down for some way to move it. But K9 must have just been chasing a mouse. There was no way that shelf was moving.

"It's bolted to the wall," Beaver pointed out, indicating a couple of anchors near the top.

Terry stepped back, his face sweating, lined with worry. "I don't see how the tunnel could be here."

But the treasure hunter wasn't ready to give up. "Don't be so quick to accept things as they appear." She walked along the shelf, examining it from all angles. "There's a way in. If the shelf is anchored to the wall, that means that the whole wall moves."

"This isn't TV," Terry said impatiently.

"I've seen all kinds of hidden rooms. Even now, there's a huge demand for safe rooms either to store valuables in or to escape to in case of a home invasion or looting. They can be incredibly well-hidden." She inched along the wall, reaching through the shelves to prod anything that displayed some variation from the wall or shelf around it. Knotholes and planks and discolorations. Like Terry, Erin thought it was too hokey to be real. The tunnel had to be a red herring. A rumor someone had started to throw people off the track of whatever it was they were really doing.

Then there was a loud click. Erin's mouth dropped open in surprise. Beaver was a strong woman, that was obvious from what Erin had seen of her body when she had taken the bulky jacket off, but she did not have the strength to move six hundred pounds of dry goods on her own. Yet she was pulling on something, and the shelf and wall were sliding forward as if on wheels. The whole section of shelving and wall swiveled around and doubled back against the wall beside it. K9 was squirming around the corner before Beaver even had it pulled all the way open, Terry calling him to stop and stay. The hole behind the shelves was black as pitch, but when the shelf stopped in its full-open position, there was another click, and fluorescent lights blinked and flickered to life.

There was a body writhing on the floor, K9 attacking and trying to get a purchase. But then Erin realized that it was Vic, and K9 wasn't attacking her, but was nosing her worriedly and licking her face. Erin dashed forward, pushing by Terry before he could process what was going on and call K9 off. Erin dropped to her knees beside Vic and pushed K9 hard out of the way. Vic's mouth was gagged and her eyes were wide with alarm. Erin levered the knotted cloth out of Vic's mouth and pulled out the rag that was stuffed inside it. Vic coughed and retched and lay on her side, breathing heavily, but no longer kicking.

"Praise the Lord," she whispered. "All praise the Lord and the Bald Eagle Falls police department."

Terry was beside Vic and worked on her hands, cuffed together behind her. As soon as he released her, Vic brought her hands around in front of her and wiped her face.

"Dog drool. I do not need a doggie face wash on top of everything else!"

Erin laughed. Tears of relief ran down her face. No matter what else she had lost, she still had Vic.

Terry looked down the narrow tunnel, swearing under his breath. Erin looked. Pallets of packages shrink-wrapped for shipping ran down one side of the tunnel. Hundreds and hundreds of white bricks.

"They really were storing it here. Using this as their shipping center or a way station," Terry marveled.

"How much is all of this worth?"

"Thousands," Terry said. "Maybe millions, I don't know."

"Enough to get the feds to listen to your requests," Beaver said, chewing her gum open-mouthed.

"Oh, dear."

Erin looked at Adele, who had caught up with them and followed them to the tunnel. She stood there, white-faced, looking at the drugs and at Vic. Terry was working on getting Vic's legs free, then she sat up. Her own face went pale.

"Adele! What are you doing here?"

Adele just looked at her, not answering. Erin looked back and forth between them. There was definitely something going on that she hadn't caught on to.

"I called Adele to come sit with me when you disappeared and Terry was trying to track down suspects," Erin explained. "Why... wouldn't she?"

Vic rubbed the insides of her wrists gingerly.

"Because her husband is the one who nabbed me."

$\mathscr{E}$rin felt her own eyes widen. She looked at Adele and knew by her sheet-white face that she had already known or guessed as much.

"I didn't have anything to do with it," Adele said, shaking her head. "I swear to you, Vic, I had no idea what he was up to."

"You didn't know that he was the one who kidnapped me, or you didn't know anything about this caper?"

Adele swallowed. Terry was watching her carefully, but didn't interrupt, letting them talk it out naturally.

"I didn't know why he was in town," Adele said. "I knew something was up, but I didn't know what. I didn't know about the drugs, or that they were going to take you. I didn't know any of it. He put on that he was only here to see me… but I… there was something different about him and I knew he wasn't telling the full truth." She gave a little laugh and shook her head. "There's one way to know for sure when Rudolph Windsor is lying, and that is that his lips are moving."

"You told me that he was just in town to see you," Terry said. "You said that he wasn't involved in anything criminal."

"As far as I knew, he was in town to see me. That was before I'd even talked to him, so how was I supposed to tell you any differently? I told you as far as I knew, he didn't have a criminal record. I left it completely open. It was up to you to find out whether he did or not."

"He does," Erin contributed. "Terry said he has a record for fraud and theft. But nothing related to organized crime. We didn't know he had anything to do with the clans. What… which clan did this?" Erin motioned to their surroundings.

"Jacksons," Vic said bitterly. "Of course. It was Aunt Angela's bakery. I don't know if anyone knew about the tunnel while she was alive. But some time after that, they started moving in…"

"This is a pretty big depot," Beaver observed. "It takes a long time to move that much dope. Engineering that door wouldn't have been an overnight job, either. They've been around here for longer than a few weeks. This operation has been going on for some time."

Vic stared at Beaver. "Beaver?"

"We think she's with DEA or something," Erin filled Vic in. "She won't say, but…"

"With an operation like this, you can bet that they know that we're here now," Terry said in a low, serious tone. "I'm surprised that there weren't guards outside or in the tunnel ready to take us out when we got too close. I didn't see any electronic monitoring, but you can be sure we set off alarms somewhere." He chewed his lip. "It's not safe for us to stay here, and we don't have the manpower to safeguard it."

"Help is on its way," Beaver said serenely, "if they're not here already. You think I would come down here without pulling my own alarm cord first?"

She stopped, cocking her head to listen. Erin tried to hear any footsteps or other sounds indicating that other people were upstairs.

"The good thing about this little storehouse is that its security relies on there being zero traffic. If you suddenly have a bunch of people coming and going into a shop that is supposed to be deserted, people get suspicious and take notice. They couldn't be seen coming in. All movement of product would have to be in the dead of night. They could process during the day, cutting, weighing, and packaging, as long as no one could see inside the store. But they could only move goods when there was absolutely no one around."

"So that's why there were no guards?" Erin asked. "And does that mean… Charley didn't know what was going on here, under her own nose? Could it go all the way back to when Angela was still running The Bake Shoppe, as long as they only operated during the night?"

"Charley might not have known. But she's a Jackson, so it's hard to be sure whether she was in on it or not."

"She was a Dyson more than a Jackson."

Beaver shrugged. "We'll keep an eye on her. I didn't see her spending any time here at night."

"Angela couldn't be here while the bakery was operating because of the contamination. So no one would have thought twice about her being here at night when everyone was gone."

"There will be an in-depth investigation."

"It was Rudolph who brought you here?" Adele asked Vic, tentative.

Vic nodded. "He's the one who grabbed me and brought me here. He talked to other guys, but he's the only one I saw enough to recognize."

Adele shook her head. "Where did he go? Did he tell you what he was doing after he left you here?"

"No. Just said he was taking care of things."

Erin had a sinking feeling in her stomach.

Vic turned to her, as if she had said something audible. "What?"

Erin took a deep breath and let it out. "Auntie Clem's."

"What about it?"

Erin took Vic's hand, more to get strength from her than to give it. "Before we left there, I smelled gasoline."

Terry looked at Erin sharply, his face suddenly gray. "What?"

Erin just nodded. Terry moved quickly, heading out of the tunnel, through the store room, and up the stairs quickly, clicking his radio to talk to the dispatcher. Erin knew she had to follow him and find out how bad it was, but she delayed. She needed a few more minutes of not knowing.

Vic moved slowly, obviously stiff from lying on the floor. Erin helped her to her feet, and the taller girl leaned on her as they walked toward the stairs.

"I'm sorry," Adele said, still ghastly pale. "I didn't know. I'm so sorry."

They walked by Beaver and stopped for a minute, back in the more familiar surroundings. The tunnel filled with drugs had been like another world. The Bake Shoppe storeroom was so like Erin's own, it was like stepping back out of the magical wardrobe.

They gave each other an encouraging squeeze, then made their way up the stairs.

Beaver had said that her people might even be there already, but Erin hadn't taken it literally. The bakery proper and the street outside were a beehive of activity, with yellow warning tape being strung up, bright lights shining on the scene, and black-jacketed figures everywhere. Erin didn't look across the street to Auntie Clem's Bakery, but instead looked for Terry and K9. She could already smell the smoke.

"How bad is it?" she asked when she saw him.

Vic was pulling on her hand, trying to get her to go to the window where they would be able to see the front of Auntie Clem's.

Terry looked grave. He shook his head. "It's bad, Erin. They're trying to control the spread. The other businesses. Some of them have residences over the stores."

"Why would someone do that?" Vic demanded. "What's the point in burning Auntie Clem's?"

Erin tried to speak around the lump in her throat. "Because we wouldn't tell them where Jeremy was. Or they knew we were getting too close to figuring out about The Bake Shoppe and were trying to distract us."

"Jeremy! Is he okay? They kept demanding to know where he was, and I said I didn't know..." Vic's eyes filled with tears. "They kept making threats, and I was so scared of what they were going to do to me. They kept describing how they were going to torture me and saying such foul things..."

Erin pulled Vic down into a hug. "It's okay, Vicky. It's okay. You're safe and so is Jeremy. There is only one person who knows where Jeremy is, and that's Willie."

Vic snuffled into Erin's shoulder. "And Willie? Where is he? What if they got him?"

"Willie's the one who called in the fire first," Terry said. "I'm sure he's probably over there now. Give him a call, but don't be worried if he doesn't answer his phone, he might be occupied with the fire."

"I don't have my phone," Vic patted her pockets. "They took it away. I guess maybe they thought that Jeremy would call. Or that he would be in my contact list. I guess... I'll just wait until Willie is done."

"No." Erin pulled out her own phone. "You'll call him now. He doesn't have to come over here, but he needs to know that you're okay."

Nodding and wiping her nose, Vic took Erin's phone. She unlocked it and called Willie. There was a long half-minute while they waited for him to answer or for it to go to voicemail, and then Willie answered. Vic looked toward the front window as she spoke to him, reassuring him that she was okay and would meet up with him once they were both free of their responsibilities.

"And Jeremy's safe?" Vic asked.

Erin couldn't hear Willie's answer, but she could see the relaxation of Vic's expression and knew he had answered in the affirmative.

"Everybody's okay."

CHAPTER 39

There wasn't a lot for Terry and the little Bald Eagle Falls police department to do once the feds descended on the town and took over the fight against the clans. He sat at the small grouping of chairs in the front section of The Bake Shoppe with the others, waiting to be consulted on any local issues.

"At least we're getting answers to some of our questions. I guess the rest will come out over the next few weeks—or months—while they investigate."

"Like who actually killed Don Inglethorpe?" Erin asked.

He nodded. "They'll have to go through his books to see if he was laundering money… he might have kept files on what was going on here… we know he had some kind of falling out with the Jacksons before he died. They wanted something from him that he wasn't willing to give."

"He'd promised Charley that she could open the bakery," Erin said. "Maybe the clan didn't want her to do that because they couldn't operate without her figuring it out."

Vic nodded. "Rudolph said Inglethorpe didn't know a good deal when he saw it. So I guess they couldn't convince him to do what they wanted him to, and they ended up killing him… I don't know, to get him out of the way?"

"He'd been over at Auntie Clem's asking me about financial stuff.

Turnovers," Erin remembered. "Uh—turnover. He went back over to The Bake Shoppe and...?"

"Maybe he went looking for some bill or insurance policy from their files," Vic suggested, "and he walked in on the drug operation. You said that they could process during the day," she said to Terry, "so maybe he walks in, and they're cutting the powder, or packaging it for sale..."

"Oh." Erin thought back to the scene she had walked into that day. A smear of flour on the counter. The door to the basement standing slightly ajar. "There was white powder on the counter, and an electronic scale. I thought Charley had been making pie."

Terry nodded. "So maybe Bo Biggles or one of the others had been processing powder. Inglethorpe walks in and realizes that the clan *is* operating out of The Bake Shoppe whether he likes it or not."

Vic shuddered. "And goodnight Mr. Inglethorpe."

～

Since Terry was the one who had suggested that they could find Rudolph Windsor by tracking Vic's phone signal, and the kidnapping was in Terry's jurisdiction, the feds agreed that he could have the first crack at interrogating Rudolph, provided a certain Rohilda Beaven was allowed to sit in on the questioning.

Terry agreed to their terms and he was the one to sweat Rudolph under the cool fluorescent lights of the police department's interview room. While it looked more like a community center multipurpose room with its nondescript carpet and lightweight tubular furniture, Mr. Windsor was looking distinctly uncomfortable waiting for the ax to fall.

He kept darting looks at Beaven, who was sitting in a chair with her arms folded, the chair tipped back on two legs, reclined against the wall. She looked casual and comfortable, a sight that was apparently winding Rudolph up considerably.

"So, Mr. Windsor," Terry said slowly, "we have a considerable number of federal charges piling up against you. Congratulations on finally making it into the big leagues."

Rudolph swallowed. He wiped his sweat-beaded brow. "Look, I'm sure we can work something out. I'm just a small fish in this operation. I was taken advantage of. I really didn't know the whole picture..."

"If you didn't know the whole picture, then how can you tell me anything worthwhile?"

"I know enough to help you. It's just that... I didn't know at the time... what they were planning. It wasn't until the end that it all started coming together and I realized..."

"You are the one who kidnapped Victoria Webster. Kidnapping is a very serious charge with heavy sentences."

"It wasn't just me. There were others involved. I can give you their names. I had to do it, because if I didn't... they would have hurt me. My family. My own life was in peril."

"Maybe you should have gone to the police."

"They were watching me all the time. They didn't trust me. That's a point in my favor, isn't it? That they didn't trust me?"

"No, it just tells me that they knew you for what you were. Somebody unreliable, impulsive, and only looking out for number one."

Rudolph rocked back and forth in his seat. "That's not the way it was... if you'll just let me tell you my story, you'll see..."

CHAPTER 40

*E*rin could tell that Vic was watching out the living room window, even though she was trying to look relaxed and casual, as if everything was perfectly normal and they were just visiting before bed like they usually did.

The truth was, Erin was watching too, and not much was making it to the lists she was working on. All of the things she had to do following the fire at the bakery. Talk to the insurers to find out when the claims adjuster was going to make it out. Decide if there was any way she could stay in Bald Eagle Falls, maybe finding a job at the General Store or one of the other businesses. Find out what she was required to do about her employees following a disaster that shut down the business. She sighed.

Vic opened her mouth to talk to Erin about it, then her head snapped around as Willie's truck pulled in front of the house. She hurried to the door and was standing on the front steps when Jeremy climbed out of the truck and ran up to her. They hugged and held each other, talking over top of one another. Eventually, Willie managed to push them into the house, and they moved apart to bring Erin and Willie into the conversation.

"Where were you?" Vic asked. "I was so worried about you. If the clan had found you…"

"Willie put me down a mineshaft," Jeremy said. He shook his head. "I mean *literally* down a mineshaft! He gave me blankets, flashlights, and food, but it was not the best camping experience that I've ever had! Man, is it dark down there! And still! Without the light, I would have gone crazy."

Erin shuddered. There was no way Willie would ever have gotten her down a hole. She'd had enough of caves and underground. She was glad that she hadn't known where Jeremy was. "Isn't that the first place anyone would look if they knew that it was Willie who had hidden you?"

"Nobody knows where all of Willie's mines are," Vic laughed. "I sure don't."

"Aren't they all on public record?"

Vic looked at Willie for his answer.

He just raised his eyebrows and smiled politely. "Where's Terry? I thought he was coming too."

"Not here yet." Erin shrugged. "I assume he'll be here as soon as he can get done at the police department. It might take some time."

"Let's get some food out," Vic suggested, "this is supposed to be a celebration."

Erin went with her into the kitchen and they worked side by side, pulling frozen baked goodies out of the freezer and arranging other finger food on platters. Orange Blossom made an appearance, yowling and begging for food. Vic flicked him a small piece of pepperoni.

"Don't give him that!" Erin protested. "It bothers his stomach and he'll keep me up all night with his... er, gastrointestinal distress."

Vic giggled.

"I'll take him to your apartment," Erin warned. "You can deal with it!"

"I won't give him any more."

Marshmallow made an appearance as well, alerted by Orange Blossom to the fact that there was food on offer. Erin gave him a few pieces of carrot and flicked a couple of kitty treats across the floor for the cat.

She gazed sadly at the cookies that were defrosting. The end of Auntie Clem's Bakery. The insurance wasn't going to cover rebuilding and replacing everything that had been lost and what she was going to owe her laid-off employees. She'd already spent the rest of her inheritance on rebuilding the garage and putting in the loft apartment for Vic. And the burglar alarm and other security equipment to keep them safe. The bank wasn't going to give her a loan when she didn't have collateral, and she wasn't going to mortgage

Clementine's house, especially not when she didn't have a regular income. She kept going in circles and couldn't find a way to get the bakery back in business.

There was a knock at the door, and she heard Terry's voice when Willie answered it. She poked her head out the kitchen door.

"Send K9 in for a cookie! He deserves it after finding Vic in the tunnel for us."

Terry told K9 to 'go get a cookie,' and the dog bounded excitedly into the kitchen. Orange Blossom jumped back and puffed up, hissing his objection to the big dog being allowed in his territory. Erin gave K9 a doggie biscuit from the cookie jar and scratched his ears and praised him, telling him what a good dog he was for finding Vic.

She washed up, and once they had everything ready, they bussed the platters into the living room. Erin was surprised to see Beaver there as well. She gave Erin an easy smile.

"I hope you don't mind me crashing your party. Officer Piper said you wouldn't mind and that there would be good food."

"Uh... no, that's fine." Erin looked at Terry. She couldn't help a little twinge of possessiveness over him. She didn't like this woman getting friendly with him and showing up with him at what was supposed to be a private celebration. "Of course you're welcome. You were a part of the rescue."

The only person who wasn't there was Adele. She had seemed deeply embarrassed by her husband's involvement in the whole thing and had retreated to her solitary cottage.

They helped themselves to the goodies while Erin got out some wine and soft drinks that had been chilling in the fridge. Beaver ended up sitting next to Jeremy and the two of them exchanged stories, laughing with their heads close together. Vic looked at Erin and raised one eyebrow. Erin shrugged back.

"So, how did it go with Mr. Windsor?" Erin asked Terry. "Did you get anywhere with him?"

Terry looked over at Beaver, who nodded at him to go on. Erin appreciated that Beaver was open to Terry talking to them about it, but didn't like their apparent ability to read each other so easily.

"It went better than I would have predicted." Terry sat forward on his seat. "I told you before that Windsor didn't have any apparent connection to the clans. He hadn't had any dealings with organized crime before, so I didn't see how he could have been involved in the drug running. He wouldn't have had enough pull as an independent operator, and he'd need a good 'in' to be involved with either of the gangs."

Erin nodded her agreement. Windsor hadn't seemed like the type to be involved with the clan. He was an outsider, from New England rather than Tennessee, and he wasn't related to anyone. He was the kind of guy who was always running his own brilliant scams but could never get ahead of the big operators.

"The last stint he served was in the Tennessee Penitentiary."

No one else saw the significance to start with. Then Vic's eyes lit up as she made the connection. "That's where Davis is."

Terry nodded. "That's where Davis is."

"Did they know each other?" Erin asked.

"They were in the same block. Apparently, they developed quite a friendship."

"So, when he got out, Davis set him up with the Jacksons?"

"Introductions were made while he was still inside. And it would appear that Davis had ideas about how to make money off of the bakery even while it was shut down."

"It was Davis's idea to use the tunnel?"

"I'm not sure whose idea it was initially. Davis doesn't strike me as an idea man, so it might have been Trenton's. But whoever it was, the boys obviously had knowledge of the tunnels."

"But Davis couldn't make money off of it if Trenton was the one running the bakery," Erin said. "If they both knew about the tunnels, then Davis couldn't use them without Trenton's knowledge, like they could when Charley was in charge. He'd have to give him a cut."

Terry nodded slowly. "Another nail in Davis's coffin. More evidence to suggest that he fully intended to kill Trenton right from the start. Joelle wouldn't have known about the tunnel."

"Good news for Charley. She can get the bakery opened and maybe not even have to split it with Davis. At least Bald Eagle Falls will still have one bakery."

"It will work out, Erin," Vic said. "Somehow we'll work it out."

Erin didn't believe it, but she didn't want to argue about it. She was mentally exhausted.

"So, is it all over?" she asked the room at large. "Is there going to be retaliation? Are we going to be targeted?"

Terry and Beaver looked at each other. "I think we'll be able to get most of the major players behind bars," Beaver said slowly. "There are always dangers with organized crime... bosses still directing operations from inside, or family members retaliating against those who put their loved ones behind bars. So it's impossible to say that it's over for sure. But my best guess... you and Vic should be safe. You didn't actually go looking for trouble. You were defending yourselves and your loved ones."

Erin breathed out. There were no guarantees, but she was glad to hear the opinion expressed by the federal agent. Maybe things would be quiet. For at least as long as it took Erin to figure out what she was doing or where she was going next.

"And what about Jeremy?" Vic asked, looking at her brother.

Beaver grimaced. She looked searchingly at the platters of food and picked out a cookie. She nibbled at it while considering her answer.

"Jeremy had certain commitments to the clan. He bailed out and betrayed the trust his family and the clan had in him. They were pretty intent on finding him before he could talk to the authorities."

"But I didn't snitch," Jeremy said. "They might have thought I was going to, but I didn't. So now that it's all over... they should just leave me alone."

"You have any plans to go back to the farm now?"

"No way!"

"My point exactly."

"What about witness protection?" Vic asked. "You could help him to change his name and get situated where no one could find him."

"For that, he *would* have to testify against them, and it would have to be something big enough for us to hang a case on. Is that what you want?"

Jeremy shook his head. "No." He looked at his sister. "No, Vic. No way. I'll do my own thing. I'm not important enough for them to be spending a lot of time and resources on."

Erin had tried to outrun her troubles before, but it seemed like it didn't matter how many times she changed her name and took up residence in a new town, she couldn't ever leave her past behind.

"You could get some *unofficial* help from an agent," Beaver said. "It would be a good idea to keep in touch with someone who knows the tricks of the trade."

A slow smile spread over Jeremy's face. He nodded. "That sounds like a good plan," he agreed.

EPILOGUE

*B*ella sat down with Erin at the library table. Erin knew she still had to go over termination pay with Bella and to apologize to her for not being able to keep the business going after the fire. The very thought of the conversation tied her in knots.

Bella had been a good employee. She was young and would be able to find work again quickly enough, though there weren't a lot of openings in Bald Eagle Falls and she might end up having to go to the city to find something.

"Vic told me how stressed you've been over the bakery," Bella said. "She said you didn't think you could find a way to start it up again after the fire."

Erin nodded, both grateful to Vic for breaking the ice and ticked off with her for not leaving it to Erin. It was Erin's job to do, no matter how much she dreaded it.

"You had insurance though, right?"

"Yes... but it's not enough to rebuild and buy everything I would need to start over again. There's next to nothing recoverable. I can't get a loan based on the property value and a business plan, not with another bakery opening any day now, one with a wider customer base. I'm not going to mortgage Clementine's house, I won't risk it." Erin was irritated by having to explain it all over again. Everybody thought the insurance company would just hand her a check and she'd be all set.

Bella didn't look dismayed by this news. Maybe she already had a new job lined up.

"What if you didn't have to rebuild? What if there was another possibility?"

Erin stared at Bella.

"What if there was another bakery that was already set up and you could just step in?"

"The Bake Shoppe?" Erin demanded. "I can't exactly walk in and take over Charley's business."

"Now that Davis has pled guilty and Charley's getting the whole of Trenton's estate, she's looking for a partner to invest in The Bake Shoppe so that she'll have the money to get a house."

Erin felt the first real glimmer of hope. "Well… I've got money I could invest, and I could help run it… but The Bake Shoppe is a conventional bakery. I'd have to give up on the idea of having a gluten-free, specialty bakery." Was half a dream better than no dream at all? She hated to think of Peter and her other precious customers having to go back to driving to the city to get second-rate factory-made gluten-free products.

"You'd have to discuss that with Charley." Bella had a mischievous twinkle in her eye, "but she figured that since that was your specialty, and you're the one with experience running a business like this…"

"You think she'd be open to making it gluten-free? Just like Auntie Clem's?"

Bella sat back in her chair, looking like the cat that swallowed the canary. "Well, that's what she *said*."

"You negotiated me partnering with my half-sister to open a gluten-free bakery without even talking to me first?"

"I know your business. I didn't want to get your hopes up with a bunch of pie-in-the-sky ideas…"

"Gluten-free pie-in-the-sky," Erin giggled, feeling giddy. "It won't be Auntie Clem's, but I think I'm okay with that."

"Oh. She did say something about your name having better goodwill than The Bake Shoppe, with all of its associations with the Plaint family and murders and organized crime activities… so she'd like to open it as Auntie Clem's…"

Erin didn't know whether to laugh or cry, so she did both, unable to contain herself, in full view of all of the patrons of the Bald Eagle Falls public library.

Did you enjoy this book? Reviews and recommendations are vital to making a book successful.

Please leave a review at your favorite book store or review site and share it with your friends.

Don't miss the following bonus material:
Sign up for mailing list to get a free ebook
Read a sneak preview chapter
Other books by P.D. Workman
Learn more about the author

Sign up for my mailing list at pdworkman.com and get Gluten-Free Murder for free!

Join my mailing list and

Download a sweet mystery for free

PREVIEW OF APPLE-ACHIAN TREASURE

CHAPTER 1

*E*rin fit her key in the lock and found herself holding her breath as she turned it. The lock clicked smoothly open and Erin pushed the door open. She turned to look back over her shoulder at Vic as she entered.

"It feels pretty weird," she said.

Vic nodded. "I know. But it's just a different location. It's still Auntie Clem's Bakery."

Erin took a deep breath in and let it out again. "Yeah... just the same."

But it didn't feel the same. She knew she should be ecstatic about being able to open the bakery again. If not for her half-sister, Charley, allowing her to become half-owner in The Bake Shoppe and to reopen it as Auntie Clem's Bakery, that would have been the end of Erin's dream. She would have had to liquidate everything and to figure out how she was going to make a living without the bakery.

Charley's offer had seemed like a godsend at the time, but Erin had become increasingly worried about how it was all going to work out. She barely knew Charley. They hadn't grown up together and their personalities were diametrically opposed. It seemed like everything Charley did rubbed Erin the wrong way, even when she wasn't really doing anything wrong.

And now they were connected not only by blood, but in the business. They had to agree on advertising campaigns, product lines, prices, and promotions. They had to agree on everything that Erin had previously set up, like the ladies' tea after Sunday services, catering for the book club at The Book Nook across the street, and the children's cookie club.

Even just stocking the kitchen had been an ordeal, since Charley wanted to use all of the equipment that had remained from The Bake Shoppe and Erin couldn't use gluten-contaminated bowls and baking sheets to make her gluten-free baking. While Charley had agreed to continue to keep Auntie Clem's Bakery gluten-free, she didn't have the understanding Erin did and thought that they could cut a few corners. Erin wasn't willing to put the health and lives of her allergic or intolerant customers at risk.

Erin turned on the lights and looked around the kitchen. It was her bakery. It was the new normal. She and Vic could continue to work together, just as they had in the shop that had burned down. It would be almost the same.

Almost, but not quite.

Vic strode into the kitchen, where she pulled a clean apron off the hook and tied it around her slim form, then put on a hat, making sure that her long blond hair was all properly tucked away. Normal, routine actions, just like she had followed every day at the old Auntie Clem's. Erin followed suit. She was considerably shorter than Vic and her hair was shorter and dark. She felt a little better once suited up. Her uniform helped to set the mood.

She went to the fridge and started pulling out the batters they had made the night before, working through her mental checklists to get everything started in the right order so that they would have the case filled efficiently by the time the bakery opened in a few hours.

"Do we have chocolate chip muffins today?" Vic questioned.

"Yes. And blueberry. And the rice bran. I'm going to work a high-protein muffin into the lineup once we've had a chance to settle back into the schedule. Not today, but maybe next week. I'm hoping we can tap into the low-carb and paleo markets."

Vic nodded, already aware that Erin had been working on it. "You're finding some low-carb recipes that don't rely on nut flours?"

They worked side by side, finding their rhythm even in the less familiar kitchen.

"I'm focusing on some of the less allergenic seeds like *sacha inchi*. It's one of the new flours out there and becoming more available. We can grind it here so that we know that they haven't been processed on the same equipment as peanuts or tree nuts."

"You're always on top of all of the new developments."

"Well, that's my job."

Vic glanced at the clock on the wall. "I thought Charley said she was going to come in this morning to help out."

Erin didn't look at Vic and tried to keep her expression neutral. "That's what she said."

"But you didn't expect her to get here, did you?"

"Uh... no. She's really not a morning person, and this is early even for morning people. Maybe if Charley came in and helped out now, and then went home and went to bed..."

Vic chuckled. "She's like a teenager. If she wants to be a business owner, she's going to have to make a few changes to her lifestyle."

Erin turned on one of the mixers, then went around to the ovens, setting the preheat temperatures. It was the coolest part of the day, but that was about to end. Once they had the ovens going, even the best air conditioning wasn't going to keep it cool.

"It's supposed to be fall, but I'll be glad when the temperature starts to drop."

"Still got a ways to go before then."

They worked in silence for a few minutes. "When do you think Charley is going to show up?" Vic asked.

Erin straightened and looked at her. "Are you trying to get me to badmouth my new boss?"

"She isn't your boss, she's your partner."

"I'd like to think so," Erin said slowly, "but I don't think that's the way she sees it. If we can't agree on things, who do you think is going to get the final say?"

"You're partners. You'll work it out together."

Erin shrugged. That remained to be seen.

"So...?" Vic pressed.

"I think we'll be lucky to see her before noon."

Vic giggled. "How about a bet? If she gets in before noon, you win. After noon, I win."

"And what do we win?"

"How about... a foot massage."

Erin shook her head. "Okay. You're on."

~

Charley didn't make it in before noon. Vic was chuckling to herself.

"I'm looking forward to that foot rub," she commented.

"I did say we'd be lucky to see her before noon. I hope nothing happened to her…"

"Nothing happened to her. She's just sleeping, like every day."

"I know… I just worry."

"She's fine. She said she was going to be here, but she hasn't got the sense of a cross-eyed goose. She's just like a kid. She's going to have to grow up if she's going to run a business."

Erin raised her eyebrows. Vic herself was barely an adult.

"I'm grown up," Vic shot at her. "It doesn't have anything to do with chronological age."

"No, you're right. She may be a few years older; she may even have been on her own for longer than you have, but she doesn't have the same sense of responsibility."

Vic nodded. There were parallels between Vic and Charley. Both had left home at an early age, rebelling against the way that they had been raised. But Charley had left, apparently, because she wanted a more exciting life on the opposite side of the law, and Vic had come out about her gender identity, transitioning to female. Despite her not aligning herself with the gender she'd been raised as, Vic still had strong moral standards and an attachment to her family. They were the ones who had forced her to leave. Erin was glad that Jeremy, one of Vic's older brothers, had recently moved into town. It was good for Vic to have contact with someone in her family. Jeremy accepted her for who she was and did his best to respect her identity.

"Think she'll show up after lunch?" Erin asked.

"Do you want to go double or nothing?"

"No. Just wondering. It's opening day, you'd think she'd at least make an appearance."

"You would think," Vic agreed.

Mary Lou and Melissa arrived together. Erin was glad to see them together more often again lately. Mary Lou needed the support of her friends more than ever, and Erin suspected that Melissa wasn't having the easiest time since she had started visiting Davis in prison. The ladies of Bald Eagle Falls were not very tolerant of what they perceived as wrong choices.

Mary Lou looked around the bakery and raised her brows. "I was expecting a better turnout for your opening day. Isn't this a little... quiet...?"

Erin shrugged, her face getting warm. "We actually didn't want to do a great big grand reopening. We didn't think it was a good idea, after..."

Mary Lou gazed at her blankly.

"Because of the deaths," Melissa piped up eagerly. "Angela was killed on opening day of Auntie Clem's Bakery and Mr. Inglethorpe was killed the night before the grand reopening for The Bake Shoppe. Were you afraid of jinxing it?"

"No," Erin insisted, though she had to admit to a little superstitious twinge over the thought of another murder around the bakery opening. So far everything had been quiet, and she hoped that it would stay that way. They didn't need any bodies to spice things up. "I just didn't want people to make that association." She looked significantly at the other patrons of the bakery, hoping that Melissa would get the hint and keep her voice down. "Even if it's unconscious... I didn't want them to think... bakery opening... someone might die..."

"That makes perfect sense," Mary Lou acknowledged.

"It's really too bad, though," Melissa said. "I wouldn't mind a free muffin..."

Erin smiled. "You buy a dozen for the Police Department, and I'll throw in a free one for you."

"You'd do that anyway."

Mary Lou and Melissa looked through the case at the baked goods on offer.

"I think... a loaf of the rustic bread," Mary Lou pointed to a hand-shaped loaf. "That would go nicely with supper. And maybe some cookies that I can throw in the freezer. We don't go through them very fast, with it just being Josh and I now, but we are starting to get a little low."

"Anything in particular, or just an assortment?" Erin asked.

"Surprise me."

Erin suspected that Mary Lou wasn't going to be eating any of them anyway. She was very careful to maintain her slim figure. Josh, on the other hand, was a teenager and could probably put away the whole dozen in a sitting without consequences.

"How are the boys?" she asked politely.

"As well as can be expected. Josh is finding high school very challenging. And Campbell... well, I don't know what to think of Campbell. He at least calls me once every week or so, which is more than one can expect from a boy his age. He says he's well, that things are going fine... but he's not going anywhere. I don't even know how he's supporting himself without any marketable skills."

"You don't know what he's doing?"

Mary Lou shook her head. "He's *finding himself*. Whatever that means."

Erin wasn't sure how to respond to that. She finished assembling the cookies for Mary Lou and handed them over to Vic to ring up at the till. She looked at Melissa. "So, a dozen muffins?"

"No, not today. Maybe on Friday. How about..." Melissa studied the display case seriously. "How about a brownie?" She motioned to the choco-late-dipped brownies that Erin had recently added to the product lineup. "Those are addictive. They should be a controlled substance."

Erin nodded. "You'd better not tell Officer Piper that. I don't want him slapping me with any fines. Or jail time."

Melissa gave one of her wide smiles, her eyes dancing. "What you and Officer Piper do behind closed doors really isn't any of my business..."

For the second time, Erin felt a wave of heat go over her face, and was sure that this time she was turning a brilliant red. She shouldn't let Melissa get to her like that. Blushing would only encourage her in the future. But she couldn't keep a dispassionate mask when she thought about Terry Piper and their relationship. They had only recently taken things to the next level with the good-looking officer, and Erin wasn't to the point where she could be casual about it.

"You mind your manners," Vic drawled, her southern accent more pronounced than usual. "Don't be teasing Miss Erin or she'll be adding something to your tea this Sunday."

Melissa responded with a blush of her own. She tittered and gave Vic the money to cover her bill. "I don't know what you're talking about, I'm sure."

It wouldn't have been so bad if Officer Handsome himself hadn't happened to enter the bakery at that very moment.

The bells jingled as Terry walked in the front door, K9 poised at his side in perfect form, as usual. Erin's heart skipped a beat at the sight of her sweetheart in uniform, but she was already embarrassed by Melissa's comments and couldn't help but feel even more awkward at his appearance on the scene. She glanced over at Vic.

"I uh, just have to go check on those cookies. Can you get K9 a biscuit and see what Terry wants? I'll be right back!"

Vic looked surprised. Erin turned tail and dashed into the kitchen, needing to get out of sight to compose herself. She ran cold water into a clean cloth and pressed it to her cheeks, trying to cool them off and remove the color. Terry would be wondering what she was so flushed about.

Not like he wouldn't wonder why she had suddenly fled at his appearance. That wasn't something she normally did.

Erin took an extra few seconds to gulp down a glass of water, then returned to the front before everyone could start to wonder what had happened to her. But that last swallow water went down wrong and she inhaled half of it into her windpipe, resulting in a fit of coughing just as she walked through the door. If she'd been trying for an unobtrusive re-entrance, she had not succeeded.

Erin turned away, coughing into her elbow, and then turned back, her face just as hot as it had been when she'd left.

"Sorry. I'm not contagious. Just some water that went down the wrong way."

"Are you okay?" Terry asked, looking concerned.

"I'm fine, really. Just some water." Erin cleared her throat the best she could, trying to suppress any further coughs. "How are you today?"

"It's a beautiful day out. Things have been pretty quiet. I'm hoping that the crime level in Bald Eagle Falls has gone back to normal."

"You think that the trouble with the clans is done?"

"Considering the fact that we managed to confiscate several millions of dollars' worth of drugs, hopefully they've decided that Bald Eagle Falls isn't the best place for a storage and shipping depot, and we won't be seeing any more of them."

"I sure hope so," Erin said fervently.

Terry nodded. "How has the first day back been?"

Erin breathed out. She blinked to clear her teary eyes and studied the officer. Taller than she was, dark haired, perfect build, and that cute little dimple in his cheek when he smiled at her. "Actually, it's been pretty nice. It felt good to get back into the routine again. When I wasn't working, it just felt... disorderly. I didn't feel like my life was going the way I wanted it to. Like things might just fall apart at any minute."

"But coming back, everything has fallen back into the old patterns?"

Erin nodded. "It feels good."

"It actually does," Vic agreed. "Unlike Erin, I actually enjoyed my time off, but I was ready to come back. The structure and the routine are good, but even more than that... the paycheck... visiting with customers... eating at regular intervals instead of grazing all day." Vic patted her flat belly. "I was starting to put on weight..."

"You were not," Erin disagreed. "You haven't put on an ounce since you moved here."

"Well, that's not exactly true. But considering I wasn't getting enough to eat before I started working for you, those first few ounces were okay. It's the ones since then that are the problem."

Erin just shook her head.

"See you later, Officer Piper," Melissa gave Terry a little wave before leaving. She did some office administration for the Police Department on a part-time basis, and quite enjoyed the prestige of her role, even if she wasn't an officer herself.

Terry nodded to her and Mary Lou as they headed out the door. "Ladies."

They were just coming up on the after-school rush when Charley finally showed her face. She rushed into the bakery through the front door, red-faced and flustered.

"I can't believe how the day has gotten away from me!" she exclaimed. "I was just doing some administrative work from home, you know, making sure that all of the advertising is lined up and that the bank has made all of the appropriate arrangements and all that..." All work that Erin had already attended to herself. "And before I knew it, it's afternoon and I still haven't made it over to the bakery! How did it go? Do you need anything?"

They were, of course, long past the point that Charley could have helped with anything, unless she wanted to take over the register during the rush or help with the cleanup after closing. Erin just looked at her.

"I was working," Charley insisted. "I was just doing it from home instead of here. It's so hot in the kitchen and that little office…"

The office was bigger than the one Erin had used in the original Auntie Clem's Bakery, which had been hardly more than a closet. With a desk fan on the heat was nearly tolerable.

"I didn't say anything," she asserted. "Things went pretty well. We had a good amount of business."

"Good. I was a little worried after we decided not to do a big grand reopening. I mean, I didn't *want* to do a big reopening, I just had some… last minute qualms. What if nobody came? What if not enough people knew that we were open for business again today…?"

"There's nothing that says you have to make all of your money the first day," Erin reassured her. "Even if opening day didn't go well, there's lots of time for word to get around that we're open and to get people in. But, nothing to worry about, it went just fine."

"Good." Charley put a stuffed shoulder bag that doubled as her brief-case down on one of the little wrought iron tables at the front of the bakery. "I'm new to this whole 'business owner' thing. I don't want to screw it up."

"That's why you've got us," Vic offered, putting her arm around Erin's shoulder to remind Charley that she was there too, part of a package deal. "We know how to run a bakery."

Charley didn't quite make a face, but her look at Vic didn't convey that she was thankful to have Vic there helping to look after things. She and Vic had never quite clicked. Erin wasn't sure whether it was a personality thing, or whether there was a certain amount of jealousy between her sister and her best friend, each of them wary of the other intruding on their relationship with Erin.

"I'm glad I've got you," Charley agreed, but her words were aimed at Erin rather than at Vic. "Whenever I start to panic about not knowing everything there is to know about the business, I just remind myself that you've done all of this before. I can't imagine how difficult it must have been for you to start up Auntie Clem's Bakery with no one to tell you how to do everything. How did you manage?"

Erin motioned Charley to move to the side so that she wasn't blocking paying customers.

"I read lots. Talked to my lawyer and accountant. Wrote out my business plan and goals and milestones…"

"You're so organized. You always know exactly what's coming next, don't you?"

Erin only wished that were true.

CHAPTER 2

$\mathcal{W}$hen they arrived home after closing the bakery, Erin saw that Rohilda Beaven's big white truck was parked in front of the house.

"Looks like Jeremy has company," she observed, and pulled around to the back to park in the garage.

"It's amazing how well they get on together," Vic said, shaking her head. "You'd think that with Beaver being older than him and a federal agent, they wouldn't have anything in common. But they get along like a house on fire!"

Erin winced at the expression. They had almost lost the house to fire once, and the original Auntie Clem's Bakery burning down was still too recent and a sore spot.

"Or like something on fire," Vic amended quickly, then tried again. "Or... like a pig and mud. They belong together!"

"They really have seemed to hit it off," Erin agreed. She unlocked the back door, pausing and calling out to warn Jeremy and Beaver that they were no longer alone. "We're home, Jeremy!"

They could hear the murmur of voices for a moment, then Jeremy's door opened, and he entered the kitchen.

"Hey Erin, hey Vic. How was the first day back?"

"It was good," Vic offered, giving him a quick hug. "Beaver's here?"

"She'll be out in a minute. We're just getting things packed up and ready to go."

Erin felt a little pang at the thought of Jeremy moving out. It had sometimes been awkward with him there, especially when he had been trying to hide out from the clans and the police. She had told him that he needed to find his own place, but she still felt responsible for him and like she might be turning him out of the nest too quickly.

"Everything is arranged at the new place?" she asked.

"Deposit and first month have been paid," Jeremy agreed. "So, it looks like I'm all grown up after all. My first place all my own."

Erin suspected that most of the money for the basement suite had been put up by Beaver, since Jeremy had just recently landed a job and hadn't likely received an advance on his paycheck. But he hadn't told her what arrangements were being made and it wasn't any of her business how he had managed to rent a place so quickly.

"It will be nice for you," Erin said. "You won't have me and all of the critters underfoot."

Orange Blossom, Erin's cat, was rubbing up against her legs meowing noisily over their conversation. Marshmallow was closer to Jeremy, and he bent down and picked up the brown and white rabbit. Marshmallow kicked his back legs, not liking to be lifted into the air, but Jeremy held the rabbit snug against his body and settled him down.

"Actually, I'm going to miss these guys. The house never seemed lonely with them around. My apartment is going to seem awfully quiet after being used to them running around here."

Erin wasn't about to offer that he could take one of them with him. She wouldn't be able to bear to part with either of them and would never separate the two. The cat and rabbit had grown remarkably close to each other.

Jeremy's bedroom door opened again, and Rohilda joined them in the kitchen. Her tall, lanky body, which always gave the impression of being slow and lazy, was anything but. She was strong quick, and graceful. She just conserved her energy until she had a need for it. She gave them a smile, chewing on a wad of gum. Her nose and lips were too big for her face and her blond hair was more like Jeremy's unruly mane than Vic's sleek, smooth hair. All together, she was not unattractive, but didn't have the type of beauty that society typically worshiped.

Erin had learned to appreciate her open, honest manner. Unlike the women of Bald Eagle Falls, whom Erin found difficult to read, with Beaver what you saw was what you got. She never put on a false front.

"Good evening," she greeted Erin and Vic. "Uneventful day at the bakery?"

Erin nodded vigorously. "Luckily, yes! I don't know what I would have done if… something… had happened. I might have a breakdown and never recover."

"Good thing we didn't have to find out."

"So…" Vic looked at Jeremy and back at Beaver. "I guess you're leaving tonight…?"

"Everything is packed up and ready to go," Beaver agreed. "Jer can sleep in his own bed tonight. I need to go back to the city for a few days, so he'll have some time to settle into his new digs. I'll be back for a day or two on the weekend." She looked at Jeremy with affection.

He grinned back at her. "I told her she could stay, but she doesn't want the commute. So, I guess I just get a few days here and there whenever she can fit me in. I feel used."

"You'd better not complain," Vic warned. "The lady is good with a gun."

Beaver grinned and nodded, chewing on her gum.

"I'm not complaining," Jeremy assured her, and put his arm around Beaver to pull her close for a moment. "I'm perfectly happy with being used."

Beaver laughed and gave him an embarrassingly passionate kiss. Erin looked at Vic and rolled her eyes.

"Did you work today?" Vic asked without waiting for Jeremy and Beaver to finish.

Jeremy pulled back from Beaver. "Yep. I don't work the long hours you two do, but I put in my time."

"What exactly is it that you're doing?" Erin asked. While he'd told her before, she never felt like she'd gotten a full explanation.

"Just keeping an eye on things," Jeremy said. "Making sure that no one bothers the crops."

Erin studied him, trying to make sense of the explanation. She knew that he was working on Crosswood Farm, but he had refused to tell what kind of crop he was guarding. It didn't seem likely that it was any of the crops that were widely farmed in the area. After all, why would fields need to be guarded against intruders? There was no reason for people to come in and steal corn or apples. What was the benefit, unless they were starving? It was harvest time, so the plants would be mature, but she couldn't see why anyone would be interested. Was there a black market for cider?

She was afraid that what he was doing wasn't quite as innocent as he made it sound.

Terry had said that they had eradicated the drug trade in Bald Eagle Falls, so Erin told herself it couldn't be anything to do with the clans. Jeremy had done his best to get away from the Jackson clan that he'd been born into. She couldn't see him giving in and just going right back to a life of crime. And she couldn't see Beaver letting him. Beaver didn't contradict anything Jeremy had said about his job, so either she knew the details, or she was satisfied that as much as he had said was the truth.

It just didn't make any sense to Erin.

"You've got to be on the lookout for poachers," Jeremy told Erin, watching her face carefully. "You'd be surprised at how much illegal trade there is around here."

"Poachers… so does that mean you are guarding animals? Not plants?"

He kept his face carefully blank. "I'm not allowed to talk about it."

"Not allowed to?"

"It's in my employment contract."

"So, your job is watching to make sure nobody steals a bunch of plants?"

He shrugged.

Erin looked at Beaver again, trying to read her expression, but she was even more closeted than Jeremy, giving Erin a cheeky smile that betrayed nothing of what she knew or didn't know about Jeremy's new job.

Apple-achian Treasure, Book #8 of the *Auntie Clem's Bakery series* by P.D. Workman can be purchased at pdworkman.com

ABOUT THE AUTHOR

Award-winning and USA Today bestselling author P.D. (Pamela) Workman writes riveting mystery/suspense and young adult books dealing with mental illness, addiction, abuse, and other real-life issues. For as long as she can remember, the blank page has held an incredible allure and from a very young age she was trying to write her own books.

Workman wrote her first complete novel at the age of twelve and continued to write as a hobby for many years. She started publishing in 2013. She has won several literary awards from Library Services for Youth in Custody for her young adult fiction. She currently has over 50 published titles and can be found at pdworkman.com.

Born and raised in Alberta, Workman has been married for over 25 years and has one son.

∾

Please visit P.D. Workman at pdworkman.com to see what else she is working on, to join her mailing list, and to link to her social networks.

∾

If you enjoyed this book, please take the time to recommend it to other purchasers with a review or star rating and share it with your friends!

facebook.com/pdworkmanauthor

twitter.com/pdworkmanauthor

instagram.com/pdworkmanauthor

amazon.com/author/pdworkman

bookbub.com/authors/p-d-workman

goodreads.com/pdworkman

linkedin.com/in/pdworkman

pinterest.com/pdworkmanauthor

youtube.com/pdworkman

CPSIA information can be obtained
at www.ICGtesting.com
Printed in the USA
LVHW040147230523
747761LV00002B/5